AN UNEXPECTED TURN

A rustling in the nearby bushes was quickly followed by two shadowy figures stepping into the glow of the campfire. Both were pointing pistols. "You boys just keep sitting and tell us what it is you're doing here," one said as he pulled back the hammer of his Colt.

"Just minding our own business," Novak said.

"Our boss don't seem to think so. He says you're here snooping around, trespassing on his property. Folks get themselves killed for that kind of behavior." Both men took another step forward. "Tell us what's your purpose."

His partner began laughing. "Don't matter to me," he said. "Let's just shoot them and be done with it." It was obvious he had been drinking while waiting to confront the intruders. He aimed his gun at Wisenhunt. . . .

RALPH COMPTON

SEVEN ROADS TO REVENGE

A Ralph Compton Novel by
CARLTON STOWERS

BERKLEY
New York

BERKLEY
An imprint of Penguin Random House LLC
penguinrandomhouse.com

Copyright © 2021 by The Estate of Ralph Compton
Penguin Random House supports copyright. Copyright fuels creativity, encourages
diverse voices, promotes free speech, and creates a vibrant culture. Thank you for buying
an authorized edition of this book and for complying with copyright laws by not
reproducing, scanning, or distributing any part of it in any form without permission.
You are supporting writers and allowing Penguin Random House to continue to
publish books for every reader.

BERKLEY and the BERKLEY & B colophon are registered trademarks of
Penguin Random House LLC.

ISBN: 9780593333938

First Edition: July 2021

Printed in the United States of America
1   3   5   7   9   10   8   6   4   2

Book design by George Towne

THE IMMORTAL COWBOY

This is respectfully dedicated to the "American Cowboy." His was the saga sparked by the turmoil that followed the Civil War, and the passing of more than a century has by no means diminished the flame.

————◆◆◆————

True, the old days and the old ways are but treasured memories, and the old trails have grown dim with the ravages of time, but the spirit of the cowboy lives on.

————◆◆◆————

In my travels—to Texas, Oklahoma, Kansas, Nebraska, Colorado, Wyoming, New Mexico, and Arizona—I always find something that reminds me of the Old West. While I am walking these plains and mountains for the first time, there is this feeling that a part of me is eternal, that I have known these old trails before. I believe it is the undying spirit of the frontier calling me, through the mind's eye, to step back into time. What is the appeal of the Old West of the American frontier?

————◆◆◆————

It has been epitomized by some as the dark and bloody period in American history. Its heroes—Crockett, Bowie, Hickok, Earp—have been reviled and criticized. Yet the Old West lives on, larger than life.

————◆◆◆————

It has become a symbol of freedom, when there was always another mountain to climb and another river to cross; when a dispute between two men was settled not with expensive lawyers, but with fists, knives, or guns. Barbaric? Maybe. But some things never change. When the cowboy rode into the pages of American history, he left behind a legacy that lives within the hearts of us all.

—*Ralph Compton*

PROLOGUE

The old man, frail and beaten down, sat at the end of the bar, his head slumped and watery eyes closed except for those moments when he would glance toward the doorway of the saloon. He was looking for someone willing to offer him a free drink in exchange for one of his tales. He was a good story-teller but worthless at much of anything else. The passing years had stolen away all his vigor and the whiskey had robbed him of interest in anything but his next drink.

Regardless of the weather or time of year, he was always dressed in the same faded pair of overalls and a flannel shirt frayed at the collar and sleeves and missing a few buttons. His beard and hair were snow white, always unkempt.

On his bony hip he wore a Colt pistol that threatened no one since it hadn't worked in years. He had no kinfolk anyone knew of, and his age was a mystery.

If he was still sober enough by closing time, he would make his way to his little shack down by the creek. If not, he slept in the alley behind the Wolf Creek Café, waking in hopes owner Irma Jean would offer him a cup of leftover coffee and maybe a piece of buttered toast before he bathed himself in the watering trough out front. He always made it a point to be at his regular spot as soon as the saloon opened, ready to get to work, telling his stories to anyone with an interest and the price of a drink.

In his stories, he was decades younger, wild as the prairie wind, quick on the draw, feared by all men and a pleasure to the women. Or, at least that's how he told them. That, he would tell listeners, was what being a member of Quantrill's Raiders was like back in the day.

In a surprisingly high-pitched voice, he would sing the praises of leader William Clarke Quantrill, recreating conversations he recalled having with the rebel leader about his fierce determination to aid the Confederate troops as they battled Union soldiers. "They called us 'bushwackers,'" the old man would say, "and you can bet your sweet bottom they hated to see us coming over the hill, guns blazing. What we were was patriots, through and through, pure and simple."

He would relive battles in little-known places like Pea Ridge and Wilson Creek along the Missouri-Kansas border where he and his fellow Raiders fought the abolitionists tooth and nail. And whipped 'em good. Back in those days, he would explain, there was a whole lot of antislavery sentiment in that part of the country. "But nobody ever had cause to question where Quantrill stood on that matter," he would tell his audience. "Me neither. Who was gonna do the fieldwork and tend the cooking and cleaning if everyone was allowed to just up and strike out on their own, belonging to no one and all of a sudden free as a bird? Think on that for a minute."

His descriptions of the guerrilla raids and ambushes carried out as the Civil War was winding down were as colorful as a dime novel. He bragged that the James brothers, Jesse and Frank, had ridden with them before they got famous leading their own gang of outlaws.

"We done all we could to help the Confederates, and were proud to serve," he said. "We got shed of a whole lot of Union soldiers, a bunch of them Kansas Jayhawkers, and a good part of the Missouri Militia."

There was, however, one infamous adventure that he rarely spoke of—unless so drunk the remorse that still haunted him was properly drowned by the whiskey. It was the reason he and other Rangers had ultimately abandoned Quantrill and fled the Midwest to hide out in Texas.

It was easy to tell that the old man wasn't proud of what happened that morning in Lawrence, Kansas, back in August of 1863.

He would always start the story this way: "God's truth is we had some folks riding with us who were just pure mean. No, worse than mean. They were evil, like the devil himself was whispering in their ear. And, Lord help us, we all got ourselves caught up in it that day, Quantrill and everybody riding with him . . ."

It was later written up in all the newspapers, re-

ferred to as "The Lawrence Massacre." Reports estimated that by the time Quantrill had persuaded other
pro-slavery groups to join in the raid, over four hundred men were armed and waiting for his signal to
attack that morning. And in a matter of four hours,
most businesses had been robbed and burned, and an
estimated one hundred and fifty civilian men and
boys had been killed. The old man was ashamed to
tell what happened to many of the women. And it all
happened simply because the town and its people refused to embrace the notion that slavery should remain the law of the land.

That long-ago morning in Lawrence, Quantrill
had gone too far with his insane attempt to bolster
the South's cause. Leaders of the Confederacy and
its military quickly condemned the murderous raid.
Shamed and afraid for their own lives, many of the
Raiders laid down their guns and quietly stole away.
The old man had been among them, adopting a false
name and settling in Wolf Creek.

He'd heard that Quantrill later made several efforts to recapture his lost glory, assembling a small
group of men who were neither disciplined nor well
trained. As they'd headed toward Kentucky early in
1864, they were tracked by a pro-Union posse and
finally cornered in a barn where they had stopped for
the night. During a shootout, a bullet ripped into
Quantrill's spine, leaving him paralyzed. He died a
week or so later, leaving his bloody exploits to the
history books.

The old man waited until another filled glass was
placed in front of him before he continued. His words

were beginning to slur, and, growing tired, he slowly rubbed a shaking hand across his forehead.

"A bunch of us wasn't no more'n kids, seventeen, eighteen years old, back then," he said. "Too dumb to know better and just looking for excitement. We thought we were doing right, but my guess is that most, like myself, regret some of what we done and would just as soon forget it.

"But there were some, the evil-to-the-bone ones, who loved every minute of it and missed it when the shooting and killing was over. Given their druthers, they'd just as soon the war had never ended. Killing was in their blood." Men like brothers Dean and Charlie Boy Ashton.

"The craziest ones I recall had earned their pay breaking horses before joining up with Quantrill. A story passed along to me was that Dean, the older of the two, was trying to get a bridle on this mustang one day and the horse plumb bit off two of his fingers.

"First thing he did was wrap a kerchief around his bleeding hand, then he pulled his pistol and shot the horse dead. After that, he went on to ride and break three other horses before the dinner bell rang.

"His brother was just about as ornery. I was told that anything that wasn't nailed down, he'd steal. And when a man once accused him of cheating in a card game up in Springfield—rightfully so, the story goes—he might near beat him to death. That done, he calmly walked out of the saloon with a big smile on his ugly face."

PART ONE

CHAPTER ONE

Texas
Spring 1866

Rays of warm Hill Country sun streamed through the grape arbors as the congregation made its way down the front steps of the Wolf Creek Family Church. Among the small group was Carl Novak, proud daddy of the young girl who had just sung her first solo at the close of Reverend Benedict's Sunday-morning service.

"I swear, that young lady has the voice of an angel," schoolteacher Dottie Rumley said as she approached Novak and his wife, her arms spread wide in celebration. "She truly does." As several others stepped forward to agree, Lucy, the center of attention, stood close by her mother, embarrassed and anxious to be freed to spend a few minutes playing with the other children before it was time to head home.

Novak, six-two, broad-shouldered, and dark-eyed, hugged his wife a bit tighter than usual and a faint smile crossed his face. A man who spoke sparingly, he rarely left his farm except to come to town for supplies or bring his family to church. He had been home from the war for a year, yet there were a few in Wolf Creek who still cast disapproving looks whenever he passed.

In their minds, he had fought for the wrong side.

When fighting first broke out between the North and the Southern states determined to secede from the Union, Novak spent long days wrestling with the issue that had so divided the country. Members of the Confederate army, many of them his neighbors, were determined to keep the practice of owning slaves alive and well. Up north, meanwhile, men were prepared to shed blood to see that the nation remained whole, the slave practice abolished, and freedom awarded to one and all.

Carl Novak was a hardworking farmer, not a politican; a self-proclaimed simple man who thought about little else but keeping his young family safe and bringing in a decent crop every season. For him, it was a plain and reliable formula for happiness handed down to him by his father. Then war broke out, raising troubling questions and causing him sleepless nights as he came to a realization that he had to take a stand.

Frieda, whom he'd married shortly after they graduated from Wolf Creek School, recognized Novak's struggle. She knew that his best friend as a youngster had been Billy Wayne Jefferson, son of a slave family that was property of the biggest land-owner in Gillespie County. Carl and Billy Wayne hunted squirrels and fished for carp and catfish to-gether, ate dinners at each other's kitchen tables, and gave little thought that they were of different color and social standing. Carl never questioned why Billy Wayne wasn't allowed to attend school with him or join his family at Sunday services. Billy Wayne, meanwhile, ignored others' cruel catcalls when they saw him riding behind Carl astride Sister, the Novak family mule. Their lives had been so simple back then, their feeling for one another genuine, their in-nocent focus on enjoying the moments they were to-gether.

That began to change as Billy Wayne grew older and stronger, capable of joining his father in the own-er's fields. Little time was left for carefree days with his friend. Carl missed that.

Now, years later, as he and Frieda sat on their porch, enjoying the gentle night sounds that settled over their small plot of land, they talked of those days past. Carl had lost track of his boyhood friend. The last time he'd seen Billy Wayne was when he attended the funeral of his father several years earlier. When Carl's mother passed a few years later, Jefferson was not among the mourners. He had vanished, along with the rest of his family.

Over the years, as he'd become more aware of the hardships his friend had endured, Carl saw the injus-tice society had forced on him, feeling guilty that he had not been more aware back when they were children.

In time, Frieda had come to better understand her husband's silent feelings than he did. When she sensed he was considering joining the war, it was she who first suggested he soldier for the Union. "It's what's right to do," she said as she leaned down to scratch behind the ears of Echo, the black-haired sheepdog sleeping at her feet. "It won't be long before things get settled and you can come back home."

It was all Carl Novak needed to hear. The decision made, he began preparations. The cotton had been picked and the soil turned, the smokehouse was filled with pork and venison, and Frieda had put up jars of vegetables from the garden. There was pay for six bales of cotton, next year's seed money, and the small savings his mother had given him before she died, carefully hidden away under the floor of their bedroom.

The following morning he had ridden over to the Williamson place, Echo following close behind, to explain his sudden plan and strike a deal with the oldest son, Lyndon, to keep watch over his wife and daughter in his absence. Though a bit slow, Lyndon was a strong, hard worker and the most trustworthy man Carl knew. Pleased with the responsibility offered him, Lyndon promised he would keep Frieda and Lucy safe, the livestock tended, and the cow milked every morning. The fifty cents a day that he was offered was agreed to with a firm handshake.

Y EARS LATER, CARL remembered their conversation as if it had occurred yesterday.
"When is it you plan on leaving?"

"Sunup tomorrow. I'm thinking I better say my goodbyes and get going before I change my mind. Frieda said tell you she'll settle up with you at the end of every week if that suits you."

"Sounds fair to me," Lyndon had replied, placing a hand on Carl's shoulder. "My pa won't understand you going off to fight with them folks that call themselves abolitionists, but I'll wish you a safe return."

THE MIXED AROMA of biscuits and blackberry muffins wafted from the farmhouse as Carl stood in the doorway of the barn that day. He inhaled a peace and quiet that was almost palpable, miles removed from what he would soon be headed to. Questions rumbled through his mind. Was he doing the right thing? Would his family, the thing he cherished more than anything else in the world, be safe in his absence? Could he really leave behind the role of contented farmer, husband, and father and become a fighter?

Frieda appeared on the front porch, waving toward him. "Breakfast's on the table," she yelled. "Lucy's waiting and says to tell you she's starving."

Inside, his daughter, still in her nightgown, gave him a peck on the cheek before taking her seat.

The parents looked on silently as Lucy hummed while she ate. Despite the fact she had not yet brushed her long auburn hair or even wiped the sleep from her eyes, she was a beautiful child. Carl felt an ache deep inside as he thought back on the unsatisfactory explanation he'd given her at bedtime. All she knew was that Daddy had to go away for a while, assuming he would return home soon and life would return to normal. Frieda, sensing his concern, reached across the table and placed a hand on his arm. "No need to worry," she said. "We're going to be just fine."

A saddlebag filled with biscuits, beef jerky, and fried cracklings sat on the edge of the stove. "I figured you'll be able to find plenty of water, so Lucy suggested we put lemonade in your canteen," Frieda said as she began clearing away the dishes. "I also pinned a little money in the pocket of your spare shirt."

Carl managed a smile. "Don't suppose you thought to polish my boots or saddle my horse," he said.

Frieda laughed and tossed a dishrag in his direction. "Some things you lazy menfolk need to care for yourselves."

What a wonderful woman he'd married, Carl thought as he rose from the table and moved toward her. He ran his fingers through her auburn hair and looked into her hazel eyes. He knew she wouldn't cry. She was too strong-minded for that. He then lifted his daughter into his arms and kissed her brow. "Promise you'll help your momma while I'm gone . . ."

He was going to tell her he loved her, but she beat him to it. "I love you this much," she said, stretching her arms as wide as she could. "More'n the whole world."

Frieda had moved to the doorway, silently holding his hat. She watched as he took his gun belt from its peg and pulled it tight around his waist. He couldn't remember the last time he'd worn it, and the weight of the Peacemaker in its holster felt uncomfortable.

T WO WEEKS LATER, in a Union camp somewhere in eastern Tennessee, he and a half-dozen strangers had enlisted and joined a regiment of soldiers who looked as wary as he felt. It was the beginning of the worst time of his life. In the endless days and nights to come, there were bloody battles at places like Tupelo, Mississippi, and Kennesaw Mountain, Georgia, and others whose names he never knew or quickly forgot. Some of the confrontations were won by the Union, some by the Confederates. In the frantic blur of war, they fought in blazing heat and bone-chilling cold, there was little sleep and food, and medicine seemed always in short supply. As the days and nights ran together, some even had difficulty remembering what the fighting was about.

The only certainty was that men died on a daily basis. Carl Novak, who had grown up a peaceful, God-fearing man, lost count of the number of faceless enemy soldiers whose lives he had taken, of those who had tried to kill him. With each well-aimed shot, each death that was on his hands, he had felt his soul slipping away. In time, only a single goal motivated him and kept him sane: to return home safely to Frieda and Lucy and let them help him forget.

I T WAS ALMOST two years before Confederate general Robert E. Lee finally surrendered, bringing the seemingly endless fighting to an end. Novak had headed for Texas as soon as the news came, feeling no joy in the fact he and the Union had been declared the winner. He was just glad to have survived, to be going home.

When his weary mare, Dawn, had forded the Guadalupe River, a sign that he was less than a mile from the farm, his spirits rose. He was thinner, a scruffy beard covered his face, and his hair hung well below the collar of the tattered uniform he wore. He was still having dark nightmares of the dead and wounded, and likely would for some time to come. He was, he knew, a different man from the one who had ridden away from his family.

As he urged Dawn into a gallop, he prayed that he could somehow recapture the warmth and gentleness of the life he remembered. He couldn't help but wonder if such a miracle was even possible.

As HE NEARED, he was pleased to see that Lyndon had done a good job taking care of the place. The cedar post fences were sturdy, there was a new roof on the smokehouse, the hay was baled, and wood was chopped and neatly stacked at the side of the house. The rich, black soil of the field had been plowed and readied for planting.

Echo was the first to see him coming, barking and happily wagging his tail as soon as the horse and rider appeared on the pathway leading to the farmhouse. Soon Carl's wife and daughter were on the front porch, Frieda waving and Lucy bounding down the steps to catch up with the dog.

Carl's feet had not even touched the ground before

he was smothered in welcoming hugs and kisses. This time, Frieda didn't try to hold back her tears. Lyndon Williamson emerged from the barn, smiling and pumping his hands in the air as he hurried to take the reins of Novak's mare. "I'll see she's fed and rubbed down proper," he said. "You go on in and visit your family. Proud you're home, Mr. Novak."

Frieda took a step back and held her husband at arm's length, smiling. "I bet you're hungry," she said.

Carl freed one hand and gently wiped the tears from her cheeks. "I'm near starved."

"You look it. But you'll not sit at my table until you've bathed, shaved your face, and rid yourself of that filthy uniform. I'll start heating water. We'll wait until later to give you a haircut."

Lifting his daughter into his arms as he moved toward the porch, Carl let out a mock groan. "You've grown up on me, gal," he said. "How old is it you are now?"

"I'm ten. My birthday was two weeks ago. Momma made a cake and Lyndon churned ice cream. Momma put a place for you at the table, even if you weren't there. When she wasn't looking, I gave Echo your ice cream once it melted."

Carl laughed and thought how good it felt. "I'm so sorry I've been missing your birthdays, little one," her daddy said. "I'll not miss anymore. That's a promise."

THE DAYS FLEW past as he reacquainted himself with surrounds that had only been visions in sweet daydreams for so long. He walked the field, breathing in the rich smell of the soil, sat on the bank of the creek, watching as squirrels played chase in the pecan trees. He visited the gravesites of his parents, pleased to find them well kept with purple iris blooming all around them. He mucked out stalls in the barn even though Lyndon's work really made it unnecessary. And in the evenings he sat on the porch, drinking lemonade, counting the stars with Lucy, and whispering thanks that he could hear no gunfire in the distance. In a barrel on the edge of the garden, the remnants of his uniform were nothing but cold ashes, burned the morning after his return.

He had no desire to venture beyond the quiet comfort of home, not even to join his wife and daughter at Sunday services. Whatever he needed from the feed store or the livery, Lyndon volunteered to fetch for him. Frieda understood her husband's reluctance to mingle among the townspeople of Wolf Creek and didn't press the issue. "I just need a little time" was Carl's only explanation, and that was good enough.

Gradually, thanks to his wife's cooking, he regained the lost weight. He and she enjoyed long, quiet conversations, mostly in the evenings and usually about their daughter or the progress of the crops, but never the war. When, occasionally, Lyndon would stop by to see if his friend needed anything, the two men would sit in silence on a bench in front of the barn for a while before Lyndon finally pulled on his hat and said he needed to be getting on back home.

It was Lucy who finally persuaded her daddy to venture into town. She had been practicing the solo the preacher had asked her to learn and would sing on Sunday morning.

Carl Novak knew it was time to come out of hiding.

CHAPTER TWO

T HE TRUTH WAS that the people of Wolf Creek—
most of them, at least—simply wanted to put the
Civil War behind them. Rather than dwelling on its
ugliness, they, just like Novak, were anxious to return
to a normal, peaceful life. The war was over, the dead
were buried and mourned, and memories were gradually growing dimmer. It was time for life to resume.

Carl was pleased that no one at the feed store, the
mercantile, or the church ever questioned his decision to fight for the Union. Nor did they ask for his
recollections of battles he'd engaged in. He sensed
only mild resentment from a few he knew had been
staunch Confederate supporters. Mainly, the world
he'd returned to was more focused on the day-to-day
challenges of life.

So, in time, he began to tend his own errands,
occasionally even taking time to have breakfast in
the café or sit among the old-timers who gathered

in the shade of the huge live oak on the town square
for their endless discussions of local politics, the need
for more rain, or the future fortunes of the town
baseball team.

He was gradually beginning to feel he belonged
again, welcomed back into the arms of his heartland.

It was mercantile owner Bill Vargus who had
called out to him one morning as he was loading pro-
visions onto to his wagon. "I'm proud to see you back
in town now and again," the white-haired old man, a
lifelong resident of Wolf Creek, said. "I can imagine
getting your life back to a normal routine is no easy
task, even with a supporting wife and fine little
youngster like you've got. I just wanted to tell you it's
good to see you out among folks." He paused for a
moment, stroking the hindquarter of Novak's mule.
"You know, if you'll let them, folks will help you get
yourself properly adjusted to being a civilian again.
We got good people here."

Carl removed a glove and extended a hand. "I
know that, Mr. Vargus. I do."

No one was more pleased to see the change in
him than Frieda. "I ever tell you how handsome you
look when you have a smile on your face?" she asked.
"The Gillespie County Fair is just a few weeks off.
Everybody will gather in the park for a picnic and
visiting. There's going to be games for the kids,
fiddling, and dancing. Mrs. Pickett will be selling
her cakes and pies. Lucy's really wanting to go. So
am I."

Her husband nodded. "Then I think we should."

She didn't bother telling him that she had already

begun sewing a new shirt for him to wear to the festivities.

S ITTING ON A blanket shaded by an ancient live oak, they listened to the constant laughter of children playing nearby, the fiddlers tuning their instruments, and the mayor yelling out an announcement to remind everyone that all proceeds from the sale of Mrs. Pickett's baked goods would go toward the purchase of new hymn books for the church. "And before you go filling yourself on brisket and sweets, don't forget to enter the Fastest Man footrace and the horseshoe-pitching tournament that will soon begin," he told the crowd.

Lucy broke away from her playmates long enough to sit a moment with her parents and ask Carl if he was going to run in the race.

"I think not," he said, reaching out to gently stroke his daughter's hair. "I'm so full of your momma's fried chicken and potato salad that I'm not even sure I can get up to walk over and watch."

Showing only mock disappointment, his daughter gave him a quick hug and was off to rejoin her friends, waving as she went.

After putting the dishes away in the wicker hamper, Frieda moved closer and took her husband's hand. "You seem to be enjoying yourself," she said. "I'm glad we came."

"Me too."

"And it seems you've begun sleeping better at night. Have some of the bad dreams gone?"

"All I've been dreaming about lately," he said, "is that we'll have us a good cotton crop." It wasn't an entirely truthful reply. There were still the sweaty nightmares of gunfire and smoke and men lying bleeding and screaming in pain, but they were coming less frequently. The war memories were growing fainter, more distant.

Sitting with Frieda, watching the celebrating going around him, he felt a warm and welcome sense of relaxation begin to flow through his body. He was considering a nap when he heard the bellowing voice of Wilson Blackwood, who had a small ribbon attached to the collar of his shirt. "Won me second place in the horseshoe pitching," he said as he removed his hat and knelt down next to Carl. "I heard you were here and wanted to stop by and say hidy."

Novak and Blackwood had been in the same class in school but had little else in common. Blackwood was the only son of the owner of the Wolf Creek Bank and had wanted for little while growing up. When his father passed following a lengthy bout with tuberculosis, Wilson returned home from a college back east and stepped in as bank president. Professionally, he had a reputation for being fair, honest, and quick to show compassion to customers with financial hardships. Personally, he was a bit of a bore, tolerated by most but really liked by few.

"I've got a little problem I'm hoping you might be able to help me with," he said. "I don't know if you recall Jesse Stillworth. He was ahead of us in school until he quit coming. Not the smartest fella you've ever met and never had much good fortune come his way. Anyway, he had this little farm over near Dink

Falls, just a few acres where he raised rabbits and chickens. Last week he was found dead in his bed by one of his egg customers. Must have just passed in his sleep. The doc says there's no telling how long he'd been dead. Apparently, he wasn't a pretty sight."

The banker gave the entire explanation without taking a single breath. Him talking nonstop and so fast was one of the reasons people avoided him unless they had money business to attend to. The women went to great lengths to stay away since he seemed to always be sweating, in sun or shade, summer or winter.

"Best I can determine, he had no living kin, so the bank is stuck with ten no-good acres of land he never even finished paying for. I was able to find a neighbor who agreed to round up his rabbits and chickens and take them off my hands.

"But he's got this milk cow that badly needs a home. I was wondering if you might—"

Carl attempted to interrupt. "Wilson, you know better than anybody I can't afford to be buying—"

"So here's the proposition I'm prepared to make. You ride over to his place and take her home, free of charge."

Frieda nodded to her husband. "I bet we could sell the extra milk."

Novak stood and shook the banker's moist hand. "I'll go have a look at her tomorrow."

Happy to have resolved the matter, Blackwood quickly doffed his hat to Frieda and was off to find someone else who might have missed seeing his proficiency in the horseshoe-throwing competition.

* * *

A S A FULL moon began to light the warm night sky, Carl and Frieda danced and the fiddlers began playing slower, softer tunes. When his wife wanted to rest, Novak extended his hand to his daughter, leading her to the center of the area roped off for the dancing. Lucy was beaming.

As they kept pace to a waltz, he kissed his daughter on the forehead. "Your dancing is about as fine as your singing," he whispered.

By the time the family was headed home, Lucy was sleeping peacefully between her parents, her head against her mother's shoulder.

"It was a good day," Frieda said as the buggy neared the farmhouse.

Carl nodded, feeling more at peace than he had in years. "Indeed it was," he said, comforted by the thought there would be no bad dreams to spoil his sleep.

I T WAS MIDDAY before he had completed his chores and saddled Dawn for the ride over to the Stillworth farm. Frieda was in the kitchen, trying to recreate Mrs. Pickett's blueberry pie recipe. She stopped kneading dough long enough to wave goodbye.

Later, Carl would bitterly regret not having lingered, having one more cup of coffee and more conversation with his wife.

He set a leisurely pace toward his destination, stopping to allow his horse a long drink from a clear spring, admiring the emerald landscape, and thinking about planting time, which was only days away. And he found himself reflecting on the dances with his wife and daughter the night before and was unaware that he was smiling as he rode.

THE STILLWORTH FARM was deserted and silent, as if all its breath had been sucked away. Novak looked at the ramshackle cabin and saw it was missing windowpanes and that rocks had broken away from the top of the leaning chimney. He decided against looking inside. Instead, he made his way past a row of chicken coops, their open doors swinging gently in the wind, and an unkempt garden as he headed toward the barn. Inside, he was pleased to see that someone had been taking care of the cow. There was hay and fresh water, and she had been recently milked. He figured that Banker Blackwood, as kindhearted as he was talkative, had hired someone to look after her.

"A little lonesome, girl?" Carl said as he scratched behind the animal's ears. Slipping a rope over her head and opening the stall door, he led her into the sunlight. "I'm going to take you where you'll have some company."

The trip home was even slower than the trip out as the cow begrudgingly followed, occasionally bawling and straining against her tether. Carl talked to her reassuringly, and made occasional stops to let her graze and rest. "Not much farther," he kept saying. "We'll be home soon."

Having not eaten since his early-morning breakfast, he was looking forward to having a slice of Frieda's fresh-baked pie.

CHAPTER THREE

THE MOMENT HE saw the screen door of the farm-house open and hanging awkwardly from one hinge, a cold shiver ran through Carl Novak's body. His throat went suddenly dry. Something, he knew, was wrong. He dropped the cow's rope and spurred Dawn, climbing from the saddle even before she reached the porch.

He raced through the empty kitchen, yelling his wife's name. It was when he reached the doorway to their bedroom that he realized why she had not responded. Frieda lay across the bed, her apron and dress covered in blood. Her body was motionless, her lifeless eyes open and focused on the ceiling. Even before he sat next to her and cradled her in his arms, slowly rocking her limp body, he knew she was dead.

He was unaware of the anguished scream that exploded from deep inside him, or of how long he sat on the side of the bed, the world around him gone dark and ugly. He didn't notice that floorboards had been pulled away in the corner of the room and his life savings taken from their hiding place.

Only when Echo's distant barking wakened him from his nightmare did his thoughts turn to his daughter. The louder he called Lucy's name, the more urgently the dog barked. Gently placing a comforter over his wife, he hurried into the yard to determine where Echo was, praying as he ran that his daughter would be with him, alive and safe.

The dog was at the entrance to the root cellar, continuing to bark and pawing at the ground as Carl raced toward him.

He found Lucy huddled in a dark corner, her knees tight against her chin. The sweet smell of damp sod filled the small room. Echo led him to the child and was licking her tearstained face when Carl knelt and gathered her into his arms. She was softly humming the hymn she had sung in church.

"Are you okay? You hurt? I'm here, little one. I've got you. Daddy's got you," Carl said.

As if she had not heard him, Lucy gave no response other than to hold tightly to his shoulders and continue to hum.

Outside, the sun was going down and a cool breeze ruffled through the trees. Carl carried Lucy to the well, pulled his kerchief from his pocket, and washed her face. As he was doing so, she held her hands out to him and he saw the blood that was caked on her palms.

She knew what had happened to her mother. Novak, who hadn't cried since boyhood, felt tears well in his eyes. In a soft voice, he asked several times if she could tell him what had happened, who had visited this horror on their quiet world. Lucy's only reply was to continue humming.

And then, even that went silent. Obviously, she was traumatized, all words and thoughts hidden deeply inside her innocent mind. "We're gonna ride into town and see Doc Turner," Carl said.

His motions were rote, achieved without thought or real plan. He went to the barn and hitched up the wagon. He lifted his frail daughter onto the seat, telling her to wait there while he went into the house. Wrapping Frieda's body in a comforter, he carried her out. As Novak he placed his wife in the bed of the wagon, Echo abandoned his spot next to Lucy to lie beside the body.

Long after they were on their way to Wolf Creek, it had still not occurred to Novak that he'd left the new cow to roam in the yard, unattended, the tow rope still around her neck.

OH, MY LORD, no," Dr. Ralston Turner said as he slowly pulled the covering away. With a hand to his mouth, he looked at Novak, then Lucy. "I'm so sorry. What happened?"

There was little Novak could tell him except for the obvious and the fact his daughter hadn't spoken a word since he'd found her.

"You get Lucy in the house and out of the chill. My daughter Belinda's inside and will see she's made comfortable. I'll be back as soon as I take care of Frieda." The doctor, who had gone off to a Boston university to study medicine, had opted to return to his heartland and assume the role of a country doctor. He also served as the county's vet and under-taker. He climbed aboard Novak's wagon and slowly headed down the street in the direction of the funeral parlor. "I'll also fetch the marshal for you," he called out as Carl and his daughter were met at the door by Belinda Turner. She was already boiling water to make hot tea for the shivering youngster.

Even before the doctor returned, word of the tragedy had begun to spread through town. First to reach the doctor's front porch was Reverend Benedict, closely followed by Dottie Rumley, Lucy's teacher. Soon, over a dozen people were milling about in the twilight, whispering prayers and keeping vigil.

Inside, Belinda had bathed Lucy's face with a warm rag and exchanged a nightgown for the soiled dress she'd been wearing. She urged the child to lie down and get some rest. Lucy's only reply was an empty, distant look and her faint humming.

W HILE THE DOCTOR examined her in the back room, Marshal Toddy Lee Woodson sat in the parlor with Novak. Such violence had been a rarity during his decade of enforcing law and order. Breaking up Saturday-night brawls at the saloon, an occasional theft of livestock, and that almost comical attempt to rob the bank by a couple of drunk brothers years earlier had been the highlights of his career. What he'd just viewed at the funeral parlor had made him sick to his stomach. A beautiful woman, a mother and wife, dead, and for no good reason. And now it was his sworn duty to see that justice was served.

"From what you're saying, it appears whoever

done this was out to rob your place," he said. "How much you reckon they got off with?"

"A few hundred dollars, maybe. Spare money we'd saved away over the years."

The marshal slowly shook his head. "Who knew about your hiding place?"

"Just me and Frieda."

"Nobody else?"

"Not that I know of."

"You got any thoughts—any at all—on who might have done this?"

Novak just shook his head.

Aside from the steady ticking of a nearby grandfather clock, the room had gone silent by the time Doc Turner entered. "She's resting with my daughter watching over her," he said. "Best I can determine, she wasn't physically harmed. She's just badly traumatized. Her mind is shutting everything out."

"Will she be okay?" Novak said.

"Oh, I think so, but it might take some time."

"She didn't tell you anything?" the marshal said.

The doctor moved to sit next to Novak. "Not a word," he said. "With your permission, I'd like to go outside and inform the folks who've been waiting that you and your daughter are okay. It's getting late and people need to get on home."

Novak nodded and waved a hand toward the front door.

In a few minutes the doctor returned, accompanied by Reverend Benedict. The pastor approached and placed a hand on the grieving husband's shoulder. "I'm sorry, Carl. So, so sorry. I can't think of anything else to say except I'm praying for you and

Miss Lucy. I know this isn't the time for decision-making, but with your blessing I'd be honored to make arrangements for a proper funeral."

"I'd much appreciate it," Carl said as he rose on unsteady legs and slowly made his way toward the bedroom. There, for the remainder of the longest night of his life, he sat at his daughter's bedside, gently stroking her hair and wondering what the dark future held for them.

THE SUN WAS just coming up as he stood on the porch, drinking a cup of coffee Belinda had brought to him. He had already been to the livery and hitched up the wagon.

"You ought to get some rest," the doctor's daughter said. "Stay here with Lucy and us today."

Carl handed the empty cup to her. "I've got chores that need doing out at my place," he said. "And I need some time alone to see if I can begin sorting all this out. I thank you for looking after my little girl. Should she ask, tell her I'll be returning shortly."

Belinda made him promise to be back by suppertime.

THERE WAS A discomforting strangeness to the farm as he drove the wagon through the gate. He couldn't remember it ever being so quiet and still. Or so lonely and uninviting.

He found the new cow happily grazing in the garden, the rope still loosely looped around her neck. He led her into the barn, where his other cow waited, and quickly milked them both, then tossed hay into their stalls. He put oats out for Dawn and the mule and scattered grain onto the floor of the chicken coop. It occurred to him that Belinda might like some tomatoes from the garden along with the milk and eggs he planned to take her. For a time he wandered the yard aimlessly, occasionally looking back in the direction of the house, which he could not bring himself to enter. He drew water from the well and splashed it on his face, then sat at the base of the large maple for a while, watching the rope swing he'd made for Lucy as it swayed in the breeze.

Finally, he got to his feet and returned to the barn. Inside, he located his pick and shovel and headed toward the spot near the creek where his parents were buried.

Next to their resting places, bathed in the fragrance of purple and yellow iris, he would dig a new grave.

CHAPTER FOUR

THE FUNERAL AT the Family Church was attended by many townspeople Carl Novak hadn't seen since he'd left for the war. The women had brought flowers from their gardens to arrange around Frieda's casket and the men were dressed in their Sunday best. The choir sang several hymns and Reverend Benedict struggled to get through his carefully prepared sermon. "She was one of Wolf Creek's brightest lights," he said as his voice broke a final time.

Carl and his daughter sat hand in hand in the front pew, their faces blank, their bodies rigid, and their minds still numbed by their sorrow. Lucy, wearing a new dress the doctor's daughter had purchased for her at the mercantile, never changed her expression, even when the choir sang.

While most of the attendees remained after the

service for a piece of one of Mrs. Pickett's cakes and the lemonade Lucy's teacher had prepared, the wooden casket was loaded into the back of Novak's wagon for its trip to the farm and the gravesite that waited. The preacher climbed aboard beside Lucy and put his arm across her shoulders. Several men followed silently on horseback to help with the burial.

I N A SHORT time it was over. At the grave, Reverend Benedict read a brief passage of Scripture, shook Carl's hand, and hugged Lucy before mounting his horse that one of the men had brought along. None who had come to help uttered a word because they simply didn't know what to say.

Only Doc Turner stayed behind as the men slowly rode off into the sunlit afternoon. "We'd be pleased to have Lucy stay on with us for a few days," he said, "while she gets on with her adjusting. Truth is, there's not much more I can do for her—she's going to be fine—but having Belinda close by might be a comfort to her."

"When will she resume talking?"

"That, I can't say. Soon, I hope, but there's no way of knowing. She's had a horrible experience, Carl, something no child should have to deal with. Right now, she's very, very fragile."

"I thank you for all you've done and for the kind offer, but she'll be staying here. Her momma's gone, but this is still her home."

As if to add emphasis to his master's statement,

Echo approached and moved to the child's side, his tail wagging.

T HE NEXT SEVERAL days passed in slow motion. Carl went about his necessary chores but put off planting in order to stay close to his daughter. He cooked her breakfasts she only pushed around on her plate, talked to her endlessly about everything he could think of that might cheer her up, and rarely let her stray from his sight. They took walks through the field and down to the creek. In its shallow waters Novak found a smooth slab of limestone ideal for a headstone. His daughter watched as he chiseled Frieda's name onto it, then, while he put it in place, Lucy picked a bouquet of wildflowers to put at its base. They checked several times a day on a mother hen that was setting, awaiting the arrival of her new chicks. And in the evenings, they sat on the porch, where he read to her until it got too dark for him to make out the words of her favorite fairy tales.

Almost daily, someone arrived with more food: a ham, fried chicken, pots of stew and soup, cobbler, and fresh-baked bread. Most of which went uneaten. The marshal had visited twice, both times to say he had no leads, no clue as to who had invaded the farm and killed Frieda.

And Lucy spoke not a word. She had finally stopped her endless humming and occasionally there was an ever-so-distant gleam in her eyes, yet she said nothing. Her dark and deep sadness tore at Novak's already broken heart.

*   *   *

A WEEK HAD passed since the funeral, and life in Wolf Creek was returning to its normal pace. The sorrow over Frieda Novak's passing was slowly replaced by shops that needed running, chores to tend, and the townspeople's own daily hardships to be dealt with.

It was early morning and Carl was hoeing weeds in Frieda's garden, stopping to occasionally steal glances at Lucy, who sat on the nearby porch steps. On the eastern horizon a bank of boiling black clouds was promising that a much-needed rain might be on the way.

It was Echo's sudden barking that caused Novak to look toward the entrance to the farm. Dismounting to swing the gate free was Lyndon Williamson. It was the first time Carl had seen him since giving him his last pay for tending the place in his absence. Only then did it occur to him that Lyndon had not been among those in attendance at the funeral.

Forcing a smile as Williamson rode toward him, Carl removed his hat. "I hope you're not here to bring more chicken soup or boiled turnips," he said.

Lyndon ignored the jest. "Just come to see how you're getting on, Mr. Novak. Thought you might be needing some help."

Lucy was running toward him, a faint trace of a smile suddenly on her face, and she threw her arms around his waist.

"I been missing you, little gal," Lyndon said.

When she didn't reply, Carl explained that she hadn't spoken since her mother's death.

Williamson's face went tight and cold. "That's what I've come to talk to you about," he said. It looked to Carl as if he was near tears. "I should have come sooner, but I'm ashamed to say it took me time to get up the needed courage."

Sensing there was something seriously troubling his friend, Carl suggested to Lucy that she go into the house and get Lyndon a cup of coffee. "Be careful you don't burn your fingers pouring it," he said as she hurried away. He then motioned for his visitor to join him on the bench in front of the barn.

W HAT HAPPENED IS my fault, Mr. Novak. I'm the one who brought all this pain and sadness on you and your daughter . . ."

A puzzled look crossed Carl's face. "Wait a minute," he said. "I don't understand what you're trying to say. You wouldn't . . ."

"It wasn't done on purpose, I swear. Your wife, she was always nice to me, treated me real good. I meant her no harm. I'm so sorry." His hands were shaking as he spoke.

He stopped talking when Lucy arrived with his coffee.

As his daughter walked back toward the house, Carl pushed the cup toward Williamson's face. "Drink some of this, then take yourself a deep breath. Collect your wits and explain to me what it is you're talking about."

Lyndon took a long drink, then a deep breath. Then he told his story.

* * *

H E HAD BEEN in the Howling Wolf Saloon the night after Frieda had paid him his wages.

"I wasn't intending to stay long," he said, "until these two fellas sat down and started talking. Said they were just passing through and had come in to wet their whistles. They told me they'd proudly served the Confederacy and seemed real friendly. They started buying me beer and asking a lot of questions, like maybe they were thinking of settling here if they could find work. Said they'd done some cowboying on a ranch up in Sunshine County.

"Truth I . . . I let them get me a little drunk. And I reckon I talked too much. Way too much."

Carl stood and brushed at his britches, then started to pace. The painful sorrow that had shrouded him for days was disappearing, turning to anger. "You tell them about this place?"

"One of them asked what line of work I was in and I told them about me working here for Mrs. Novak while you were off fighting for the Union."

"And . . . ?"

"They made some remarks I didn't appreciate. And I told them so."

"What kind of remarks?"

"Saying things like any man who hooked with the North had to be a traitor." Lyndon wiped at his eyes with his kerchief, then began shaking his head. "I told them you were the finest human being I've ever known, Mr. Novak. Swear to God, I did. And I told them if they were going to continue their belittling of you, saying you must be a coward or worse, I was taking my leave.

"They apologized and ordered another pitcher of beer."

Novak kicked at the dirt. "Did you tell them there was money here?"

"They asked if I was paid decent for my work and I told them Mrs. Novak was more than fair to me."

"How did they know where it was hidden?"

"I guess I must have told them. One morning, I was sitting in the kitchen, waiting to get paid. She left the bedroom door open and I saw her lift some boards from the floor and pull out this little metal box. Then she came back in, gave me my wages, and offered me another cup of coffee and one of her sweet rolls. She sat and talked with me a bit, about how anxious she was for you to get home."

Carl's rage boiled to a point where he wanted to lash out at the distraught young man sitting in front of him, to pull him to his feet and give him a beating. Instead, he turned away and calmed himself. "Did they tell you their names? What did they look like?"

"I don't recall getting their names. Could be they were brothers, but I don't remember them mentioning being kin. I'm just guessing on that. The only thing that stuck in my recollection was that one of them was missing a couple of fingers on one hand. He laughed about it when I asked and said a wild mustang bit them off."

Williamson buried his face in his hands and sobbed. "I got your wife killed, Mr. Novak. I'm fully to blame."

Carl looked down on the young man and finally reached out and put a hand against his arm. The rage hadn't disappeared, only refocused toward two nameless men who had destroyed his world.

"I'll need you to come with me and tell this to the marshal," he said.

Across the yard, Lucy sat on the porch, stroking Echo's back as she watched her father and her friend. Again, she was softly humming.

CHAPTER FIVE

MARSHAL WOODSON WAS wiping mud from his boots as the two men entered his small office. A downpour had begun just as Carl dropped his daughter off at the doctor's home in town. "Miss Belinda's been asking about you and wanting to see you," he told Lucy. "You two can visit a bit while I run some errands. I'll be back soon, and when the rain lets up, we'll head on back home."

The marshal nodded as Novak and Williamson walked in. "If there's a muddier street in Texas than the one right outside this door, I want no part of it," he said. "Got myself caught in it when I was returning from the café. Don't get me wrong. I'm glad for this sorely needed rain. I just wish so much of it didn't have to fall on me."

He shook droplets from the brim of his Stetson before placing it on a nearby rack. "You fellas don't look like you're here to confess to rustling any cattle, so what is it I can do for you?"

"Lyndon thinks he knows who killed Frieda," Novak said.

"And who might that be?"

Williamson took a step toward the marshal's cluttered desk, buried his hands in his pockets, and began retelling the events in the Howling Wolf. Neither Woodson nor Novak spoke as the nervous young man recounted his evening spent with the two strangers.

"You recall seeing them after what occurred out at Carl's place?" the marshal finally asked.

"No, sir. That night was the only time I ever saw them."

Woodson scratched at his beard and shuffled a stack of papers on his desk. He looked at Novak, then slowly moved his head to focus on Lyndon. "So, what we've got is a couple of thirsty, nosy men passing through . . . no names . . . no telling where they came from or where they were heading . . . and one's missing a couple of fingers. Interesting as the boy here's story might be, it ain't much to go on."

Sensing the marshal's lack of enthusiasm, Novak spoke up. "They said they had worked on a ranch up in Sunshine County."

"Don't reckon these were the types who might be inclined to lie a bit, do you?"

Carl felt his anger slowly return, like a slow-boiling kettle. Outside a clap of thunder brought a curse from Woodson as he turned to the lone window in his office.

"Seems we've been a bother, wasting your valuable time," Carl said as he grabbed Lyndon's arm and led him toward the door.

"You boys ought to stay until the rain lets up," the

marshal said. "I've got coffee I brought over from the café."

"No thanks," Novak replied as he shoved his hat tight onto his head. "I've got things to do."

Having removed his muddy boots on the front steps, Carl sat in the doctor's parlor, watching as Belinda and Lucy drew a multicolored picture of a rainbow. He shifted in his chair occasionally, embarrassed at having realized there was a sizable hole in one of his socks. It was something his wife would never have allowed to happen.

A mixture of emotions raced through his mind as he watched his daughter carefully select the colors she planned to use. How he wished to hear her burst out in laughter, to call his name, to recite some silly nursery rhyme or break out in song. Just speak and return to being the innocent and happy ten-year-old she was such a short time ago.

Mixed with that wish was the image of two faceless, nameless men whom he had already come to hate. It was like a hammer beating against his chest, the blows growing faster and increasingly painful.

"I'm going to start us some supper," Belinda said as she watched Lucy add a yellow half-moon to their drawing. Outside it was growing dark and the rain continued to beat against the side of the house. "No telling when Daddy will be able to get home. He left this morning to go out to Gil Brewster's place and tend some ailing sheep. He might wind up bedding down with them in Gil's barn if the weather doesn't soon improve."

"I've already imposed . . ."

"No way am I letting you two leave this house tonight," Belinda said. "Lucy can sleep with me and you can take Daddy's room. If he does show up, there's a bedroll and extra pillows in the front closet."

Carl didn't argue, instead tucking his foot and frayed sock out of sight.

S LEEP FOR NOVAK was impossible. After supper he had read Lucy a story before tucking her in. Then he lay in the dark room next door, listening to the rain, his mind racing. Several times he left the doctor's bed and stood by the window, watching puddles grow in the street outside.

By the time the rain ended and the sun peeked from behind the church spire, he had reached a decision.

When Lucy left the breakfast table to go dress, Carl reached across the table and took Belinda's hand. "I've got another favor to ask before we head to the farm," he said.

Her reply was a warm smile.

"In a couple of days, after I make some arrangements, I'm going to be gone for a while. Can't say for how long or exactly where it is I'm going. But I can't take Lucy with me and was wondering if she could stay with you for a bit. I'd appreciate it if you would think on it and talk it over with the doctor. I'll gladly pay."

"You'll pay nothing. And I can tell you right now that my daddy would love having Lucy around. He's always wanted a granddaughter. We'll take good care of her."

"I thank you kindly," Carl said.

"I've got only one thing that we'll need from you—a promise."

"What's that?"

"That you make sure you come back safe to us and your little girl. You know she loves you very much."

Novak nodded. "I know," he said. "I just wish she could tell me so."

F OR THE NEXT few of days he made ready. Aside from seeing that all was in order on the farm and fumbling through a weak explanation to Lucy about why she would be staying at Dr. Turner's house for a while, there was really little to do. The barn was clean, ample hay piled inside and the oat barrel filled. He had folded clothes for his daughter into a duffel bag, filled a basket of vegetables from the garden, and taken them into town to Belinda.

He had set aside his displeasure with Lyndon Williamson and his foolish mistake and ridden over to ask that he again look after the place in his absence. "I'll need to wait on paying you until I can sell my crop," he said. "In the meantime, help yourself to the smokehouse and whatever comes ripe in the garden. You'll also have plenty of milk and coffee's on the shelf over the stove. Just make yourself at home."

He cleaned the Peacemaker he hadn't touched since his return home and began wearing his gun belt to get familiar with its weight against his hip. And even as he did, he wondered if his plan was nothing more than a fool's errand. The doubt, however, was overshadowed by a palpable and powerful need to do something to avenge his wife's murder.

On the foggy morning he planned to leave, he rose early and paid a visit to Frieda's grave, then returned to the barn to saddle Dawn. Waiting for him were Lyndon and a young man he didn't recognize.

"Morning, Mr. Novak. I want to introduce you to my friend Cy Butler. He and his pa got a little place over near ours. They just came here after the war ended."

Butler nodded and removed his hat to reveal a shock of flaming red hair that matched the row of freckles running across the bridge of his nose. He was muscled and tanned, signs of a strong work ethic. "Pleased to know you," he said.

"Cy here is going to be looking after your place," Lyndon said. "I can vouch for him being trustworthy, hardworking, and good people. I've told him what'll need doing. Also, his uncle Milton will be coming out shortly to help see that your planting gets done. I've done explained about you not being able to pay right now and took it on myself to mention you've got an extra milk cow you might like to have taken off your hands. He says him and his family are getting weary of drinking goat's milk and would welcome a change."

Butler nodded. "If the cows haven't been milked this morning, I can tend to it."

Carl gave no reply as he stared at the bedroll strapped behind Lyndon's saddle and the leather scabbard that held a rifle Lyndon had borrowed from his father. "Maybe you should tell me what's going on."

"I'm riding out with you."

"I don't think that's—"

"I've done had this argument with my pa," Lyndon said. "No need you and me having it, too. I've got things to make up for as best I can. I owe you that, so I'm going. I'll either ride alongside you or trail behind, that'll be your choice to make."

Novak checked to see that Dawn's bridle was in place, then stroked the horse's neck for several seconds. Finally, he looked up at Lyndon and smiled. "I'll be glad for the company," he said.

T HE SUN WARMED the early morning and burned the fog away as the two men rode side by side. The air was sweet with the smell of cedar and wildflowers as they settled into an easy pace, stopping occasionally to let their horses drink from the pools left by the recent rain.

"I'd admire to hear what plan you've got, Mr. Novak," Lyndon finally said as they were climbing back into their saddles.

"First," Carl said, "is to have you stop addressing me as 'Mr. Novak' and call me by my given name. Beyond that, the best I can say is we're heading up into Sunshine County to start looking and listening."

CHAPTER SIX

THE SETTLEMENT OF Cinco Gap loomed in the distance just before noon. After camping for the night in a shallow ravine, eating a supper of the fried bread and canned peaches Lyndon's mother had sent along, both men were anxious for some stove-cooked food and hot coffee.

Novak had said little during the first day's ride, choosing to focus on the terrain ahead while keeping his thoughts to himself. Though dozens of questions swirled in Williamson's head, he opted to respect his companion's silence. The only sounds were the clicks of their horses' hooves against rocky ground and the grackles that flew from tree to tree, branch to branch, engaged in a high-pitched cawing argument.

Only as they neared town did Carl speak. "It's not likely we'll learn anything of use until we get up into Sunshine County," he said. "That's still another good day's ride. But, so you'll know, we need to be careful of the manner in which we go about asking questions.

We don't want to come off sounding like lawmen or bounty hunters chasing down some outlaws. Should anyone inquire, we're just two out-of-work cowboys looking for someone who'll offer us a payday."

"I figure on letting you do the talking," Lyndon said. "I'm going to be too busy eating me some ham and eggs."

THE OLD FARMER who sat in the corner table of Miss Bessie's Café & Bar finishing up his biscuits and gravy made it clear there would be no work found in Melton's Chapel. "You boys have come to the wrong place," he said with a chuckle. "What few folks that's left here are wanting to hightail it out as soon as they can. The ones not thinking that way are mostly like me, too old and stove up to do anything but stay and sit, counting the days until the Maker calls our name."

As he spoke, Bessie took their order. "I got nothing fancy," she said. "There's a few biscuits left, and some cream gravy I can warm. Got plenty of eggs I can fry up."

Carl smiled up at the rotund, sour-faced owner. "Got any coffee to go along with that?"

"Coffee, I've got," she said. "Don't recall seeing you folks before."

Novak's reply was more for Lyndon's benefit, a lesson on how to respond and make inquiries. "We're headed north," he said. "An old war buddy of mine said he found work breaking horses for some rancher up that way. We're hoping to catch up to him and see if his boss is still hiring. Could be, he came through here. A kind of ugly-looking old boy who has a couple of fingers missing on one hand."

Bessie glanced toward the old man in the corner and saw he was shaking his head. "Don't think he ever stopped in here," she said as she tossed a frayed dishrag over her shoulder. "Best I get to cooking . . . so long as you boys got money to pay."

"We've got money," Carl said, digging into the pocket of his britches.

B EFORE MOUNTING THEIR horses, they looked down the dusty street of the dying and dingy town. Aside from the café and bar they'd just left, there was a feed store with a rusting tin roof, what appeared to have once been a bank, now boarded up, and a small grocery and dry goods store. The only sign or sound of life was a blacksmith down the way, pounding on a stubborn wagon axle.

"If this place don't make a man homesick," Carl said, "I can't think of what could."

"I saw what you done in there," Lyndon said, "how you made conversation and asked questions. Watching and listening to you was almost as good as Miss Bessie's breakfast."

Novak was pleased to have made his point.

For the remainder of the day they continued their journey, occasionally stopping at a farmhouse or cabin. Saying they were in need of directions, Carl always managed to mention that he was looking for an old friend. None he spoke to could remember a man with missing fingers.

"We're not far enough west yet," he told Williamson

as they rode away from a little farm where goats and chickens ran free and three little girls played in the shade of an ancient oak. After he waved to them as he passed, Novak's thoughts turned to his own daughter.

And again doubts entered his mind. He knew the danger of his uncharted mission and again questioned whether avenging Frieda's death was worth the risk of Lucy growing up without either parent. He was no gunfighter, no great marksman. And now he was putting Lyndon at risk as well. The negatives were overwhelming, yet masked by the anger that drove him. So long as he maintained the burning hatred he felt toward the men he was searching for, he would continue his search. But he needed to explain his concerns to the young man who had insisted on coming along.

That evening, as they made camp, he watched Lyndon poking a stick at the embers of the campfire. "Collard greens and cold corn bread don't match Miss Bessie's cooking," Williamson said, attempting to draw the sullen Novak into conversation.

"Lyndon, we need to have ourselves a serious talk."

"I ain't going back, Mr.—Carl."

"Just hear me out and then do yourself some hard thinking."

Sensing the argument Novak was about to make, Lyndon got to his feet. "I can figure what you're thinking and planning to say," he said. "I'm no fighter, never went off to the war like you, and I'm not as smart as most folks. Truth is, I can't rightly say how much use I'll be to you if . . . when . . . we catch up to the fellas we're looking for. But you can rest assured I'm gonna do my best. I got amends to make and a feeling of shame that gnaws at my insides every time I think on what I done. So, don't go trying to get me to turn tail and head back. Not until we've finished what needs doing."

Lyndon's speech took Carl by surprise. He picked up a dead branch, tossed it onto the fire, and began to idly draw circles in the dirt. Finally, he nodded. "Then I reckon we'll keep on riding," he said.

Soon they were sleeping. Lyndon snored and Carl dreamed, not of past war battles or angry revenge, but of his wife. In his dream, they were dancing.

T HE LANDSCAPE CHANGED dramatically as they continued northward. The lush rolling hills were behind them, replaced by flat stretches of hard-packed black dirt and thorny mesquite bushes. The air seemed drier and the sun warmer.

It was Lyndon who first saw the riders on the horizon. Though they were still a distance away, it appeared to be two men, leading four horses that weren't saddled.

"If it wasn't for the fact we're out here ourselves, I'd say this is a strange part of the country for people to be traveling," Novak said, brushing back his coat to make sure his sidearm was visible. "We'll approach them, all nice and friendly, but don't go letting your guard down." He stepped up Dawn's pace to put him a stride in front of Williamson.

As they approached the riders, one waved his hat and yelled, "Howdy. You fellas got yourselves lost?"

He was small and bony, missing a tooth in front. Maybe eighteen or nineteen. The other was a spitting image. Brothers, most likely.

"Oh, I figure we'll know where we're going once we get there," Novak said. "Where is it you boys are headed?" He was looking at the trailing horses, each with nothing but a halter, as he spoke. "Fine-looking animals you got there."

"Taking them down south to a man looking to buy them," the other rider said. "Our pa just passed, and since we've got no use for extra mounts . . ."

"Your pa used two different brands, did he?" Carl said. Two of the horses had linked triangles on their hindquarters, the others, a boxed number seven.

The smile quickly disappeared from the stranger's face as he clearly struggled for an explanation. "My recollection is Pa bought them off some rancher friends while we were away in the war." He quickly tried to change the subject. "You boys wouldn't have any extra coffee, would you?"

"Sorry," Carl said as he continued to examine the horses. "We're running low . . . I particularly admire that big mare."

The riders were growing nervous, their hands slowly moving toward their scabbards. "You law?" one asked.

Novak laughed. "You see us wearing any badges?"

"Then I reckon we'll be on our way. We've still got a long ride."

Novak waited until they were well out of earshot before turning to Lyndon. "Horse thieves," he said.

For the next several miles he stole glances back in the direction they had headed. He said nothing about it to Williamson, but wanted to make sure the two men didn't decide to turn back and try to take their horses.

By late afternoon they had begun to see long stretches of barbed wire fence and longhorns lazily grazing in the distance. "I'm pretty sure we've arrived in Sunshine County," Novak said after taking a long drink from his canteen. "We'll find us a place to bed down for the night, then go calling first thing in the morning."

THE OWNER OF the Broken Spur was not hard to spot. Jeb Sampson's britches were neatly creased, his boots had a shine, and a corncob pipe was clenched between his teeth. He was not standing at the corral to await his turn at branding the new calves, just watching. His bulging stomach was indication that he much preferred a hearty breakfast to saddling up for an early-morning ride out to the pasture.

Still, he was friendly enough, smiling at the visitors. "You boys haven't come back to steal more of my horses, have you?" he said, ending his question with a booming laugh. A few feet away, there was the sizzling sound of hot iron on flesh, then a calf's plaintive bawling as it was released. "Climb on down and tell me what you think of my crop of newborns, then state what brings you to the Broken Spur."

Novak began his practiced explanation, saying he and his partner were looking for work and had been told by a friend to try some of the ranches up this way. Even before he could mention missing fingers, Sampson was shaking his head.

"I can barely afford the help I've got," he said. "Haven't done any hiring in a while and don't expect I will anytime soon. What little help I've got has been with me since they were teenagers. To be plumb honest with you, things are a might tight. You could have better luck up in the north part of the county. There's bigger spreads there. Maybe try the Running X or the Bar 99. Most likely, they're what your friend was telling you about."

Novak tipped his hat. "We appreciate your time," he said, noticing the newly burned brand on one of the calves. "And sorry to hear your horses got stole. If some of your boys were to ride due south, they just might catch up with the two fellows who took them."

Lyndon was smiling as they left. "What caused you to tell him who stole his horses?" he said.

Carl shrugged. "My guess is they took off with his best broodmare. If she was mine, I'd be wanting her back."

"You figure there'll be shooting if they catch up to them?"

"Wouldn't surprise me. But that's not the fight we're looking for."

If they did find it, Williamson knew full well, there would definitely be shooting—and probably killing. As he thought about it, he didn't know if he was excited or more scared than he'd ever been.

Over the next two days they visited three more ranches with no success. Weary and discouraged, they arrived in the town of Cinco Gap late in the afternoon and immediately went in search of the livery. "Our horses have earned themselves a bucket of oats and soft hay to rest on for the night," Carl said.

The owner was dozing in a rocking chair out front as they arrived. Wakened by the approaching horses, he quickly got to his feet and rubbed at his eyes. "What is it I can do for you folks?" he said. "Looks like you been hard traveling." He scratched at his beard and spat tobacco juice out into the dusty street. "Prine Livery at your service. Name's Earl Prine."

"We'd like our horses fed and tended," Carl said.

"Yes, sir, you've come to the right place. A stall and a bucket of oats will cost you thirty-five cents each. If you're of a mind to bed down with your horses, it'll cost a half dollar. You can wash the trail dust off in the trough out back. Morning coffee's free till the pot's empty." Pointing up the street, he told them the location of the café and saloon.

"I'm both thirsty and hungry," Novak said as he removed Dawn's saddle. "My suggestion is we whet our appetite with a beer, then see about us some supper."

Williamson's thoughts flashed back to his drunken night in the Wolf Creek saloon. "Maybe I'll just help Mr. Prine get the horses settled and meet up with you later," he said.

THE DIMLY LIT saloon smelled of stale beer, day-old coffee, and lingering cigar smoke. It was anyone's guess when the spittoons had last been emptied or the floors swept. Still early, the only patrons were four men, three elderly and one who looked to be in his twenties, sitting at a table toward the back of the room, playing poker.

Weary and discouraged, Carl stared glumly at a jar of hard-boiled eggs and pickled pig's feet floating in brine while waiting for his beer. His thoughts bounced from his daughter back home to what he and Lyndon might do next. Neither possibility lifted his spirits.

"Mister, you seem a million miles away," the bartender said as he carefully lined up clean glasses along a nearby shelf.

"Just a little tired," Carl said, removing his hat and setting it on the stool next to him.

The conversation was ended.

He lost track of time, sipping at his warm beer, daydreaming. Perhaps he was, in fact, on a fool's errand. Could be it was time to turn back and be with his little girl, tend his farm, and get on with living as best he could. Maybe, just maybe, the anger would eventually go away little by little until he would someday feel whole again. It seemed maybes were all he had.

O VER AT THE poker table, loud cursing suddenly broke out. The oldest member of the group was on his feet, waving a bony finger in the face of the young player. "You've been cheating all afternoon," he said, "and I'll thank you to return my money and get on out of here."

Even before he completed his sentence the accused was on his feet, his hand on his holster. The other players sat in silence, watching the exchange. It

was when the old man threw a half-full glass of beer
across the table, that the other drew his pistol and
cocked the hammer. "Killing you over a two-dollar
wager seems a bargain to me, old man," he said, smiling to show a row of crooked, yellow teeth. By the
slurring of his words it was obvious he was drunk.

Without thinking, Novak was on his feet and rushing toward the table. "Whoa," he said. "Let's think
about calming things down before somebody gets
hurt. No need to—"

The young cardplayer turned his pistol toward
Carl. "I'd just as soon drop you as well," he said,
"even though this ain't none of your business."

Novak moved closer. "Hey, take yourself a deep
breath and give me the gun before you get yourself in
more trouble than you've got need for."

In reply, the gunman squinted one eye in an attempt to aim, then pulled the trigger. The bullet
nicked Novak's shoulder and ripped away a piece of
his shirt before burying in the wall. Ignoring the
burning sensation of his wound, Carl took a step forward and knocked the shooter to the floor with a
single punch. He then placed a boot against the
young gambler's neck. Instinctively, he started to
reach for his own gun but thought better of it.

When the marshal entered, the shooter was still on
his back, cursing and screaming, trying to push Novak's boot away.

Normally, Marshal Del Wisenhunt paid no attention to bar fights until much later in the evening. But
the bartender had run into the street, frantically waving his arms and yelling for help, as the marshal was
on his way home for supper.

He surveyed the situation while hitching up his pants. "Seems you boys started your serious drinking a little early," he said. Moving Novak away, he reached out to the young man and helped him to his feet. "A bit wobbly, ain't you?" he said. "I got a place down the street where you can sleep it off."

Turning to Novak, he saw that a trickle of blood had stained his sleeve and held out his kerchief. "Don't need you bleeding all over my jail cell," he said.

Novak was surprised to realize that he recognized the man. It was the gravelly voice more than the marshal's physical appearance. "I know you, don't I?" he said. "You were the law in Wolf Creek back in the day."

Wisenhunt took a step toward Novak, giving him a long, silent look before replying. "Yep, that's where I was born and raised," he finally said. "Wore the badge there long before I wound up at this godforsaken place." He made no mention of how he had allowed himself to be seduced by the promise of higher pay to keep the peace in Melton's Chapel, or how sorely he regretted the decision. "You're Jeb Novak's boy, I'm guessing. Me and him, we were once friends. You were still wearing short britches . . ."

"You're arresting me?"

"Seems only fair, at least until we get this sorted out. I got two cells, so you won't be sharing with your friend here." By then, a deputy had arrived. "Take 'em and lock 'em up," the marshal said. "I gotta get home and eat my supper."

By the time Wisenhunt returned to his office, the three other poker players were waiting. They began speaking all at once as he hung his hat and made his way to his desk. In short order it was clear to the marshal that the instigator of the ruckus had been Bobby Ray Shelton, just as he expected. The no-good son of the town's attorney-at-law was quite familiar with the inside of Wisenhunt's jail.

"The boy's got too much money and too little sense," the marshal said. He turned and shouted in his direction. "You could have got somebody killed, you idiot. Me and your daddy, we're going to have us a long talk about what needs to be done about you when he comes around in the morning."

Bob Ray only moaned and turned his face to the wall. His jaw ached, his throat throbbed, and he felt like he was going to throw up.

Wisenhunt took the keys from his desk drawer and opened Novak's cell. "Don't think I've had the pleasure," he said. "I hope you'll excuse the confusion. I didn't honestly figure you was at fault in any of this. Just had to be sure." He extended his hand. "I got some black tar salve we can put on that shoulder. Appears to be only a flesh wound, but you don't want to allow it to get infected."

Carl introduced himself, then undid the blood-spotted bandanna and handed it to the marshal. "Sorry to have soiled it," he said. He knew he should be enraged at being thrown in jail but found himself liking the chubby little lawman.

"You wanting to file any charges against the boy? Honest truth is, I'd dearly love to throw the book at him if it didn't involve so much paperwork. Even if I did, his rich daddy would probably find a way to get him found not guilty."

"Naw, I'm just passing through and got other things I need to do."

"I can at least offer you a cup of coffee. My deputy just brewed it." As Wisenhunt spoke, he heard another loud moan from the cell. "Bobby Ray, if you make a mess in there like you done the last time you was here, you're cleaning it up," the marshal called out.

CHAPTER SEVEN

Y OU HAVEN'T BEEN fully honest with me about looking for cowboy work," Wisenhunt said. He and Novak had gone through a half pot of coffee while they sat on the office steps, enjoying the evening breeze. "My guess is you've come this way because you're looking for somebody. Not that it's any of my business, of course. Unless you figure on breaking the law."

"What makes you think I'm looking for anybody?"

"In my years as a lawman, I've come to have a pretty good feel about people. It's part of my sworn-to duty. You got an angry look in your eyes, boy, even though it don't rightly suit you. I'm guessing right, ain't I?"

"I don't even have a name," Novak admitted. To his surprise, he was suddenly eager to share his grief.

Wisenhunt interrupted only once. "Lost my wife, too," he said. "Giving birth at her age was too much.

Buried her and our little boy together. The midwife women did all they could, but . . ." His voice trailed off. "That was a long time ago."

"Does it still pain you?" Carl said.

"Every day, every night."

There was a long silence before Novak continued. He talked of the funeral, of burying Frieda, of his troubled daughter, whose lyrical voice had gone mute, of the two unknown men who had forever changed his life. It was when he mentioned that one had fingers missing that the marshal got to his feet.

"Don't reckon the name Ashton, Dean Ashton, has any meaning for you," he said.

Novak shook his head. "Who's he?"

"Him and his brother, Charlie Boy, spent time in my jail more than once back when they were working out at the Bar 99. Mischief-making, mostly, but they seemed capable of a lot worse. Some folks, you can tell, are just bad people. And as I recall, Dean, the oldest, had a couple of fingers gone."

"They still at the Bar 99?"

"Last time I had them locked up, the foreman came in, pitched them their wages through the bars, and told them their jobs were done and not to come back. Though I have my doubts, someone out at the ranch might know where they were headed. If you like, I'll ride out there with you in the morning and we can do some asking."

As the marshal spoke, Lyndon came running toward them, bits of livery straw still in his hair, his shirttail flapping. "I woke up and seen you weren't bedded down in Dawn's stall," he said, his voice more high-pitched than usual. "A fella down at the saloon told me you got yourself thrown in jail." He looked at Novak's bloodstained sleeve. "You hurt?"

Carl smiled. "I'm fine," he said. "Actually feeling better than I have in a while." He introduced Lyndon to the marshal and recounted their conversation about the Ashton brothers.

Wisenhunt shook Lyndon's hand. "Speaking of the saloon, I best get down that way and see what fools are fighting and tearing up furniture. You boys go get you some sleep and we'll meet up at the café in the morning. The old man who does the cooking makes the finest bowl of grits you'll ever taste."

T HE FOREMAN OF the Bar 99 whittled a chew from his plug of tobacco. Tall and tanned with steely blue eyes, he was a man who had spent his entire life working outdoors. He had an easy smile that belied the fact the workers under his watch viewed him as a tough and demanding taskmaster. Everyone called him Boss.

"I've got no idea which way they might've headed," he said, "but good riddance. Last I seen of them was when they came to collect their belongings. Dean gave me a cussing like I never heard before, then they just rode off. My guess is they went looking for another ranching job.

"When they were of a mind, they were good workers, especially when it came to breaking horses, but they spent way too much time looking for ways to make trouble. Wasn't anybody in my crew who cared for them, I'll tell you that. Truth is, I made a mistake

when I suggested to the owner that he hire them, let
the fact they'd just finished fighting in the war cloud
my judgment."

Carl made an effort to hide his disappointment.
Once again, he was looking down a cold trail with no
idea of what direction it might lead.

"My last word on the matter," Boss said, "is that
they most likely headed for the nearest saloon that
wasn't the one where the sheriff arrested them. Mood
they were in, I'd figure getting drunk and doing some
fighting was high on their list of things to do."

"Junction Valley," the marshal said as he turned to
Novak. "That's the closest town to Cinco Gap. Maybe
a half day's ride. When I get back to the office I'll
send a telegram to the marshal there and see if he's
had any dealings with your friends."

"Not my friends."

"Just a figure of speech," Wisenhunt said as he
nodded thanks to the foreman.

A S THEY RODE back toward town, Lyndon tried to
improve Carl's sour mood. "Least we've got
names now," he said. "We're gonna find them."

When Carl didn't reply, Wisenhunt tried to help.
"It's been my experience in matters of this nature
that patience is a man's best friend. You take one step
forward, another back, but keep on going, even if
progress comes in small drips. Look on it this way:
Yesterday, you didn't even know who it is you're after.
Tomorrow, God willing, you'll find out something
more. And the next day, who knows?"

It didn't take as long as the marshal suggested.

Late in the afternoon, he hurried down to the livery, waving a telegram. Carl and Lyndon were grooming their horses with brushes borrowed from the owner.

"The Junction Valley marshal's seen 'em," he said with no attempt to hide his excitement. "They got thrown in his jail just a couple of nights ago after pistol-whipping the saloon owner, who wouldn't continue serving them."

"They still there?"

"Far as I know," Wisenhunt said. "I say we head that way at daylight. I've already told my deputy I'll be leaving him in charge for a spell."

"I'd say we go now," Carl replied, tossing aside his brush and reaching for a saddle blanket. He had no reservations about riding through the night.

"Like I told you . . . patience," Wisenhunt said. There was a no-argument firmness in his voice. "We'll head out at first light. I'll not have my horse stepping in a gopher hole he can't see and breaking a leg. Get some rest and I'll see you boys in the morning."

D EAN ASHTON WAS pacing back and forth in the tiny jail cell. Five steps one way, five steps the other, cursing under his breath. His brother, wearing only his long johns and socks, was stretched out on the wooden bunk, eyes focused on the ceiling.

"Put your boots on," Dean yelled. "Your feet stink so bad it's making me plumb dizzy."

As Charlie Boy obeyed, his brother continued to walk back and forth. "I've got a plan for how we can get out of this stink hole," he said. They had been locked up for three days and the marshal had told them they would remain in custody until the circuit judge made his monthly visit. Marshal Jackson couldn't say when to expect him. He had mentioned that there was every chance that when he did arrive and hear what had caused the barkeeper to still be unconscious and near dead, their next stop would be Huntsville and the state prison.

"I ain't going to no prison," Charlie Boy said for maybe the hundredth time, barely holding back tears.

"Shut up and listen to what I've got to say." Dean knelt beside his brother and whispered his escape plan.

F OR A MAN whose schemes had rarely, if ever, been successful, this time Dean's worked like a charm, thanks to the marshal's less-than-bright son, who worked as the night jailer and cleanup man. It was also his duty to see that coffee had been brewed by the time his daddy arrived in the mornings.

It was well after midnight when the elder Ashton began banging a fist against the bars and calling for help. He said his head was starting to bleed again from where he'd been hit with the butt of pistol while being arrested. "And I got me a fever something fierce," he screamed.

The noise finally woke the young jailer. He took a pistol from the desk, put it in the waist of his pants, and made his way back to where the cell was located. He could see that Charlie Boy was on the cot, apparently sleeping. He pointed a finger at Dean. "Keep raising this kind of ruckus and you'll wake your brother . . . and half the people in town," he said.

"I'm hurting bad, real bad."

"Nothing I can do. I'll see about fetching the doctor once it gets daylight. If my daddy says it's okay."

"Maybe you could just bring me a drink of water and a damp rag for the fever?"

When the jailer returned carrying a tin cup, Charlie Boy was no longer on the cot. Instead, he'd moved into a shadowy corner of the cell. As the jailer attempted to hand the water to Dean, the younger Ashton grabbed his arm and jerked it sideways. The sound of a bone breaking was drowned by a pained scream. Dean placed a hand behind the jailer's head, jerked it toward the cell door, and repeatedly pounded his forehead against the iron bars until he was unconscious.

"The keys are on his belt," Dean said as he reached to get the jailer's pistol.

In minutes they were out the back and into a dark alley. Charlie Boy kicked at a stray dog that yelped and ran toward the street. The jailer, still unconscious, had been locked in his own cell.

"I was told," Dean said, throwing the ring of keys to the roof of the marshal's office, "that our horses are being kept in the corral out back of the livery."

"What about our saddles?" Charlie Boy said.

"No time to take the risk of hunting for them. What we've got to do is get ourselves out of here before we're seen. We can steal us some saddles once we put some distance between ourselves and this godforsaken place."

THE MARSHAL'S FIRST hint that something was wrong came when he saw his morning coffee hadn't been brewed. He was cussing his son as he walked to the back and saw him lying in the cell, moaning and cradling his broken arm. Suddenly more concerned than angry, Marshal Jackson went in search of the spare jail key.

While he was rummaging through his desk drawer, rancher Pete Stanley burst through the front door. "I've come to report a robbery," he said as he tried to catch his breath. "Somebody broke into my barn during the night and made off with a couple of my finest saddles."

Jackson shook his head and rubbed at the stubble on his chin. "Well now," he said, "ain't this day off to a great start."

The doctor arrived to see to the injured jailer just ahead of Carl, Lyndon, and Wisenhunt. The marshal was sitting behind his desk, nervously drumming his fingers as the new visitors explained their reason for traveling to Junction Valley.

"If it's the Ashton brothers you're looking to see, they're gone," Jackson said. "Lord knows where. First jailbreak I've had since taking on this job." He explained what they had done to the local bartender, then to his son. "They're mean and crazy, you can believe that. If I can find them, you'll not likely get a chance to talk to them . . . 'cause I'm gonna shoot 'em dead, then feed 'em to the hogs."

CHAPTER EIGHT

THE STANLEY RANCH was seven miles to the east of Junction Valley, five hundred acres stretching along the banks of the winding Cabbott Creek. Having calmed somewhat, the cattleman agreed to join Jackson and his visitors for breakfast before heading home. Sitting across from Novak, staring at his untouched grits and bacon, the marshal was thinking out loud. "At least we can figure which way they're likely headed," he said. "For what reason, I don't have the slightest notion except for them wanting to get as far from here as they can. If I can get a posse rounded up and ready to head out, we might be able to pick up their trail before they get too far."

"Don't worry yourself about a posse," Carl said. "You stay put and keep watch over your boy. We'll go after them. That's what we came here for."

"I've got boys who could ride with you," Stanley offered.

"Thanks, but the three of us can travel faster,"

Carl said. "We'll do our best to see your saddles are returned. Along with those who stole them."

"If you bring them in—dead or alive—I'll see to it you receive a proper reward," Jackson said. He stood, tipped his hat to the waitress, and headed across the street to the doctor's office.

For the next few minutes, those remaining watched Lyndon finish off his scrambled eggs, then pull Jackson's plate across the table and start on it. "Son, you must have yourself a hollow leg," Wisenhunt said.

T HEY REACHED CABBOTT Creek just before noon, after briefly stopping at Stanley's ranch house, where the cook prepared them a sack of tortillas and jerky to take along. "And there's sweetened lemon water in this canteen," the plump Black woman said, handing it to Lyndon.

The owner urged them to wait a few seconds longer as he went into the house and returned to the porch with a rifle and a pouch filled with shells. "This might come in handy if you can't get close enough to use your Peacemaker," he told Novak.

"I'll see you get it back . . . along with those saddles."

"If we'd stayed much longer," he told Wisenhunt, "our horses couldn't have taken the load."

Cabbott Creek was rock-bottomed, its swift-running water shallow and clear. While their horses drank, Wisenhunt and Novak walked along the bank, hoping to find hoofprints. "Don't know about you," the marshal said, "but I'm just playacting. I don't know get-from-come-here about tracking."

"Neither do I," Carl said as he knelt to look at faint indentations in the sand. "This could be them, or a couple of mighty big mule deer, for all I know."

"Good that the Ashtons don't know our limitations," Wisenhunt replied. "Our best bet is to try and think like they might be doing. From what I know of them, that shouldn't be too hard, considering they're both stupid. I'm betting they went into the creek here and walked their horses upstream or down for a ways, figuring that'll throw us off their track."

"Which way, you think?"

"Dean's most likely to point with the hand that's got all its fingers. So, I'm guessing they're headed west. Again, I'm just pretending to know."

L YNDON HAD BEEN watching Wisenhunt with great interest. He nudged his horse's ribs to position himself alongside the marshal. "Mind if I ask you a question?" he said as he looked over at his traveling companion's badge.

"Ask away."

"Someday," Lyndon said, "I'm thinking I might like to be a marshal. I was wondering what a job of that nature requires."

Wisenhunt smiled and repositioned himself in his saddle. "It ain't that hard," he said. "The way I see it, a man has to have no talent whatsoever at farming or ranching, no sense of business or money, and be foolish enough to tangle with men who are drunk, angry, mean, and usually bigger than you are. Small ambition don't hurt neither. If you've got all those qualities, you got yourself a halfway good chance of being a marshal one of these days."

Williamson was still trying to determine whether the marshal was jesting or serious when Novak stopped and pointed toward the horizon. "That ain't from no chimney," he said. In the distance a plume of black smoke was slowly rising into the late-afternoon sky.

ALL THAT REMAINED of the small cabin was the soot-covered porch where a pair of smoldering boots sat next to what was once the front door. The rest was just embers and a memory. As they viewed the destruction, a muffled sound came from a nearby cottonwood. An elderly man, wearing worn overalls and barefoot, was tied to the trunk, struggling to spit a soiled sock from his mouth.

Carl quickly removed the gag, cut away the bindings, and helped him to his feet.

"I was taking me a short nap," the man said. "Been working in the barn since sunup. All at once these two fellas rode up and commenced to beating on me and cussing a blue streak. All for no reason except meanness. They tied me up and proceeded to steal everything they could find out of my cabin. Then they set fire to it and made me watch it burn down. One of them said I was lucky they didn't shoot me in the head."

While Lyndon hurried to the well to get the old man a drink, Wisenhunt and Novak surveyed the heartbreaking damage, troubled by the fact the still-frightened old man had been forced to watch his life go from having very little to having nothing.

"I guess we now know which way they headed," Wisenhunt said.

They helped the old man into a barely standing barn and made him a bed of clean straw and a couple of well-worn saddle blankets. Lyndon offered him a drink of what was left of the sweet lemon water Stanley's cook had given them.

After a time, the old man's breathing came easier and he was able to get to his feet and walk to a window. Looking at the charred remains, he suddenly let out a loud curse. "They even burned up my only good pair of boots," he said, his voice breaking as he made the observation.

"The men who did this say anything about where they were headed?" Novak said.

"Last I seen, they were headed out toward the pasture. I could hear them laughing as they rode off. If I was younger, I'd—"

"We'll handle it," Wisenhunt said.

The old man, seemingly energized by his anger, put out a gnarled hand. "We ain't been properly introduced," he said. "I'm Dickie Ralston. Been living on this property since I was a little boy. My folks raised me in that very cabin. What used to be a cabin."

Novak introduced himself and his companions and explained they were trailing the men who had burned his home.

"Wasn't for this bad leg and my failing eyesight, I'd be proud to ride with you," Ralston said.

When Carl asked if it would be okay if they camped at his place for the night, Wisenhunt shot him a puzzled look. He waved him to distance himself so they could talk. "We can't waste time staying here," he whispered. "The Alstons are getting farther away every minute."

"I know . . . I know," Carl said. "But we can't leave the old man until we're sure he's okay. He's been beat up pretty bad. I don't want to be responsible for leaving him here and him dying alone in the middle of the night. If he seems okay in the morning and can maybe suggest somebody who can come look after him, we'll be on our way."

Wisenhunt studied Novak's face and nodded. "You're getting that patience business figured out," he said. "Maybe even better than me."

Lyndon returned from the back of the barn, where Ralston had been building a new shelf to hold his meager collection of tools. "Your cow appears to need milking," he told the old man. "I wouldn't mind having something to drink other than well water."

"I'd appreciate it, young man. Help yourself. And there's a few taters and onions left in the garden that you're welcome to dig. I'd do it myself, but I'm feeling the need to lie back down."

By the time he woke, Wisenhunt and Williamson had built a campfire, found a cast-iron pot in the ruins that was still usable, and were cooking milk and potato soup.

Carl and the marshal alternated watching over Ralston through the night, listening to the rattling of his shallow breathing and the pained moans he uttered each time he moved. "If he makes it through the night and we can get him to a doctor in the morning, he could survive," Wisenhunt said.

At first light, Lyndon called out to his companions. "You've gotta come see this," he yelled from the doorway of the barn. Outside, people were arriving, some on horseback, others in buggies and driving wagons. A few of the women had baskets of food in their laps.

Among those arriving was the town doctor. "We got word of the fire," he said, "and came straightaway. Where's Dickie?"

"In the barn, still sleeping," Novak replied. "He rested fairly well through the night."

Even as he spoke, men were unloading spades and rakes and beginning to clear away the rubble of the burned cabin. The doctor hurried to Ralston's side and began examining the blackened eye and numerous bruises to his frail body. He called out to one of the women, asking that she prepare a pallet in the bed of one of the wagons so his patient could be transported into town.

"It's good you boys were here to tend to him," the doctor said. "Otherwise, I 'spect we'd be here to make arrangements for a burying."

"He going to make it?" the marshal said as he was handed a biscuit by one of the women.

The doctor nodded. "I'm going to see to it. It'll be a while before he's fully mended, but he's ornery enough to keep on living. You boys happening by most likely saved his life—and we all thank you for that. One of his neighbors has said he'll be welcome to stay at his place until he's back in good health and his cabin can be rebuilt. Don't worry, he'll be well taken care of."

Ralston was sitting up, a faint smile on his face, as he became aware of the activity out in his yard.

Novak knelt next to him. "You're mighty lucky to have such good friends," he said.

The old man's smile widened. "That's one of the Good Lord's gifts that can't be stolen or burned down," he said.

Soon Novak, Lyndon, and the marshal watched as two neighbors helped Ralston into the wagon bed for his ride to the doctor's office. "We best be on our way," Carl said.

Several people stepped forward to shake his hand. "You boys go find the men who did this to him," one said.

Wisenhunt, hardened over the years by witnessing man's inhumanity to man, could not get the image of the battered and bruised old farmer out of his mind as they rode westward. He was beginning to share the hatred Novak had been feeling since finding his wife murdered.

"These boys we're after," he said, "sorely need killing."

CHARLIE BOY HAD stripped naked and was sitting waist-deep in a spring-fed pool. Dean, having removed his britches, dangled his bare legs in the cool water.

"We're gonna be needing us some money soon," the elder brother said. "That old man was broker than we are." They had found only seven dollars and a pocket watch missing its minute hand hidden in a coffee can in Ralston's cabin. "He was such a waste of time, I'm proud we burned his place to the ground. We shoulda killed him and been done with it."

"I'm not really that fond of killing," Charlie Boy said as he batted away a bothersome dragonfly, "but I do like money. Where we gonna get us some?"

"You let me worry about that," Dean said. "This friend that we're headed to see works for a man I'm told is richer than you can imagine. He has folks rustle livestock to sell at the stockyards up in Fort Worth. We discussed it when we were in the war together and my friend told me there was always room for another hand. Soon as we can get ourselves hired and steal some cattle, maybe some horses, we'll be sitting pretty."

The wealthy man Dean mentioned was Rafe Tompkins, a half Mexican, half Anglo who had grown up on the border, dirt-poor and without mother or father. As a young man, he rode with a notorious bandito gang that pillaged and struck fear up and down the Rio Grande. But having grown weary of paltry wages and taking orders, he decided to strike out on his own. With a half-dozen followers, eager for the riches he promised, he set up his operation in an isolated box canyon near the abandoned Fort Lewis in West Texas. His encampment had quickly grown into a small village of tents, a water well, a chow hall watched over by a full-time cook, corrals, barn, and a workforce that was constantly growing. Business was good as his men stole from farms and ranches owned by men too fearful of having their families terrorized or their homes set afire to alert the law to Tompkins's activity.

Those who worked for him delighted in the power they represented and the fear they struck.

"What I'm told," Dean said as he pulled on his

pants, "is that he's a fair-minded man to work for so long as you show him proper loyalty. Word is he's got a temper, and those who he gets displeasured with seem to just quietly disappear. So, little brother, you would do well to remember that if we're able to get ourselves hired."

"How long before we can get there?"

"Three, four days, if these horses don't play out."

"Maybe we can steal us some new ones."

"That was my thinking as well."

CHAPTER NINE

TRY THOUGH HE did to hide it, Rafe Tompkins walked with a slight limp, the reminder of a long-ago cantina fight over a señorita whose attention he and another man both sought. He'd never shared the story, but the result of the drunken episode was that he was stabbed in the leg and the other man got the girl. It was one of the few battles Tompkins ever lost.

In truth, he was the eventual winner when, later, he shot and killed the man who had scarred him for life.

He was sitting on the top rail of the corral, peering from beneath a floppy sombrero at the small herd of longhorns that had been brought in sometime after midnight. It pleased him to see they were all well-fed, in good health, and had survived the torchlit drive and dark crossing of the Concho River. They had once belonged to an unsuspecting rancher miles to the south.

"That's top-dollar beef," he said to his foreman.

"A couple more runs and you can be heading up to Fort Worth."

Tompkins had designed a unique approach to cattle rustling. First, a scout would be sent out to locate ranches where herds were spread over numerous pastures. The grazing land that was the greatest distance from the headquarters and bunkhouse would always be the target of a late-night theft. On the off chance there was a cowboy riding the distance fences, he would be dealt with by a knife-wielding Chicano who had been hired for just such dirty work. Then a team of three or four men would cut fences and use torches to light their way back to the canyon. It was all done quickly and quietly, and only the following day would the ranch owner realize his cattle were gone and the throat of one of his employees had been slashed.

Once the stolen herd—always small and manageable—reached Tompkins's corrals, the brand of the original owner was obscured by burning a series of interlocked circles onto the animals' hindquarters. Later, when the collection of stolen cattle reached a satisfactory number, they would be driven to Fort Worth, where a number of unsavory buyers waited.

It was an efficient plan Tompkins was proud of.

He was putting a match to his first cigar of the day when one of his men escorted the Ashton brothers toward him. He ignored them for several seconds as sweet-smelling smoke rings rose from beneath his sombrero, then motioned for them to dismount. "You boys lose your way?"

"No, sir," Dean said. "We been headed here for the better part of a week, hoping we might get hired on." Then, thinking it might enhance their standing, he added, "We'd have been here sooner if we hadn't got thrown in jail for a time."

He thought he saw the hint of a smile beneath the floppy hat.

"Done cowboying before, have you?"

"It's all we ever done. Breaking horses, tending cattle. We're hard workers."

Tompkins looked at the hand Dean was using to hold the reins. "Not having enough fingers ain't a problem?"

Ashton laughed. "A mustang and me got kinda crossways back in my younger days."

"How come you're not still working your last job?"

Finally, Charlie Boy spoke. "We were just wanting to move on, see us some new scenery."

Tompkins silently studied both men for several seconds. "Go up to the house and get you something to eat while I think on it," he finally said before turning his attention back to the activity in the corral.

THEY HAD JUST finished a second helping of flapjacks when the foreman, an older but fit-looking man who was going bald, entered. "I'm called Trey Newsome," he said. "I keep watch over things for the boss."

"Mr. Tompkins?"

"Yep, he's the head man. Told me to say start-up wages are fifty cents a day, plus meals and boarding. You'll be seeing to the cattle, keeping the horses groomed, the barn clean, and whatever other chores I can come up with for you. If that's of interest, go tend to your mounts and pick yourself a bed in the bunkhouse."

Dean's quick smile masked his disappointment in the tasks they would be assigned. "Sounds good," he said, "real good."

As they were walking their horses toward the barn, Charlie Boy whispered, "I thought you said we were gonna be cattle rustlers, making a lot of money. A half dollar a day ain't—"

"I figure we've gotta work our way up," Dean said. The explanation satisfied his brother.

CARL NOVAK KNEW they were getting closer. They had visited another small farm that had been robbed, this time of two horses and a widow woman's egg money. Apparently in a rush, the thieves hadn't taken time to either harm the elderly owner or set fire to anything.

"Looks to me like they've got a destination in mind," Wisenhunt said. Then he made an observation for which he was immediately sorry. "They don't exactly pick fair fights, do they? Women and old folks."

Novak jerked to look his way but said nothing.

They were weary of the travel, of chasing after ghosts. Though now certain they were on the right trail, they still didn't know where it was leading them. All three were feeling anxious as they attempted to determine what lay ahead.

"Way they've been stealing," Carl said, "they're in bad need of money. So, likely they're looking for a ranch owner who's hiring. We're getting into the part

of the country where there are some big spreads, so
my best bet is that's where we should be looking. Far
as we know, they're good at little other than cowboying." He looked over at the marshal. "That," he
added, "and doing harm to those not capable of fighting back."

Lyndon, aware of the tension that was building,
suggested giving their horses a rest. "If we was to
stretch our legs a bit," he said, "I'm guessing we'd all
feel better. We've also got some of those tortillas
left."

Wisenhunt and Novak both chuckled at Williamson's peacemaking effort. "I think that's a good
idea," Carl said.

The marshal gave Lyndon a good-natured slap on
the back. "Boy, has there ever been time in your life
when you wasn't hungry?"

While Dawn nibbled on tufts of grass, Carl wandered to a nearby rocky outcrop and sat. His thoughts
bounced from the mission at hand to his daughter back
in Wolf Creek. Was she missing him? Had she begun to
speak—maybe even sing—again? How long before
things would return to normal and he would see her?
In a matter of seconds, he found himself going from
anger to sadness and back again.

He was shaken from his thoughts by an unfamiliar
voice.

"Thought I seen some fellow travelers," the rider
said as he approached. He was a young man with a
black goatee and hair that was tied back in a ponytail
that reached well below his shoulders. He sounded
friendly, but his smile quickly disappeared when he
saw Wisenhunt's badge.

He shifted his oversized chaw of tobacco from one side of his mouth to the other. "Y'all hunting down outlaws?"

"Could be," the marshal said. "What's your purpose for being out here in the middle of nowhere?"

The visitor struggled for a quick reply. "On my way to visit kinfolk at a ranch down the way," he finally said. He looked suddenly nervous and, without thinking, slid a hand toward his holster.

"Maybe you can be of assistance," Wisenhunt said, making a show of feeling his pistol handle. "We're on the trail of a couple of brothers, one who's missing a few fingers on one hand. Maybe you've seen them during your travels."

The visitor shook his head, a little too quickly. "Nope, can't help you."

"I suppose you got a name."

The rider again hesitated for a split second, then said, "Hugh . . . Hugh Longley."

"Where you from, Mr. Longley?"

"I work for a cattleman out by Fort Concho."

"A big spread?" Carl asked as he walked up. "One likely to be hiring?"

"Place I work's a pretty small operation," he said. "Can't say if the boss is hiring or not, but I'm guessing he ain't." As he spoke, he began moving his horse away. "I best be getting on," he said, tipping his hat. "You folks travel safe."

Hugh Longley was not even out of sight before Wisenhunt said, "That fella seemed awful nervous when he seen I was the law. And even more so when I asked him about the folks we're looking for. That special instinct I told you I've got makes me wonder what he wasn't of a mind to tell us. You see the look in his eye when I mentioned that one of the folks we're looking for ain't got all his fingers?"

Novak watched Longley disappear on the horizon.

"You and Lyndon set us up a camp here," he said. "Seems a nice enough spot. Maybe shoot us a rabbit or two for supper. I think I'll follow this Longley for a bit, just out of curiosity. Your instinct seems to be wearing off on me."

When the marshal tried to argue they should all go, Novak quickly convinced him that a lone rider was less likely to be spotted.

It would be a while before they saw him again.

L ONGLEY'S PACE WAS leisurely. When he approached a ranch he would seek out the highest nearby vantage point, ride to it, then just sit and look, as if memorizing the geography. Sometimes, he would make his way to the back side of the property, slowly riding the fence line as if he was taking a shortcut to some particular destination. Occasionally, he seemed to write something in a little book, but Novak couldn't be sure. He had to remain at a distance to not be seen and had no binoculars for a closer look.

During the afternoon he saw Longley follow the same routine at another ranch, clearly a more prosperous one, with cattle grazing in every pasture. Only when he saw that ranch hands, armed with rifles, were riding the fence line did he spur his horse and ride away.

As the sun began to set, Novak watched Longley ride into a dense grove of oak trees to make camp.

Oddly, he didn't make a fire to cook dinner or boil coffee. From his own hiding place, Carl sat in the darkness throughout the night, watching for any sign of movement. None came until first light.

For a second day, Longley repeated his movements. Then he suddenly disappeared behind a small ridge. Wary of getting too close, Carl pulled Dawn to a stop and dismounted, shading his eyes from the sun in an attempt to see where Longley had gone. As he did so, a rifle shot rang out from behind him and pinged off a nearby wall of rock. Novak grabbed his horse's reins and was pulling it to cover as another shot raised a puff of dust near his boot.

"Who's shooting?" he yelled.

"The fella you've been following." Longley fired off another shot. "I've known you were trailing me since early yesterday. You ain't much good at it, are you? I've just been waiting for the right time to put an end to it so I can get on with my business."

Carl slipped his rifle from its scabbard and checked to make sure it was loaded. Its heft and the coolness of the barrel felt foreign to him. He'd not fired a long gun since the war. Crouched behind a boulder and trying to determine the location of his attacker, he yelled out again. "This keeps up, somebody's going to be killed."

The answer was another shot that raised more dust a few feet from where Novak was hiding.

He fired blindly in the direction the sound of Longley's voice had come from.

"Ain't much of a shot, are you?" Longley was laughing. "Can't properly trail, can't shoot . . . What is it you figure on doing?"

"I've got no disagreement with you. I was just curious to know if you're acquainted with the folks I'm looking for."

"The brothers? Yeah, I've seen 'em."

"Where? That's all I'm asking."

"What you're asking is to get yourself killed. Probably would have been by them if you hadn't poked your nose into my business. Now I guess I'll have to do it for them." He fired another shot that zinged a few feet over Novak's head.

Taking stock of the situation, Carl recognized his disadvantage. Longley was on higher ground and knew exactly where he was. To each side of the boulder where he was hidden there was nothing but open ground. He was pinned down.

"I got all the time in the world and plenty of ammunition," Longley called out. "But if you would consider saving us some time and showing yourself—"

He was interrupted by another shot from Novak.

Longley's next taunt was called out from a slightly different location. Obviously, he had freedom of movement, another advantage.

The back-and-forth shots sporadically continued throughout the day. Carl's legs began to cramp as he remained in his crouching position. He was thirsty but his canteen was on his saddle and he'd sent Dawn out of the line of fire. The extra rifle ammunition was in the saddlebag, and his pistol, he knew, was of no use.

Twilight was approaching when the shots and conversation from the hillside ended. Novak imagined Longley making his way toward him, seeking a better location from which to bring the confrontation to an end. Aside from the sounds of birds coming to roost, there was only a still silence. The soon-to-arrive darkness would definitely work in Longley's favor.

The next voice Carl heard was gravelly and welcome. "Put down your rifle so you don't go shooting your friends in the dark," Del Wisenhunt called out.

From the shadows, three men slowly appeared, two holding guns, the third holding his bleeding head. Novak got to his feet and lifted his arms in celebration. "Can't say how happy I am to see y'all," he said.

The marshal gave Longley a shove forward so he was only a few feet from Novak. "I'm guessing if you aim real careful, you ought to be able to shoot him dead from there," Wisenhunt said. All of Longley's bravado was gone as he kept his eyes on the ground.

"I'd be satisfied just to have him take a seat and answer some questions."

"Might take a bit of pistol-whipping," the marshal said, "but I figure we can make that happen."

Lyndon was busy gathering wood for a fire as Wisenhunt explained. "After you took out, me and the boy got to talking and decided we'd follow along, whether you wanted our help or not. We kept our distance so you wouldn't know, but never let you out of our sight. Sometimes, we could see you and this other fella both when he'd stop to admire somebody's cattle.

"It was when we heard all the yelling and shooting that we decided to get ourselves more involved. Sneaking up on our friend here was easy, him being so interested in smart-mouthing at you. It was Lyndon who pulled off his boots and crept up behind him in his bare feet and bashed his head in with a rock. I figured for a minute he'd killed him. We had to wait a good spell for him to wake up before we could get him on his feet and come check on you. You ain't shot, are you?"

The smile still hadn't left Novak's face. "I'm fine."

Longley was still bleary-eyed when the marshal knelt in front of him. "I'm thinking you've got three choices," he said. "You can tell us where we're going to find Dean Ashton and his dimwit bother, then ride out of here to Mexico or up to Indian Territory, never to be seen again. Two, I can arrest you and put you in jail for attempting to murder an innocent traveler. Or, three, I can put a bullet between your eyes and end that headache you're suffering right now. Was it me choosing, I'd have done shot you."

"They just hired on to do odd-job work for a man named Tompkins," Longley said. He attempted to get to his feet, but the lingering dizziness caused him to fall to his knees and begin vomiting.

"Where is it we're going to find this Tompkins's place?" Novak said.

"Just a short way out of Fort Lewis," Langley mumbled after running a sleeve across his face. "But you ought to know he don't like strangers visiting." Before he could say anything else, he passed out.

Wisenhunt was watching Lyndon as he sat by the fire, happily admiring the Winchester they'd taken after subduing Longley. "Boy needed himself a proper gun," the marshal said, nodding his approval.

He suggested they tie up their prisoner and get some rest before heading to Fort Lewis. "I guess we could take turns keeping watch over him, but I doubt he's in much shape to cause any trouble. We'll fetch him his horse in the morning and send him in his way."

Soon after daylight, they helped Longley onto his horse and watched him slowly head north. Still in pain, he was hardly riding high in the saddle. And since he'd betrayed his boss's trust, he knew better than to consider returning to the canyon. Instead, he planned disappear into Indian Territory.

The sun had just risen above the treetops when the marshal, the boy, and Novak began their ride west. In an effort to lure Carl from his silence, Wisenhunt tried to make conversation. "What was it you done in the war?"

"When we weren't in battle, I mostly did cooking."

The marshal smiled. "That's about what I would have guessed. You ever kill anybody?"

"Hey, my chili wasn't that bad," Carl said. His mood was improving.

CHAPTER TEN

RAFE TOMPKINS LOOKED out the window of his cabin again and cursed loudly when he still saw no signs of his scout. Though there was no one in the room with him, he was talking in rapid sentences. "He knows full well we've got us a schedule to keep," he said just before biting his cigar in half. "I've got a good mind to fire him when he shows. Send him on his way." His tolerance, like his temper, was short.

After checking the yard one more time, he did what he always did when he was angry. He opened his safe, pulled out a strongbox, and counted his money. The exercise calmed him, even more than a bottle of whiskey.

Hugh Longley was like a son to Tompkins, a young man he planned to one day turn the running of his business over to. The anger he was displaying was but a mask for his growing concern. He had raised Hugh since finding him huddled beneath an overturned wagon after a Comanche raiding party had tortured and killed his parents. That had been almost fifteen years earlier, when Tompkins was making his way north from border country to establish his cattle rustling enterprise.

Trey Newsome entered the dimly lit room, firewood cradled in his arms and anticipating his boss's mood. "You want me to go looking for him?" the foreman said. He knew the answer before asking.

"Yes, but do we even know which way he was headed?" Tompkins said.

Newsome had long resented the young scout's arrogance and independence, his unwillingness to share his plans or even make conversation with any of the other hands. Over the years, the trusting Tompkins had given Longley favorite son status and free rein to seek out locations for their nighttime raids.

"Last time he rode out," Newsome said, "he headed north. Since he doesn't like us raiding the same ranches too often, he likely went south, maybe east, this time."

"Go find him," Longley said.

Anticipating the order, Newsome had already saddled his horse and picked two men to accompany him on the mission. "We'll find him, boss," he said. He stopped short of saying "alive or dead."

In truth, he wouldn't mind the latter.

NOVAK WAS IDLY tossing rocks into the shallow creek where they had stopped to let their horses drink. Wisenhunt and Lyndon were on their knees, washing their faces in the cold, swift-moving water.

"Now that we've got an idea where the Ashtons are," Carl said, "we need to do more careful planning." He looked down at the marshal. "What's your thinking?"

"Our purpose here can't be known," Wisenhunt said. "We need us a good reason for being out this way. Something people are likely to believe." Getting to his feet, he removed his badge and stuffed it in his pocket. "Don't figure it's wise to be seen as a lawman from here on."

It was Lyndon who came up with the story they would tell. "We don't look like cowhands needing work," he said, careful not to look in the middle-aged marshal's direction as he spoke. "Maybe we're related and headed to New Mexico to lend our sister a hand on the farm she's attempting to run since her husband just passed. We could say she sent us a letter . . ."

The young Williamson's imagination surprised Novak and the marshal.

"Then that's our story," Carl said, nodding his approval. "You got any other smart ideas to share?"

"Yeah," Lyndon said. "I'd like for us to soon find someplace where we can get something to eat."

THE CAFÉ IN the community of Bent Tree was called just that—The Café.

"Been riding all day," Wisenhunt told the woman who owned the place, "and I'm hungry enough to eat the legs off this table."

"We're headed to New Mexico," Lyndon said.

The owner clearly didn't care. "I've got beans and

corn bread, some cabrito, half a jug of sweet tea, and one piece of apple pie left," she said.

"Bring it all quick as you can," the marshal said, "and give the boy here the pie. He recently earned it."

When she brought their meals, she surprised the men by taking a seat at the table. "Mind me joining you?" she asked. "Ain't had many folks to talk to today."

"Business slow?"

"Ever since the soldiers over at Fort Lewis quit chasing Indians and went home. When they shut down, I should have done the same. Some days I don't have enough customers to make it worth firing up the stove."

"You cook mighty good," Lyndon said as he reached for another helping of cabrito.

"How far is it to this Fort Lewis?" Wisenhunt asked.

"Maybe a half day's ride if you hurry. Close enough so soldiers used to come over for their dinner and supper pretty regular. I served beer in the evenings, which they liked more than my cooking." She smiled at Williamson. "I thank you kindly for the compliment, young man."

"Ever get a customer named Tompkins?" Novak said.

A sour look crossed the woman's face. "Him, I could do without. Same for those who work for him. Whenever they come in, they act like they own the place. Got no manners, cussing and spitting their awful tobacco juice on my floor."

Lyndon reached for more corn bread as she refilled their tea glasses.

"He got a pretty big herd?"

"I couldn't say. Don't recollect him ever speaking except to order his food. All I know is he's got a place somewhere out past the fort."

Since Novak didn't want their travels to find them in an unknown place when it got dark, he asked if there was someplace in town to stay for the night.

"There was a little hotel on the other end of town, down past the feed store. Don't know for sure if it's still open since the friendly ladies who came to visit the soldiers have gone back to wherever they came from."

She got up and began clearing away their dishes. "If you boys do decide to stay over, come on back in the morning. I'll fix you something better than left-overs. I got ham and eggs and red-eye gravy and can cook up some biscuits. "

As they were leaving The Café, the marshal spoke. "There ain't much I won't do or at least try," he said, "but I'll not be spending the night in a deserted whorehouse."

Instead, the three men paid fifty cents to bed down in the drafty loft of the livery. At Lyndon's urging, they returned to The Café early the next morning for breakfast.

THEY REACHED THE old fort midmorning. The limestone structure was a sad sight, empty and forgotten. Roofs of outbuildings were falling in, the corral fences dilapidated. Tumbleweeds piled against the front wall, as if begging to be allowed in. The constant wind made an eerie music as it blew through open doorways and empty windows. Once the home of a hundred or more soldiers whose purpose was to protect new settlers from Indians and any other dangers they might face heading west, it had been abandoned when there was no more threat.

The only sign of life was a lonesome donkey tethered to the edge of a well and the faint sound of someone singing.

As the riders got closer, a middle-aged man, wrapped in a ragged blanket and wearing handmade moccasins, appeared. Somewhere behind a tangled beard was a smile.

"Howdy and welcome," he called out. "Welcome to Fort Lewis, or what remains of it. Help you fellas with something? I can shoe them horses or soap your saddles. Coffee's hot inside. Ain't checked my traps yet today, but if I got rabbits, I can cook a chili that'll curl your toes and make you wish to kiss your momma. I'm called Bubba Joe. Last name don't matter."

The isolation had obviously driven the man insane.

"We're just passing through," Novak said.

Before anyone asked, the man was telling his story: "I was headed out west where all that gold is. Gonna stake me a claim and get myself rich. But my wagon broke down just as I arrived here and I decided to stay for a few days. Lotta space, nobody to bother you. Longer I stayed, the better I liked it. Just decided to stake my claim right here." He explained that a family of settlers occasionally passed his way, needing his help to repair a broken axle or mend the canvas on their wagon. "I'm always happy to see folk. Did you say you need new shoes for your horses? Or some coffee? There's a mail carrier who rides this way from time to time and he brings me coffee makings and a sack of beans." He pointed in the direction of his donkey. "I was just going to roust ol' Isabel and go run my traps. Hoping to catch some rabbits."

"We're looking for a place run by a man named Tompkins," Wisenhunt said.

"I make the best chili this side of—"

"Tompkins," Wisenhunt gruffly repeated. "You know him?"

"He needing help with his horse?"

Novak wearily tipped his hat and thanked the man for his time. "We best be going. Good luck with running your traps."

As they rode away, Lyndon was shaking his head. "That poor man is blind bat crazy. Guess being alone will do that to you."

"It ain't so much the being alone," Wisenhunt said. "It's the wind. Blows out here night and day, never stopping, filling the air with dust and sand and all manner of seed pollen. It's the wind that'll make a man crazy."

DEAN AND CHARLIE Boy were in the barn, mucking out stalls, when the three strangers arrived. Leaning against their pitchforks and looking out the window of the stockroom, they couldn't make out what was being said. In a matter of only minutes, the visitors were on their way.

"Probably somebody looking to hire on and do our jobs," Dean said.

"They're welcome to mine," his brother replied. He had been in a foul mood since they agreed to work for Rafe Tompkins.

CARL WAITED UNTIL they had distanced themselves from the canyon before speaking. "A strange-looking setup," he said. "Hid away like it is, only a few cattle but lots of pens and a lot more workers than necessary milling around. Everybody I could see had a pistol on his hip. And that fellow in the sombrero made it pretty clear he didn't like us being on his property. Didn't even pretend to be friendly. Wasn't nothing that felt right about the place."

"I tried not to look like I was being nosy," Wisenhunt said, "but just glancing around as you and him talked, I didn't see nobody who was missing any fingers."

"You reckon that man believed our story?" Lyndon said.

"Probably not," the marshal replied. "Most likely, he figured we were poking into his business."

"I'd like to find us a spot we can sit and just do some watching for a bit," Carl said. "I got a feeling we've come to the right place. Just can't figure what its purpose is."

TOMPKINS ALSO HAD questions. "No way those boys just happened to stop here," he said to the two cowboys he'd summoned to his cabin. "Follow after them and see if you can figure what they're up to."

His men didn't have to travel far.

O N A NEARBY hillside, a grove of young oaks offered what Novak judged to be an ideal spot to hide and view the activity in the canyon.

"We ain't exactly equipped to set up camp," Wisenhunt said after again cursing himself for leaving his binoculars hanging on the wall of his office. "Still, I think we might learn something if we stay after dark to see what's going on."

It was almost midnight, the moonless sky black and the air chilled, when Novak stood to try to stretch the cramps from his legs. "I doubt if we were to build us a small fire it would draw any attention, far away as we are." Lyndon quickly got to his feet and went in search of kindling and fallen branches. Soon the mesmerizing crackle of a campfire broke the silence as the men huddled around its warmth.

They took turns keeping watch over the darkened canyon, and it was Lyndon who first saw the tiny firefly-like lights dancing in the distance. By the time he waved Carl and the marshal to his side, the lights had moved closer. "Torches," Wisenhunt said. "Riders carrying torches to light their way."

As they reached the entrance to the canyon, it became clear what was happening. There were faint grunts of cattle and an occasional slap of a rope against a horse's hindquarters. A small herd was being moved toward one of the empty pens.

"Cattle thieves," Novak whispered. "Tompkins and his men are rustling cattle."

"Sounds about right," said Wisenhunt.

They watched silently as a dozen stubborn long-horns were locked away and the torches doused.

Lyndon, who had been speechless, said, "I've got some personal business needs tending."

"Ought to take your new rifle with you in case you meet up with a bear out there in the bushes," Wisenhunt said, then suggested to Novak that they return to the warmth of the campfire. "We've learned something," he said, "but I don't know how it figures into what we came for."

"Patience," Novak said.

A RUSTLING IN the nearby bushes was quickly followed by two shadowy figures stepping into the glow of the campfire. Both were pointing pistols. "You boys just keep sitting and tell us what it is you're doing here," one said as he pulled back the hammer of his Colt.

"Just minding our own business," Novak said.

"Our boss don't seem to think so. He says you're here snooping around, trespassing on his property. Folks get themselves killed for that kind of behavior." Both men took another step forward. "Tell us what's your purpose."

His partner began laughing. "Don't matter to me," he said. "Let's just shoot them and be done with it." It was obvious he had been drinking while waiting to confront the intruders. He aimed his gun at

Wisenhunt and was preparing to shoot when something cold was pushed into his back.

A nervous voice demanded that he drop his weapon. Lyndon, having heard the intruders, had crept up behind them and shoved the barrel of his rifle between the cowboy's shoulder blades. "If there's killing to be done," he boldly announced, "I'll tend to it."

The first shot to echo into the night was unintentional. As the suddenly sobering cowboy attempted to holster his gun, it went off, the wild shot grazing Wisenhunt's thigh. Lyndon's sudden reflex was to fire his rifle, wounding the stunned gunman in the shoulder.

As he fell, moaning in pain, Novak was fast to his feet, wrestling the pistol from the hand of the other man, who was momentarily distracted by the shooting of his partner. He mumbled something about "not signing on for this" before Novak hit him in the face with the butt of his own gun. Instantly unconscious, he, too, crumpled to the ground.

Young Williamson was in shock, shivering, his rifle now dangling at his side. "Never shot nobody before," he said.

"Good you did," Wisenhunt said as he limped over and put an arm around Lyndon, "otherwise, me and Carl would likely be dead as doornails."

Novak approached and looked at the marshal's wound. "You fit to ride?"

"I'm okay," Wisenhunt said as he dabbed a kerchief at his wound. "Mostly, it just ruined a good pair of britches."

"Then we best be on our way . . . now."

Lyndon looked at the two men lying on the ground. "What about them?"

"They'll be found soon enough," Carl said. "Your rifle shot likely alerted everybody in the canyon, stolen cattle included."

With Dawn and Novak leading the way, they were soon galloping into the night. Once they put some distance between themselves and the canyon, they allowed their tiring horses to slow to an easier pace.

"Well," Wisenhunt said, "I don't figure we made ourselves any friends on that visit."

"I'm just glad there wasn't nobody killed," Lyndon replied.

Novak smiled. "You done real good," he said. "I'm proud to be riding with you. Soon as we get to town, I'm buying you the biggest breakfast you've ever had."

PART TWO

CHAPTER ELEVEN

HUGH LONGLEY WAS unrecognizable, his once-proud goatee untrimmed, his hair disheveled, and his eyes watery and hollow. He had been aimlessly roaming the Indian Territory for days, sleeping in the open, bathing in streams, and wearing the same clothes he'd had on when he was issued his ride-away-or-die ultimatum.

His decision had turned his life into a raging disaster, his future into storm clouds of doubt. His days as a scout and cock of the walk back in the canyon were history. He was a weaker man than he'd ever dared think, exchanging the betrayal of his boss for his life, and he was beginning to wonder if he'd made the better deal.

By now, the men looking for the Ashton brothers had likely found them and learned of Rafe Tompkins's cattle rustling enterprise. The man wearing the badge who had threatened to kill him might even now be planning to make arrests and shut the business down. The idea of someone who had raised and mentored him sitting in a jail cell, waiting to go to prison, was impossible to consider.

First, the depression had overwhelmed him, then it had slowly changed to revenge-seeking anger. Longley decided to head back to Texas.

Two days later he was sitting in a run-down road-house just north of the Red River, feeling sorry for himself and getting drunk, when he heard a familiar voice.

"I was beginning to think you were dead," Trey Newsome said as he pulled up a chair. "Seeing you, I'm not sure you ain't."

"What are you doing here?"

"The boss sent me out looking for you. I've been wandering all over and finally figured you either went south to Mexico or came up here to be with the Indians. I flipped a coin and here I am."

"You here to kill me?"

"Can't say I'd mind it, but my orders were to find you and bring you back. State you're in, I don't see you putting up much of an argument about it."

Longley pushed his empty glass aside and made a feeble attempt to smooth his hair as he waited for word about things happening back in the canyon. When the foreman made no mention of men looking for two of Tompkins's hired hands, or a marshal being made aware of the boss's business, he let his shoulders slump in relief.

"I can't go back," he said, turning away in an attempt to hide a tear that was slipping down his cheek. "I done something there's no forgiving for." Then in a burst he related the encounter that had led to his disappearance. He spoke rapidly, as if, if he didn't do so, he would never get his confession told.

Newsome's only response was to try to hide a slight smile. At last, he had an advantage over the boss's golden boy. "Didn't nobody come calling before I left to find you," he finally said. "Maybe they haven't located the place yet. Seems to me the thing for us to do is get you sober and go see if we can beat them there."

Longley stood on wobbly legs, looking for his hat. "I can sober up while we're riding," he said.

I N THE FRONT room of Tompkins's cabin, one of his cowhands had his arm in a sling, still in pain after the camp cook dug the bullet from his shoulder and stitched the wound with fishing line. She seemed to enjoy her work and, despite his pleas, had refused to give him whiskey during the procedure. "Go ahead and faint if you're of a mind, but you're getting none of my liquor," she'd told him.

His companion sat nearby, staring at the floor with the one eye that wasn't swelled shut. There was an ugly bruise that ran from one side of his forehead to his jaw, and two teeth were missing.

"Worthless," Tompkins bellowed. "Sorry and flat-out worthless. I keep sending folks out to do a job and they either disappear on me or get themselves shot and beat up." He briefly fell silent as he moved closer to the two, bending down so his face was only inches from theirs. "If I had my druthers," he said, "they'd have killed you both."

Neither could give him any real indication of why the three trespassers had been watching the place. "It seemed like they were looking for somebody," one of the men said just before Tompkins slapped him in the face.

Tompkins began pacing, puffing frantically on his cigar. "It's those new boys," he finally said. "They're the cause for all this trouble. Go out to the barn and fetch them. Bring 'em to me."

In just minutes the shamed and battered cowboys returned. "Boss, they're gone," one said in a voice that was barely a whisper.

WHERE WE HEADED?" Charlie Boy yelled, kicking his bootheels into his horse's ribs in an effort to keep up.

"Far away as we can get," Dean said. "We'll figure us a destination once we've put some distance between us and what's going on back at the canyon." Since watching the three men talking with Rafe Tompkins earlier, he had felt uneasy. Then, when he learned that two workers had been found shot and beaten by the same visitors, he became certain they were looking for him and his brother. Once his sombrero-wearing, hot-tempered boss figured it all out, he would take a sizable bite out of their hides. Or worse.

It was time to run.

They rode until their horses were bathed in sweat and could go no farther. When they finally stopped in the shade of a towering cottonwood, Charlie Boy looked at his brother and saw something unfamiliar. Dean was scared.

"Did you recognize any of those men who came to visit the boss?" he said.

Dean shook his head. "No, but if I had to guess, they were looking for somebody who broke out of jail. Us. And if they came this far, they're not returning home until they get satisfaction." It didn't occur to him that the pursuit might have to do with other, more serious crimes they had recently committed.

"We can't just keep heading nowhere," Charlie Boy said. "You're the smart one. You've got to make us a plan."

"I'm thinking on it," Dean said, kicking at the ground.

Feeling the need to try to calm his brother, Charlie Boy said, "Since yesterday was payday, at least we've got no cause to rob anybody."

Dean, lost in thought, ignored the observation. "Abilene," he finally said. "We'll go to Abilene. If I'm right, it'll only be a couple of days' ride. The town's got enough folks for us to get ourselves lost in the crowd. It's a cattle town, so likely there will be plenty of jobs."

"I ain't cleaning out no more stalls," Charlie Boy said.

Normally, such an innocent statement would have eased the tension they were dealing with. Not today, however, not now. Both men would have been more at ease had they been aware that the men they were worried about were headed in another direction, being chased themselves.

THEY'LL BE COMING after us," Carl Novak said, "none too pleased about how we treated their friends."

"We didn't kill nobody," Lyndon said.

"No, but we might have to now, just to keep our own bacon out of the fire," the marshal said as they neared Fort Lewis. He pushed his hat back on his head and looked over at Novak. "You thinking what I'm thinking?"

"I don't much like the idea of putting Bubba Joe in harm's way."

"Way I see it, it can't be helped."

THE SECOND FLOOR of the old fort was a gray maze of dust and cobwebs and stacks of discarded furniture. A Confederate flag, soiled and ragged, hung on one wall and a nest of startled raccoons scattered when the men reached the top of the stairs.

Bubba Joe, delighted that the men had returned, remained downstairs, boiling water to make coffee. As his visitors discussed their plan, he happily talked to himself about more company coming. He'd obviously not understood when Novak attempted to warn him of the danger that was soon to arrive.

Wisenhunt selected a chair that was still in working order and moved it to the window facing east. "They'll be coming from out yonder," he said, pointing toward the horizon, "and there's nothing but a few scrub mesquites marring the view. We'll be able to see them well before they can get close."

"How long you figure?" Novak said.

"Most likely, they're done on their way."

"How many?"

"Too many," Wisenhunt said as he reached into his

pocket for his badge and pinned it back onto his vest. Then he placed his rifle on the windowsill to wait.

J UST AS THEY could smell the aroma of coffee being brought up the stairs, a faint cloud of dust appeared in the distance. "That's them," the marshal said. Soon there were small black dots. "Looks like five or six." He squinted, using a pointed finger to count. "No, I think there's eight."

Novak felt his hands shake as he gripped his rifle. He was having flashbacks to his days in the war, recalling the slow-motion minutes that always preceded battle. "How close we gonna let them get?"

"They'll soon see our horses and know we're here, so they won't make it easy. If I was them, I'd split up and head in from two directions."

Lyndon held his rifle to his chest as he approached the marshal. "Where is it you want me to be?"

"Go downstairs and keep watch over Bubba Joe. Stay with him and see he's protected, unless you hear me calling for you."

Young Williamson hoped the relief he was feeling didn't show. He'd had his fill of shooting at people.

S HORTLY, THE RIDERS were in range.

Wisenhunt fired the first shot and let out a cheer as a man slumped in his saddle, then fell to the ground. "Now there's just seven," the marshal yelled. Return fire peppered the wall of the fort, one shot zinging over his head and burying into the wall behind him.

The oncoming horses broke from their cluster as Wisenhunt's second shot missed its target. "Best you start shooting," he called out to Novak. "I can't do this all by myself."

Carl aimed at the closest rider and pulled the trigger. To his surprise, he saw a gun fly away and the rider grab his chest before falling backward out of the saddle. His frightened horse began galloping away in the opposite direction.

It was obvious Tompkins's men hadn't discussed any plan of attack. In the open space, with nothing to shield them from the shots coming from the fort, they had ridden into an unfair fight. The marshal moved to another window and could see two men trying to approach from the opposite side. He fired off two quick shots, the second hitting one of the riders in the forearm as the other turned and rode to safety.

After two more were shot, the others turned their horses and fled. In just twenty minutes it was over.

"What's left of them are heading home, tails tucked between their legs," the marshal said, adrenaline raising his voice an octave. "We flat ran 'em off."

Lyndon had run up the stairs. "You think they'll be back?"

"No time soon," the marshal said. "Unless they're wanting to collect their dead."

As he spoke, Novak was on his way into the yard. The man wounded by Wisenhunt writhed in the dust, holding his hand to his bleeding arm. He looked no more than eighteen.

"Get to your feet," Carl said, pointing his rifle at the frightened young man. "Come inside and we'll see about stopping that bleeding. Then we're going to have ourselves a talk."

T HE WOUND WAS cleaned and kerosene poured over it to prevent infection. The bullet had gone through the fleshy part of the arm, damaging no bones. Wisenhunt donated his bandanna as a wrap.

"You got a name?" Novak said.

"I'm called Jeb."

"Were you told to come and help kill us?"

"That's what Mr. Tompkins wanted."

"Why, just because we roughed up a couple of his boys who attempted to ambush us?"

Jeb shrugged. "I can't for sure tell you. I just do what the boss says."

Wisenhunt joined the conversation. "I reckon that includes stealing other folks' livestock."

Jeb shrugged again.

"You work with a man who's missing fingers on one of his hands?" Novak asked, squeezing Jeb's injured arm.

"Yeah . . . You're speaking of Dean Ashton. Him and his brother recently hired on. I've seen them at chow a few times but can't say we're friendly. Truth is, I don't much like either of them, especially the older one. I was glad to see them go, to be honest about it."

Novak rolled his eyes, then looked up at the ceiling. "You're saying they're gone. When? Where?"

Jeb was sweating and his arm was starting to throb. "I've got no idea," he said as his voice grew weak. "All I was told was they took off the day after we got our pay." He asked if it would be okay if he lay down for a while.

Carl's fists were clenched and he was grinding his teeth as he walked outside, trying to determine what to do next. The closer he got to those he was looking for, the farther away they seemed to be. And the questions that had begun haunting him returned. Was he doing the right thing? Was it all worth it?

The sun was going down and the air was beginning to cool, a faint hint that fall wasn't too far away. After a while he looked out toward where Tompkins's men had come from and saw four horses, still saddled, patiently waiting for riders who would never come. Somewhere nearby, he knew, were men who had died for no good reason.

He went back inside and found Wisenhunt and Williamson sitting at the kitchen table, drinking coffee. "Finish up what you're doing and come with me," he said.

"What?" the marshal said.

"There's dead that need tending to."

THE FOLLOWING MORNING, the injured cowboy slowly rode into the canyon, four tethered horses following behind. Tied across each saddle was a body.

Rafe Tompkins was briefly speechless as he listened to what his hand had been told to say. "They said tell you they've got no fight with you and wanted me to bring these men back for proper burying. Told me to say they killed them only because it was made necessary."

Tompkins removed his sombrero and slowly walked past each of the lifeless bodies. "Well, I'll be . . . Somebody fetch some shovels and start digging graves while I try figuring all this out."

A T THE FORT, Novak and his partner were saying goodbye to Bubba Joe. He apologized for not having time to linger but said his traps needed to be checked. He wanted to have chili cooked if any other visitors stopped in. Carl said he understood, shook the man's hand, and mounted his horse.

They rode away slowly, Carl and the marshal side by side, Lyndon following. "Think we've heard the last of Tompkins?" Novak said.

"Absolutely not," Wisenhunt said. "Soon as we get the business we came for done, I'm coming back with whoever I can get to join me—sheriffs, other marshals, maybe even a couple of those Pinkerton fellas—and putting his cattle thieving to an end. Right now, though, we need to focus our thoughts on where it is we're going."

"And where might that be?"

Neither had an answer.

CHAPTER TWELVE

EVEN WITH THE last rainstorm of spring flooding its downtown, Abilene was alive. People stood in the canopied doorway of the downtown café, waiting for tables to empty so they could have lunch. Cattle drivers, stopping over on the way to Fort Worth or out to New Mexico Territory, filled both saloons. Once the sun broke through, the wooden sidewalks were busy with women doing shopping or going to their church and book club meetings. Dogs barked, roosters crowed, and the bells of the Sacred Church of the Holy Father were ringing.

"I'm liking this place even if I haven't seen much of it yet," Charlie Boy said as they rode along the mud-rutted main street.

"What I like," Dean said, "is don't nobody here know us."

Trail-weary as they were, and with Tompkins's pay in their pockets, their first stop was the nearest saloon. Then they located a small, cheap hotel that had a corral in back where customers could keep their horses. For the first few days they ate heartily, alternated drinking at both of the saloons, and rested. With each passing day, they found themselves looking over their shoulders less and less.

Only when their money began to run low did they venture down to the stockyards in search of short-term work. Dean got a job unloading bales of hay and feeding cattle, while Charlie Boy found himself back in the role of barn cleaner. "It's only for the time being," Dean said. "We'll soon find ourselves the right outfit to sign on with."

All in all, things were going well. They were sleeping indoors, a hot bath and a shave cost only twenty-five cents, the food at the café was a huge improvement over what they had been served by Tompkins's cook, and living anonymously was a great comfort.

It lasted for the better part of two weeks. It was Dean, the more outgoing, fun-loving of the two, who first felt a growing need for some excitement. One evening, after they had received their pay, he convinced his brother that they should pool their money and visit one of the local gambling houses.

"What you're meaning is I get to come along and watch you play cards with my money," Charlie Boy said. There was little enthusiasm in his voice.

"Hey, I'm feeling lucky," his brother said.

SINCE THE RAINS had made fields still too wet to plant, farmers had come to town for supplies and a few hands of poker with the visiting cattlemen.

Though it was still early in the evening, the whiskey was flowing freely.

Dean was already tipsy when he ignored his brother's advice and invited himself into a game.

A man wearing loose-fitting overalls and a flannel shirt stood and waved a hand at the chair where he'd been seated. "If it's the most unlucky spot in the whole town you're wanting, you can sit here. I'm broke and heading home."

The three men who remained laughed and welcomed Dean to the table. "That, of course, is assuming you've got money in your pocket," the eldest of the group, a cattle buyer, said as he pushed a half-full whiskey bottle across the table. A smiling waitress quickly put an empty shot glass in front of the newcomer.

Soon Dean was drinking and betting with equal abandon. He was fast becoming drunk and broke. Charlie Boy was getting angry. "Come on, brother, it's time we got out of here," he said.

"You boys brothers?" the buyer said.

"Yep," Dean, distracted from mentally counting the money he had left, said.

"Y'all cowboys?"

"That's right. Deal the cards."

Shuffling the deck an extra time, the cattleman shook his head. "Maybe you ought to sit out a few hands . . . until your luck turns a little better. I make it a rule never to take a man's breakfast money, so why don't you relax and just visit. Have another drink."

Dean felt he was being talked to like a child but said nothing.

"What outfit you boys ride for?"

Charlie Boy jumped into the conversation. "We're looking for jobs right now," he said.

"And before you came here?"

Dean, already embarrassed by his dismal efforts at five-card stud, was feeling ignored. "We had jobs working for a rich man who wasn't exactly a law-abiding sort," he said. "About half-crazy, wore a big sombrero, always smoking a cigar . . ."

Another of the players, a wrangler wearing a leather vest and an aging black hat pulled low on his forehead, looked across the table and slowly nodded. "Bet his name's Thomason . . . or Tompkins," he said.

"You know him?" Dean said.

"Friend of mine worked for him back in the day, rustling cattle. He's got stories about as wild as ones you've most likely got. One I recall was about him once getting so mad at one of his men that he tossed him into a gravel pit full of rattlesnakes."

"That's Mr. Tompkins, all right," Dean said, spilling his drink as he reached for it with his bad hand. "He's still got that mean temper and is still stealing cattle. The old fool's made himself twice-over rich."

By the time the bartender rang a bell to indicate it was closing time, the whiskey bottle was empty and Dean had to be helped to his feet by his brother. In an attempt to impress the others at the table, he had spun a series of yarns, some he'd heard from others, some he made up. "That little box canyon is the strangest place I ever worked," he said as Charlie Boy lifted him from his chair. "And, like I was saying, its well hid unless you know where to find it."

It took little urging from his listeners for him to divulge the location.

B ACK IN THE hotel, Dean was spread-eagled on the bed, laughing at some private joke playing in his head while Charlie Boy pulled off his boots. Raising up on his elbows, Dean turned serious for a moment. "Brother," he said, "I'm mighty sorry about losing our money."

Charlie Boy glared down at him. "Unless I'm a whole lot dumber than either of us thinks," he said, "I'm betting that ain't all you're going to be sorry for."

Already snoring, Dean didn't hear a word he'd said.

A SIDE FROM THE still-drunk Longley falling off his horse as he and Trey Newsome forded the Red River, he was feeling better. Though he'd lost his hat and probably ruined a good pair of boots in the knee-deep water, he was on the mend. The fog had begun to lift from his mind and he was no longer seeing two of the man he was riding with.

By the time they were on Texas soil, they had agreed on a plan. Newsome convinced him that to try to run from Tompkins was useless, that it would be better to face the boss and hope he was in a forgiving mood.

Privately, the foreman hoped Longley would be tarred and feathered.

"Even if those men you told have found their way

to the canyon," he said, "it's not likely they'll cause a great deal of trouble. All they're wanting is those two we made the mistake of hiring. Once they've ended their business, they'll be gone. You'll find a way to make this right."

Longley wasn't completely convinced but did like the idea of no longer running and hiding. "Reckon what I ought to say?" he said.

Newsome was enjoying Longley's discomfort but tried to show concern. "If it was me," he said, "I'd tell it to him just like you told it to me. How these men said they would shoot you dead if you didn't provide them the information they were after. I can't see anybody not understanding a predicament like that. My guess is Mr. Tompkins is going to be pleased to see you're safe and in one piece." He gave Longley the most sincere smile he could muster. "Between you and me, I'd have done the same thing you done."

The welcome was hardly what Newsome had promised.

Rafe Tompkins was sitting on his porch, looking mad at the world, when they rode in. The scowl on his face only got worse as Longley dismounted and walked toward him.

"I'd about decided you was dead," Tompkins said. "Not that it would have been any great loss. You got any idea the misery you've caused?"

"I just came to tell you how sorry I—"

Tompkins interrupted the attempted apology. "I've done buried three men and got two others so beat up they can't hit a lick," he said. "All because of those people you sent here. I never figured you to be so dumb."

Newsome was still astride his horse, enjoying the rant. Longley was wishing he hadn't been persuaded to return.

Finally, Tompkins waved an arm in disgust and turned to go inside. "Go on and get out of my sight," he yelled. "Get down to the bunkhouse and make yourself presentable while I decide what I'm going to do with you." He was halfway through the door when he turned. "What happened to your hat?"

Longley had decided honesty wasn't working. "Ain't sure," he replied.

Tompkins let the door slam behind him before breaking into the closest he could manage to a smile.

I T WAS TWO days before Longley was summoned back to the boss's cabin. He fully expected to be told to gather his belonging and leave. Instead, he entered the living room to see a man he didn't know sitting across from Tompkins, a glass of whiskey in his hand.

Tompkins was in a good mood. "This fella here is named Jonesy Blake," he said, "and he risked near getting his head blown off by one of my guards to bring some interesting information. You know those boys we hired, the brothers your friends were looking for when they threatened you?"

Puzzled, Hugh nodded.

"Well, he knows where they can be found." Turning to Blake, he encouraged him to retell his story.

Drawing out the moment as best he could, Blake told about the poker game, of Dean Ashton getting drunk and telling tall tales. "He's maybe the worst cardplayer I've ever met," he said, "and I'm not comfortable repeating some of the things he said about Mr. Tompkins here. All I come to say is I know the location of this property is supposed to be a secret and he was blabbing his fool head off about its whereabouts. It just occurred to me that you folks ought to know."

He'd not gotten around to asking Tompkins for a job as his reward.

"Thanks to this man being so neighborly," Tompkins said to Longley, "I can now see a way for us to solve at least one of the problems that you've stirred up. We're going to hunt these sorry brothers down and skin their hides."

Longley shuffled his feet and waited to hear the boss's plan.

"My friend Jonesy here has agreed to help out. I'm going to pay him a proper bounty fee for leading us to where they are. You and Newsome are going to Abilene with him. Once you return and convince me that things have been taken care of, we'll call everything even." For the first time since Longley's return, Tompkins smiled at him. "We'll start out fresh, forgetting past mistakes. Tend to this business, then come on back and start scouting for cattle again."

"You saying you want them killed?" Longley said.

"I'm saying you do whatever you think best. Go tell foreman Newsome the plan and you boys get ready to be on your way. I figure Jonesy is anxious to get back to Abilene."

As Longley turned to leave, his boss had one final

instruction. "See to it you get yourself a decent hat before you leave," he said.

D EAN ASHTON KNEW he'd made a serious mistake when his brother recounted the night at the poker table. His head throbbed, his eyes watered, and when Charlie Boy suggested they walk over to the café for breakfast, he felt he was going to be sick to his stomach.

"You had no call to be talking about what goes on back in that canyon, much less telling total strangers the location," Charlie Boy said. "And it's you always calling me stupid."

Dean closed his eyes, trying to recall the men who had been sitting at the card table the night before, trying to determine which of them might profit from the information he had let slip. If anyone, he finally decided, it had to be the young one who wore the big black hat and never said a word. If he even gave his name, Dean couldn't remember it.

In the days that followed the incident, he tried to forget it and convince himself that nothing would come of his letting his mouth run. It would have been easier if Charlie Boy hadn't continued to dwell on it.

"I'm thinking as soon as we get us another pay-day," he said, "we ought to move on. Find us another place where there won't be people looking for us."

The matter was beginning to grate on Dean. "And where might that be?"

"We could give some thought to going over into New Mexico, maybe Taos or Santa Fe. I wouldn't mind seeing that part of the country. Maybe we could change our names and quit telling people we're brothers."

"We're as safe here as we're going to be anywhere," Dean said. "Trust me on it and quit worrying so much."

I N TRUTH, THE notion of participating in a manhunt didn't appeal to Jonesy Blake. All he'd wanted to do was gain Rafe Tompkins's favor and maybe get himself hired on as a cattle rustler and finally earn a decent wage. But he'd allowed himself to be talked into the plan before he'd known what was happening. Now he was faced with the possibility of having to kill just to get a job. If he'd had more time to think it over, maybe he could have simply thanked Tompkins and turned him down. He cursed the evening he and his friends had invited the stranger into their card game.

Now it was a matter of making the best of a bad situation. Somehow he had to make riding with Tompkins's foreman and Hugh Longley work out. How could it be his fault if they just weren't able to find the men they were sent to deal with?

"Where do we start looking for these two?" Newsome said as they made their way across a lengthy stretch of West Texas flatland.

"Like I told your boss, I only seen them that once, when we were playing poker in the saloon. I've got no idea where they came from or where they went."

"What was the place called?" Newsome said. He was warming to the idea of beginning their search for the Ashton brothers in a saloon.

"It's called the Branding Iron Bar."

"Whiskey any good?"

"I'd say it's passable . . . and fair priced."

Hugh Longley had said little since they left the canyon. He, too, had reservation about the trip. He knew he could be killed in a confrontation with two men he was certain were flat-out crazy.

Also, Trey Newsome had no use for him and was probably already working on a plan to see that he never returned to his job as Tompkins's scout.

By the time they reached Abilene and tethered their horses to the hitching post in front of the Branding Iron, his concern had grown.

The saloon was empty except for the idle bartender, who was reading a dime novel, and an elderly man who had been lazily sweeping in the same spot for half an hour. The rains had gone and farmers were back in their fields, plowing and planting, and on the edge of town trail camps were breaking up in anticipation of the final stage of cattle drives headed on to Fort Worth. The business of whiskey drinking and cardplaying was on the decline.

"Don't look like the most popular place in town," Newsome said as they entered. He was already reaching into his pocket for money to buy a drink.

For the next two days, he seldom left his seat at the bar while Longley and Jonesy Blake nervously waited. The foreman was feeling no rush to complete his boss's assignment. Aside from the bottle in front of him, his main concern was what to do about Hugh Longley.

CHAPTER THIRTEEN

"I SEEN THEM with my own eyes," Charlie Boy said as he rushed into the hotel room. "They were walking into the saloon. Two were men we worked with back in the canyon, the other was who you lost all our money to, playing poker. They're down there right this minute. And I'm guessing they're looking for us."

With his job feeding cattle abruptly ended, Dean had been spending a great deal of time sleeping. He had just wakened and his brother had to repeat his news before it fully registered. His eyes roamed the cluttered room they would soon have to vacate since their money was again running low.

"I'm telling you, we need to be getting on our way," Charlie Boy said. "Sooner the better."

Dean was focused on a row of empty bean cans lined along the windowsill. Due to growing financial concerns, they hadn't been eating well for several days and his stomach was growling. He would also like a drink, but not badly enough to chance running into the men his brother had just described. Finally, he broke his silence with a stream of curses. "I wish folks would just leave us be," he said as he searched for a missing boot. "I'm plumb worn out from running. I ain't . . . we ain't . . . doing it no more."

"What are we gonna do?"

"If they're here figuring to kill us, we do it to them first."

I T HAD BEEN Jonesy's suggestion they camp in one of the fifty-cents-a-night tents down by the stock pens rather than spend their traveling money on a hotel room. Newsome had quickly agreed, figuring that would leave more for buying whiskey and the hot meals served in the café.

Jonesy, meanwhile, had mentioned that he had cowboy friends he could bunk in with for free. Mostly, he just wanted to get away from Newsome and Longley and try to figure a way out of the mess he'd gotten himself into.

T HERE WAS ONLY a silver sliver of a moon on the night the Alston brothers chose to deal with their situation.

For two days Charlie Boy had kept constant watch on the three men. Mostly, it had meant hiding in an alley across the street from the Branding Iron, watching them go in, then, hours later, finally come out. It was always the tall one, Tompkins's foreman, who walked unsteadily and had trouble getting on his horse. A few times they stopped at the café but most often rode straight to the stock pens and their tent.

"Don't seem they're in any big hurry to find us," Dean said after hearing his brother's latest report.

"From what I can tell," Charlie Boy said, "it's the foreman in charge and he's of a mind to enjoy himself a little partying before they tend to what they're here for. But I figure we can count on them coming for us pretty soon."

"I've had me an idea," Dean said.

"Hope it's better than the ones you've been having." The remark earned Charlie Boy a hard slap across the face.

Dean spread a handful of coins on his pillow and began counting. Handing the money to his brother, he said, "Rather than buying yourself biscuits and gravy, go down to the hardware store and see if they've got dynamite like farmers use for busting buried rocks and tree stumps. If you have enough money, buy us two sticks. And a box of matches."

T HEY ARRIVED AT the stock pens well before closing time at the saloon and found a waiting place behind a barn where visiting cowboys stowed their saddles. Charlie Boy had purchased two sticks of dynamite and some matches and they crouched in silence, watching the tent he'd seen two of the men enter the night before.

"They'll put their horses in that little corral over there. Last night, the tall one was so drunk he even forgot to take off the saddle. I felt sorry for the horse."

Dean had no sympathy for the discomfort of any

animal. His only concern was the mission at hand. When his brother told him that one of the men wasn't staying in the tent, he considered saving one of the sticks of dynamite until they could locate him. Then he'd decided to tie them tightly together and toss both into the tent. What was going to happen to those who were sleeping would surely scare the other into running.

There was a chill in the air and Charlie Boy was shivering and growing anxious as the night got even darker. He was relieved when he finally saw the men arrive. "That's them," he said. The foreman was so drunk he stumbled and fell as he dismounted. He mumbled a curse, picked himself up, and staggered into the tent, leaving Hugh Longley to tend the horses.

"How long you figure on waiting?" Charlie Boy said.

"Until we hear snoring."

The wait wasn't long.

THE ASHTONS CREPT along a row of vacant tents until they reached the edge of the one they had watched Newsome and Longley enter. The doorway flap hadn't been closed, and near the entrance they could see the faint outline of a pile of boots and britches. Newsome's snoring had grown louder.

Dean took a deep breath and nodded his head, signaling his brother to strike a match; then he lit the dynamite and tossed it into the darkness. The two sticks bounced once on the wooden flooring and landed on Newsome's bedroll, causing his snoring to briefly turn to a quick series of grunts.

Neither Newsome nor Longley was awake when the explosion came. Dean and Charlie Boy were already running back toward town. Only when they reached what they assumed was a safe distance did they briefly stop to look back. Dean couldn't stop laughing as an intense orange fire lit the night and shreds of burning canvas floated into the darkness. The tent was engulfed in flames and burning boots had been scattered in several directions. The only sound was the cracking of tentpoles before they fell into the rubble.

B Y DAYLIGHT, A small gathering of early risers had arrived and were silently examining the smoldering aftermath. The oily smell of charred canvas hung over the still morning. A couple of curious youngsters were quickly sent away by their fathers.

Once the area had cooled, the town doctor pulled on his fishing waders and made his way into the ashes. It was not the first time he had been required to walk through ashes, and after ruining a good pair of boots checking for survivors of a cabin fire, he'd learned his lesson.

Shortly, he announced that two people had died in the fire. Had it not been for the faint smell of gunpowder, he would have assumed they had accidentally set fire to the tent themselves.

Word of the fire soon reached Jonesy Blake and the wranglers he was bunking with. "Weren't those boys killed the ones you came back to town with?" one of his friends asked.

Blake didn't answer. He was too busy thinking of getting out of Abilene as quicky as possible.

Back at the hotel, the Ashtons were having the same thoughts. Bathed in sweat and still breathing hard, they were hurriedly gathering their belongings into saddlebags.

"Where is it we're going?" Charlie Boy said.

"I recall you saying you wanted to have a look-see at New Mexico," Dean replied.

His brother left to saddle their horses.

I T WAS TWO weeks before word reached the canyon that Trey Newsome and Hugh Longley were dead. The news had been delivered by two of Tompkins's men who had taken a small herd of stolen steers to Fort Worth for sale. While visiting some of the saloons in the city's Hell's Half Acre area, they had overheard several people talking about the fire out in Abilene that had claimed two lives.

Their deserted horses and the fact they had been living in the tent encampment were sure signs they weren't locals. After several cattlemen mentioned seeing Newsome and his friends drinking in the Branding Iron for several days, then suddenly disappearing, it wasn't difficult to put two and two together.

The canyon crew members wondered how Tompkins would react to the latest wave of bad news. Instead of launching into the public tirade they expected, he boarded himself up in his cabin and opened a bottle of whiskey. Alone, he cursed his dead foreman and wept for the loss of his scout.

In his solitude he reached two decisions. He would avenge Hugh Longley's death, no matter what the cost. To do so, however, would require someone far more talented at such matters than any of the cowboys on his payroll.

He knew exactly who to reach out to.

CHAPTER FOURTEEN

THE LONE STREET of Bent Tree was empty except for two stray dogs waiting to see if the café owner would put any breakfast scraps on her back porch. Carl Novak sat alone on a bench in front of the livery, watching the sun rise, waiting for Lyndon to wake up and the marshal to return.

Frustrated by the fact they still had no solid information on where the Ashton brothers might be, Wisenhunt suggested a long shot. "I'm thinking what's been going on out at that cattle rustling place has something to do with who we're looking for," the marshal said.

"Another one of your lawman's instincts?"

"All I'm saying is there's no use us just sitting here, growing older by the day," he said. "I'm going to ride back to the canyon and see if there's anything happening that might be of interest."

Novak immediately argued against it, reminding the marshal what had happened the last time they attempted to spy. "If you're going to be stubborn about it," Novak said, "you're not going by yourself."

"One person won't draw as much attention as three," the marshal said. "I'm going to take another route and come up on the canyon from the other side. My guess is they're still checking the hiding place we used before." He smiled. "Besides, the way I figure on going this time will allow me to avoid the fort and that crazy fella."

By midmorning, he was on his way.

D EL WISENHUNT HADN'T been honest about his intentions. He had watched Novak's resolve slowly slip away in recent days; he seemed to be haunted by doubt that justice for the death of his wife would be possible. He was talking more and more of the child he'd left in the care of the doctor's daughter, of how he missed her and felt he was on the verge of failing her. The marshal saw a wounded man whose life seemed to be vanishing. Carl Novak, he feared, was on the edge of becoming lost and beaten. Even Lyndon was concerned by the growing depression he sensed in his friend.

They had to find and confront the Ashton brothers. Soon.

Wisenhunt had decided to take matters into his own hands. He wasn't going to hide and watch the canyon in hopes of learning something that might lend promise to their search. He was going to ride directly into it, nonchalant as you please, and attempt to reason with a man he hoped to one day put behind bars.

On the morning he arrived he was quickly met by two riders pointing Winchesters. Even before they approached, the marshal had his hands in the air, signaling surrender. He made sure his badge was in plain sight.

He was roughly ushered into Tompkins's cabin and shoved toward a single chair in the middle of the room. The two men stared silently at each other for a minute before Tompkins spoke. "You being law," he said, "you're lucky you're not already dead. Still might be soon, but first I need my curiosity satisfied."

While his men watched, rifles still at the ready, Rafe Tompkins walked to a nearby table and poured two glasses of whiskey, handing one to his unexpected and unwelcome visitor.

"Now suppose you tell me what you're doing here . . . all by your lonesome." He took his time lighting a cigar.

"We've got common business to discuss," the marshal said.

Tompkins cursed. "That's grade-A bull and you know it. All we need to discuss is you causing my men to be dead."

"They were only killed before they could kill us, like I expect you told them you wanted done. Am I right?"

The marshal got no answer.

"You having me shot won't mean much to nobody. I'm fat and getting old, and my rear end aches just from the ride here. I ain't got the energy or eyesight I once had, and most important, I just don't much care what you decide to do to me."

He sipped at his drink, then continued. "I'd prefer you hear me out first. I've come to talk about a couple of men you made the mistake of hiring a while back. Brothers. One with fingers missing."

Tompkins leaned forward in his chair and puffed on his cigar. "Now, I will admit to wanting those two dead," he said.

"That's exactly the same feeling me and my friends have."

In a calm, quiet voice, Wisenhunt told why he and his partners had been searching for the Ashton brothers. He told how Novak's wife had been murdered and explained how it had caused a pretty little girl to lose her ability to speak even a single a word. He described the sorrow people of Wolf Creek had expressed at the funeral. And he tried to explain the overwhelming effect the tragedy had on the man he had come to West Texas with.

"In my years of keeping the law, I've seen killing that made sense and a lot that didn't. What those boys did to a fine lady named Frieda Novak—who you've never even heard of—is the kind that needs justice done.

"Seeing as how they've caused you grief as well, I'm here to ask for your help."

For a moment, Tompkins was silent, his thoughts flashing to the loss of a young man who had been the closest thing to a son he'd ever had. He could understand how this man Novak was feeling. Shifting in his chair, he nodded toward the two men holding rifles. "You boys can go on," he said.

He waited until they had left before nodding to

the marshal. "I got word recently that they're out in Abilene," he said. "Killed two of my best men who I had looking for them."

"So, we're thinking alike," Wisenhunt said.

"Strange as it might sound, I'm of a mind to have us join up. For the time being."

For the first time since entering the room, the marshal smiled. "That's what I came to hear," he said. Then, after a pause, he added, "But once this is over and done, I intend to see you're put in jail for being a cattle thief."

"Or die trying," Tompkins replied.

They shared another drink as they discussed a plan. "I've tried to run them down with men I've got working for me," Tompkins explained, "and they ain't done anything but get themselves killed. Can't say it's been all their fault, though. They're cowboys, not gunfighters. So, I've reached out to someone I figure can get the job done. He should be here in a day or two."

"A hired gun?"

"The best."

Wisenhunt contemplated the line he was crossing, joining forces with men who had no respect for the law he'd long ago sworn to uphold. He was surprised that the irony didn't trouble him more than it did.

"We'll be wanting to travel with him," he said.

T HE DAY THE marshal returned to Bent Tree, he was followed by a buggy and two other riders. Speechless, Novak and Lyndon remained seated on their bench as they approached.

"Let me introduce you to our new partner," Wisenhunt said as he dismounted.

Rafe Tompkins lifted his sombrero and stepped down from the buggy. "Pleased to finally meet you boys," he said. "Got anything worth drinking?"

CHAPTER FIFTEEN

S AM LIBBY DIDN'T look like a man who made his living killing people. He was less than six feet tall and dressed more like someone who worked at a bank than a hired gun. A black leather vest covered a white shirt that was buttoned just beneath his clean-shaven chin. His polished boots showed no sign that he'd traveled all the way from Laredo. When he spoke, which was seldom, it was in short, whispered sentences. The last time he'd laughed was when he was a baby. It was his cold, blue eyes that told all one needed to know. If, as the story goes, they're the window to a man's soul, they showed that Sam Libby most likely didn't have one.

He had arrived the day after Tompkins's visit.

"We've been waiting for you," Novak said, extending his hand. "When will you be wanting to head out to Abilene?"

Libby ignored Carl's attempted handshake. "Now," he said.

* * *

T HE RIDE TOOK two days, during which Carl and the marshal gave up attempting to make conversation. Only Lyndon persisted.

"How many men you reckon you've killed?" he asked.

Libby's answer was a cold look that suggested he might like to immediately add one more to whatever the count might be.

Without speaking a word, he made it clear he wasn't pleased that Rafe Tompkins had insisted he allow the marshal and the others to accompany him.

It was only when they arrived in Abilene that Libby became talkative. He questioned workers at the stock pens, in the saloons, the café, and on the streets. He made no attempt to hide his purpose or to vary his questions. "I'm looking for a man who's missing some fingers on one hand and has a brother tagging along with him. Their name's Ashton," he would say. Whether he came across as friendly or intimidating, Novak wasn't initially sure, but people were always quick to respond.

A local horse trader said he didn't know the men but might know somebody who did. "Check with a fella working down at the feed store. I'm told he was friendly with those strangers who got themselves blown up over in Tent City. Calls himself Jonesy."

"That his last name?"

"Couldn't tell you."

Jonesy Blake was loading corn onto a wagon as two more able-bodied men than he stood by watching. He had a sack balanced on his shoulder when Libby and his party approached.

"I need you to put that down and talk to me," Libby said, then began to gruffly explain that he was looking for someone. Novak quickly decided it was not Libby's friendliness that got people to talk.

Blake's eyes never met his visitor's as he listened to the description of the Ashton brothers. Being reminded of the deaths of Trey Newsome and Hugh Longley sent a cold shiver down his back.

Libby took a step closer, his face just inches from Jonesy's. "I'm waiting to hear what you've got to say."

"I made a big mistake that got me mixed up in all this," he said. "I got too ambitious and it near got me killed and ended up with me working at this lousy job." He recounted his visit to the canyon and his travels in search of the same people Libby was looking for. "Closest we got was finding them hid out here," he said. "I wasn't no witness, but I'm betting it was them who blowed up that tent."

Impatient, Novak jumped in with a question, displeasing Libby. "Know where they are now?"

"The owner of the Greenleaf Hotel came asking the same question a few days back. Seems the Ashtons took leave in the middle of the night without making full payment for the room they'd rented."

"He have any notion which way they were headed?" Libby asked, regaining control of the conversation.

"Told me he once heard them talking about going over into New Mexico Territory, which is fine with me. If your intention is to find and kill them, I'd be much obliged. For now, the farther away they are, the more likely I am to keep breathing."

Blake's news disappointed Novak. "Seems they stay two steps ahead of us," he said. "It's like we're chasing ghosts."

To his surprise, Libby gave him a friendly slap on the shoulder. "Men like these," he said, "are easy to track. They're broke and not real smart. They'll leave a trail a mile wide. You can trust me on that. You ever been to New Mexico?"

Novak shook his head.

"Ain't nothing but jackrabbits, dust storms, and open range," Libby said. "We'll get us a good night's rest, then head that way."

Standing nearby, the marshal smiled. As much as he hated to admit it, he was beginning to like Sam Libby.

H E WAS RIGHT about the Ashtons leaving a well-marked trail.

At one farm where Libby and the others stopped shortly after crossing the border, they learned that a smokehouse had been raided and two freshly washed shirts had been stolen from an old lady's clothesline.

Later, they were greeted by a ranch owner with a bandage wrapped around his head. He'd been pistol-whipped, then had his shotgun and a bag of silver dollars taken from his cabin.

"They also took two of my best horses," he said, "leaving the ones they rode in on. Both are so wore out and broke down I most likely should have just shot them and put them out of their misery. But since they've already been so mistreated, I think I'll see if I can get them well enough to finish their lives in peace out in the pasture."

Before they left, Novak and Williamson cleaned the cut on the rancher's forehead and put on a fresh bandage. In turn, he offered them chicken soup and leftover corn bread, then filled their canteens from his well.

"Just like I told you," Libby said as they rode away. "They're leaving us signposts pointing where they're going. It won't be long now."

"I hope when we do catch up to them," said Lyndon, "we can bring that man's horses and shotgun back to him. He seemed a nice fella."

A T DUSK THEY made camp in a gully that protected them from the blowing sand and any strangers who might be passing. Lyndon gathered wood for a fire and the marshal led the horses to a small patch of grass on the bank of a shallow stream.

Then he and the marshal watched as Libby took a tin cup and a small pouch from his saddlebag and headed toward the water where the horses were leisurely drinking. After washing himself, he filled the cup and returned to sit by the fire, spreading the contents of his pouch on his saddle blanket—a straight razor, a bar of soap, a comb, and a small dollar-sized mirror. His traveling companions watched in silence as he shaved, combed his hair, then spit-polished his boots with a bandanna.

"You planning on going courting tonight?" Wisenhunt finally asked.

Novak and Lyndon chuckled but Libby gave no response, just gathered his grooming items and put them away.

Later, after the campfire had burned down to embers and Carl and Lyndon were asleep, gently snoring, the marshal returned from a visit to the privacy of nearby bushes and joined Libby. "Me, I don't do much sleeping these days," he said, "but a young man like yourself ought to be getting some rest."

"Nothing but bad things happen when you're sleeping," Libby said.

For the next several minutes they sat in a silence interrupted only by the faint night sounds of birds settling in to roost, crackles from what remained of the campfire, and small animals foraging in the dark.

"I realize you ain't much of a talker," Wisenhunt finally said, "but I've got a question that's been weighing heavy on me since we first met."

"What's that?"

The marshal stirred the coals with a stick before he replied. "Probably it's none of my business, but I'm wanting to know what it is that causes a man to take up your line of work."

When he got no reply, he continued. "In my days I've seen a good amount of killing. Way too much. I've known outlaws who killed so they could steal, men getting drunk and killing over nothing more than the dealing of a card. Crazies who claimed to hear voices in their heads. Brothers killing brothers in war and men going on a rampage just because their woman didn't have their supper on the table when she was supposed to. And I've never been smart enough to make much sense of it."

Libby turned to face Wisenhunt. "It's a job, one I'm good at and get paid well to do. The way I see it, there's people who need killing. Doing away with men like the ones we're chasing won't harm anyone but them and just might make the world a little better place."

"You saying what you do is a calling?"

"Nope, just a job," Libby repeated. "Now I'll thank you to say good night."

Wisenhunt wasn't satisfied, so he continued. "You know it ain't going to end well, don't you? Somewhere, someday, there's going to be somebody a little faster on the draw, or hiding, waiting to shoot you in the back. Or maybe somebody like me will decide enough's enough and see to it you wind up sitting in a prison cell or getting hanged."

Without a reply, Libby got to his feet and slowly walked away, into the darkness. The marshal returned to poking at the campfire, his question unanswered.

L YNDON WAS ALWAYS the first up in the morning, busying himself rekindling the fire and doling out portions from the bag of oats he'd brought along for the horses. As he had done for the past several mornings, Wisenhunt complained about not having any coffee. "It ain't decent for a man to start the day without something to get his juices to flowing," he said.

"How much longer you figure until we catch up to them?" young Williamson asked.

"I got no idea. That's a question better put to our friend Sam."

Lyndon shrugged. "He don't ever bother talking back when I speak to him."

Saddling his horse nearby, Libby overheard the conversation. "It depends on how often they stop to cause more misery," he said, "but even with them on fresh horses, I'm guessing we're not too far behind. A day, maybe two."

Wisenhunt slapped his hat against his thigh. "Lordee mercy, if that didn't sound like him giving us a full-out sermon."

Libby turned away to hide a smile, He was beginning to enjoy the marshal's good nature.

CARL NOVAK, MEANWHILE, had not warmed to Libby, keeping his distance and avoiding conversation as much as possible. While he accepted the fact this stranger hired by Rafe Tompkins was better suited to achieve the goal of finding the Ashton brothers than he was, this was not Libby's fight. It wasn't his wife who was killed, his heart doing the suffering, his daughter left back in Wolf Creek, scared and speechless.

They'd not discussed it, but at some point Novak planned to make it clear to Libby that when they did catch up with the Ashtons, it would be him who did the killing, not a hired gunslinger.

IT WAS NOT difficult for Sam Libby to remember the first man he killed. He'd been just a boy, living with his older brother, a goat farmer, after their parents had passed away. The second or third time his friend Ruby arrived at Wayside School with a black eye and a large bruise on her arm, he knew something had to be done. Her father was well known as the town drunk and a notoriously mean one.

The night after Sam saw the newest marks Dan Scoggins had left on his daughter, he borrowed his brother's shotgun, rode his mule to town, walked straight to the saloon, and, without a single word, blew Ruby's daddy's face into red, greasy pieces. A bloody eyeball, someone later recalled, had stuck on a nearby mirror.

Though not in the least remorseful, Sam left that night after returning the shotgun. It was the last time he'd had a place to call home.

He had wandered through South Texas, working at odd jobs and keeping his past a secret. On his nineteenth birthday he was sworn in as a deputy sheriff in the border town of Los Rios, but the job lasted only a few months. His boss, the sheriff, had become ill at ease over the fact Libby was inclined to shoot lawbreakers when a simple arrest and a night in jail would have sufficed.

The fired deputy's only argument before turning in his badge was that he hadn't killed a single man who didn't deserve it.

It had been a wealthy rancher, weary of having his prize cattle stolen, who first offered him money for his services. In short order he had dispatched the cattle rustling ringleader and three of his followers to their eternal reward and had more money in his pocket than he'd ever dreamed of.

Libby had found a profession. He bought himself a rifle, a pearl-handled Colt, a faster horse, and was in business. He practiced his shooting until he could regularly knock a penny off a fence post from twenty yards away. His reputation steadily grew, to a point where he was even given a nickname—the Caretaker. He didn't much care for it, yet liked the job that went with it.

By the time he was hired by Rafe Tompkins, he was thirty-four years old and couldn't have answered Lyndon's question even if he'd wanted to. He'd long since lost track of the number of men he'd killed.

CHAPTER SIXTEEN

⌒

THEY WERE TWO days into New Mexico Territory
when they were surprised to see a riderless horse
limping in their direction. The mare's mane and tail
had been singed and a blister on one ear was oozing
blood.

"There's been a fire someplace," Novak said as he
stopped and slowly scanned the horizon. Just over a
nearby hilltop he saw faint clouds of smoke floating
into the otherwise clear morning sky. Lyndon was
already at the injured horse's side, talking to it gently
and trying to determine what aid he could give.

When they reached the crest of the hill, they could
see a burning building in the distance. "Appears
they've left us another sign," Sam said.

They slowly rode closer, the injured horse following at Lyndon's side.

It wasn't much of a place, just a small adobe house,
a smoldering barn, an outhouse, and a garden with
nothing but a half-dozen rows of cornstalks. There

was also a pen for chickens that were, at the moment, frantically clucking. A milk cow, having escaped the blaze, stood in the shade of the lone tree in the yard. Beside her, tethered to a low-hanging limb, were two horses, still saddled and looking as if they were dreading their riders' return.

"They're still here," Libby whispered as he pulled his rifle from its scabbard. Novak and Wisenhunt, their bodies suddenly tense, already had their pistols drawn. "Reckon what their fascination is with setting things afire?" the marshal said as they quietly dismounted and looked for the most protected route to the house.

"You go back a ways and see to it our horses don't bolt," Sam told Lyndon. "If there's shooting, I don't want them harmed or running away. We'll need them to get us out of this godforsaken part of the world once our business is tended to."

As Lyndon frowned at his dismissal and stroked a hindquarter of the injured horse, Libby signaled for Novak and the marshal to make their way to a position behind the outhouse. "I can hear yelling going on inside," Wisenhunt said as he crouched and followed Novak across the outer edge of the yard.

Libby, meanwhile, was making his way to the back of the house.

He had almost reached a small window when Lyndon accidentally touched the injured horse's burned ear, causing it to cry out in pain. The other horses immediately reacted, nervously rearing and stomping the powdered ground.

In the house, Charlie Boy left his chair and hurried to the window. "Somebody's out there," he said.

His brother slowly eased back the hammer of the pistol he had been pointing at the man and woman seated at the kitchen table.

T HEY HAD RIDDEN up on the isolated place earlier in the day, tired, hungry and ill-tempered. They saw little evidence of any measure of prosperity, the most they hoped for being a meal and maybe a few needed supplies.

What they would soon learn was that the elderly couple who came into the yard to greet them made corn whiskey for a living, selling jugs to neighbors and a saloonkeeper who sent a wagon fifteen miles to pick up a load on the first of every month.

"You boys headed west, are you?" the man said, squinting into the early-day sun.

"Just seeing the country," Dean answered.

The woman, holding tightly to her husband's arm, smiled and invited them in. "I've got coffee on the stove and there's plenty of biscuits left from breakfast," she said.

As everyone sat at the table, Dean surveyed the sparsely furnished house and was about to decide there was little, if anything, to steal when the man first alluded to the business he was in.

"You boys care for a little taste before you head out? Maybe give your coffee some kick?" he said. "So happens, I make the best corn whiskey in the territory." As he spoke, his wife was taking a clay jug from the kitchen shelf and placing it in the center of the table.

The man was obviously proud of his product and

was soon bragging unabashedly about the quality of his home brew and the growing number of customers who came to buy it. "I'll soon be needing to plant me a bigger cornfield," he said.

Dean took his pistol from its holster and placed it on the table in front of him. "I'm proud to hear business is good," he said. "I surely am. Where is it you keep all the money you've been making?"

The woman put a hand to her mouth to muffle a cry.

"Could be I was a bit misleading," her husband quickly said. He stuttered slightly and his hands were shaking, causing him to spill what remained of his coffee. "Truth of the matter is—"

The elder Alston picked up his gun. "I asked polite as I know how to without hurting nobody. Where . . . is . . . the . . . money?"

"We ain't got none. I swear. What profit we've made so far has gone to buying supplies and making payments on this place. I just traded six quarts to get us a half-decent milk cow. See, we ain't been here long . . ."

Dean ignored the rest of his explanation and told Charlie Boy to start searching the house. "Tear up what's needed," he said. "Just find the money."

The woman was crying. "Like my husband just said, we ain't got none. No cause to tear up our things."

Dean was drinking the old man's whiskey straight from the jug by then. "If one of you don't tell us, and soon," he said, "I'll be sending my brother out to burn down your barn. And if that don't persuade you, I'll not bother telling you what'll most likely happen next." He was fast getting drunk and angry.

"Ain't no money," Charlie Boy said after searching the kitchen and the couple's bedroom.

"Gotta be. Go out and look in all the outbuildings
for a hiding place. See if you can find any spot where
a hole's been dug up to bury something. If you don't
find anything, set fire to the barn." He handed his
brother the remainder of the matches they had
bought in Abilene.

After no success, Charlie Boy dutifully set the
barn ablaze. In the house, Dean ordered the woman
to bring another jug to the table and light a fire in the
fireplace to warm the room. Though badly shaken,
her husband couldn't help but ask Ashton's opinion
of his brew.

"Better than passable," he said. "You got my com-
pliments."

"I appreciate that. Now, if you would kindly not
kill us I'd be even more grateful. I've got orders need
filling before Saturday-night dancing."

Dean glared at the old whiskey maker. "Just shut
up until you're ready to tell me what I want to know."
His words were beginning to slur.

Charlie Boy returned to the house and pulled up a
chair. "Brother, I don't think they're lying," he whispered into Dean's ear. "They really ain't got no
money to steal. So, we've got no cause to kill them,
right? Maybe it's time we be on our way."

Dean's only reply was a crazy grin, then another
long drink from the jug. Outside, the barn, made of
old and brittle timber, was crashing in on itself. A
horse had busted out of its stall and was running for
its life, smoke streaming from its mane and tail. A

Jersey cow lumbered out, her udders full and swaying from not yet having been milked.

And Dean just kept grinning, drinking, and waving his pistol. Until Charlie Boy alerted him there was someone outside. He immediately told the woman to remove the jug of whiskey from the table and start bringing his brother coffee. "Bring him lots . . . and be quick about it," he said.

The urgency in his brother's voice didn't immediately register as Dean clumsily attempted to wrestle the jug away from the woman. Only when he realized he couldn't recall Charlie Boy ever sounding so assertive did the fog lift slightly. "What is it makes you think we've got company?" he said.

"I just know." He was taking the man's shotgun from its place above the front door as he spoke. "I'll be needing some shells," he yelled.

S AM LIBBY HAD reached the corner of the house and crawled on hands and knees to the nearest window. Without curtains, it provided him a good view of the scene playing out in the kitchen. He could see that two men were seated at the table and a woman was standing at the stove, pouring coffee into a tin cup. He was preparing to take aim, assuming the two men were those he was after, when another person came into view, holding a shotgun.

Libby slowly slid down beneath the windowsill. This was not going to be as easy as he had hoped.

As he contemplated what to do, the sudden sound of a shotgun blast came from the front porch. Charlie

Boy had rushed outside and fired a shot into the air before he began to yell. "I know you're out there," he said, "so show yourself or get gone. This here's private property." For emphasis, he fired a second shot from the double barrel.

No more than thirty yards away, the marshal had a good line of sight to the porch and immediately recognized the man with the shotgun. "That's the little brother," he told Novak. "My opinion is he's near harmless and will only do whatever bidding his brother Dean tells him to."

A nervous smile crossed Carl's face. "Then we've got them. Finally. Let's move in and get this done."

"Patience," Wisenhunt said. "We'd be wise to wait and see what brother Dean's up to first. He's the crazy one we've got cause to be concerned about." He moved back behind the outhouse and frowned. "Phew . . . I wish we'd picked us a hiding place that didn't smell quite so ripe."

Novak ignored the marshal's attempt to lighten to mood. "Reckon where Libby is?" he said. Then he fired a wild shot in the direction of the house.

Too late, a hand grabbed his pistol and pulled it away. "That was a fool thing to do," said Libby, who had made his way through the cornstalks to where they were. "We've got a problem. And now it just got bigger."

"What?" Wisenhunt asked.

"There's others in the house," Libby said.

The marshal glared at Novak. "I warned you to be patient," he growled. "Now it could be innocent folks are going to get harmed."

His chastising abruptly ended when another shot,

this one from a pistol, was fired from the house. In the doorway two people were standing. An elderly woman, clearly terrified, was still holding a coffee cup as she served as a shield for the man who had fired the shot.

Dean Ashton sounded almost sober as he called out, "There's folks in here who are going to get hurt real bad if this keeps up." He fired two more shots that thudded into the outhouse door before he disappeared back into the house and shut the door.

Inside, the old man had fainted and was lying spread-eagled on the floor. Released by Dean, the woman hurried to her husband and was soon bathing his face with a damp cloth and trying to get him to take sips of whiskey.

Dean laughed. "I guess we know who it is wears the pants in this house," he said.

Charlie Boy wasn't amused. "People are going to get killed, Dean," he said. "Maybe us."

Growing more sober by the minute, the elder Ashton placed a hand on his brother's shoulder. "Not today," he said. "I got us a plan."

Charlie Boy knew better than to respond.

THE STANDOFF WENT on for much of the day. One of the brothers would occasionally fire a shot from a window to keep the men pinned down and Libby would reply, always aiming his rifle at the rooftop so no one inside would be hit.

"I suppose it ain't often that famous manhunters find themselves hiding behind an outhouse, getting themselves shot at," Wisenhunt said. "I'm anxious to hear your thoughts on what it is we should do. 'Cause my old legs are getting stiff as a board."

Novak hadn't spoken since firing his impatient shot. "I've already made one mistake," he said, "so I'm not inclined to offer suggestions. But I've got to say I don't want harm to come to the folks whose place this is. They've done nothing wrong except to let the wrong folks into their house."

He and the marshal were surprised when Libby readily agreed. "I don't want to cause anyone to be killed who shouldn't be," he said.

"So, what do we do?" Novak said.

"Much as I hate saying it, we've got no control of the situation unless we just rush the place and shoot everything that moves. Since we're agreed that's not a choice, we're at the mercy of a full-out crazy man."

INSIDE, DEAN WAS outlining his plan to his brother. "Now that the old man is awake and returned to his senses, we're getting out of here. He'll ride back of me, you take the old woman."

Emerging onto the porch again, shielded by the wife, he called out. "Here's what's going to happen so nobody gets themselves shot," he said. "We're gonna be leaving now, taking these folks with us. First, though, I want you to show yourself and drop your weapons—all of them—on the ground. Then back away. Once you've showed your good faith, we'll mount up and be gone. If you try following us, you'll be causing the deaths of two real nice folks, one of them being the best whiskey maker in the county."

The sound of Ashton's voice infuriated Libby.

"I'm going to kill him so dead there won't be nothing left to say grace over," he said, "but not now. He's got a good plan and we've got no choice but to go along with it."

"Patience," the marshal added, nodding his approval.

"What if he starts shooting us once we've surrendered our weapons?" Novak said.

"I figure he's already thought about that and realized he couldn't kill us all before he wound up dead himself," Libby said. "We'll just take our chances."

The end of the confrontation came quickly. Charlie Boy gathered the weapons while Dean pointed his rifle at the men, who stood side by side, their hands over their heads.

"Now," Dean said, "I'll thank each of you to loosen your belts and let your britches fall to your ankles. Don't want you boys chasing after us."

Both brothers were laughing as they and their terrified hostages galloped away.

It was left to Wisenhunt to assess the situation. "Now, ain't we a pitiful-looking bunch," he said as he kicked at the dirt, then pulled up his pants.

T HEY WAITED IN hopes that Lyndon would bring the horses, but when he didn't arrive, they started walking back toward the grove where they had told him to wait.

It was Novak who saw the boy leaning against the trunk of a tree, the injured horse gently nuzzling his face. When the men got closer, they could see that the front of Williamson's shirt was soaked in blood.

"Thank God he ain't dead," Wisenhunt said as he put his hands to Lyndon's face and looked into his eyes. Pulling the bloody shirt away, he could see where a bullet had entered just below his rib cage and exited from his lower back.

"Get him on a horse and we'll take him back to the house," Novak said. "Under the circumstances, I don't think the owners will mind us briefly moving in."

While Sam stopped the bleeding and the marshal fed Lyndon sips of whiskey to dull the pain, Novak found a half-full tin of black salve in a kitchen cabinet. "Not certain what it is," he said, "but it looks like medicine."

"Best we can do," Libby said as he began to smear the tar-like substance onto the wounds. Lyndon cried out in pain and reached for the whiskey glass Wisenhunt was holding.

It was a while before he could tell them what had happened. "I was just tending the horses like I'd been told," he said, handing the empty glass back to the marshal. "All of a sudden these two horses came toward me, running like they was in a Fourth of July race. My best recall is there were two people on each horse. And as they rode past, this one man pulled his pistol, let out some kind of wild yell, and shot me. Never even slowed down to take aim."

Wisenhunt cursed and threw the empty glass against the wall. "They've bought themselves some time," he said.

Libby was equally upset. "At least," he finally said, "we know which way they headed."

Lyndon was becoming more alert, sitting up, and in less pain. He reached for one of the biscuits that had been left on the table, then examined the bandage wrapped around his abdomen. "I'm guessing my shirt's ruined," he said.

Then he turned his attention to a greater concern. "Reckon there's some of that salve left that we can doctor that burned horse with?" he asked.

CHAPTER SEVENTEEN

THE NEAREST DOCTOR was ten miles south in Bois d'Arc Hills, a small silver-mining town Sam Libby had once visited. He'd done business there years earlier, chasing down a man who had kidnapped the wife of a bank president on Galveston Island. Unlike his current assignment, it had been easy. The kidnapper was shot and killed as he was leaving a saloon and the woman returned safely to her husband. It had, Libby remembered, required a long, hard ride, but a generous payday made it worthwhile.

It was Wisenhunt who insisted that Lyndon see someone with experience treating gunshot wounds. "Don't want him getting infected and dying on us," he said. "He's got a fever and needs someone to stitch up the holes in his side and back." Neither Libby nor Novak argued.

After feeding the horses and milking the old couple's cow, Carl found a serviceable wagon and offered to make it comfortable. Lyndon, however, insisted he could ride—if they took their time making the trip.

"First farmhouse we come to," Novak said, "we need to make somebody aware the cow needs seeing to. I've done promised Lyndon we'll take the horse with us."

Weighing on them all was the necessary delay in searching for the brothers. Sam was angry and impatient, pacing through the house and muttering curses. Carl was slipping into a dark depression, sitting alone on the porch when the marshal joined him.

"Things don't always go the way we plan," Wisenhunt said.

"If I hadn't been such a fool and fired that first shot, we might have figured a way to end this yesterday," Novak said. "Now we've got ourselves an even bigger mess to deal with. The Ashtons rode away laughing at us, those old folk are likely to be killed, and I caused Lyndon to get shot." He buried his face in his hands.

"So," the marshal aid, "what you need to do is get your head up, put a smile on your ugly face, and see to it we make things right. We'll catch up to those two soon enough, then you can get back to your little girl and forget all this nonsense. First thing, though, we need to see that the boy's going to be okay."

Novak looked at Wisenhunt and a faint smile emerged. "Patience, right?"

"Yes, sir. Works every time."

T HE BOIS D'ARC Hills doctor stepped away from the table where Lyndon lay bare-chested. He had just applied sulfur packs to the wounds and stitched them up. "Lucky thing," he said, "is no ribs were broken and I see no signs of muscle damage. He'll have himself a scar to brag about, but soon as his fever breaks he'll be fine. It's a good sign he said he was hungry."

As he spoke he was reaching for his hat and medical bag. "Now, where's this horse he's wanting me to have a look at?"

While the doctor was carrying out his dual role as doctor and veterinarian, Libby was visiting the office of the local mining company, hoping to find a map of the territory. He had promised to meet the others at the café down the street from the doctor's office.

They were finishing ham and eggs and red-eye gravy when he arrived. After asking a waitress for coffee, he handed a package to Lyndon. In it was a new shirt he'd stopped into the dry goods store to buy. "See to it you don't let this one get ruined," he said.

Lyndon was at a loss for words.

After the waitress cleared their dishes away, Libby unfolded the map he'd borrowed and spread it on the table.

Pointing with the spoon he'd used to stir his coffee, he said, "This is where we were . . . and this is the way they went when they left. The question is, where is it they're headed?" He studied the map for a minute as the others sat silently.

Novak finally spoke. "What's your thinking about the old couple they took with them?"

"They can't do nothing but slow them down. Once they're convinced they have no need for them, they'll either set them loose or kill them. With any luck, we'll find them somewhere along the way . . . dead or alive."

"My experience," said Wisenhunt, "tells me these boys aren't the kind to do much sleeping under the stars and living off the land. They're town folks. They'll be headed someplace where they can find a friendly saloon and somebody they can rob or who's willing to give them work."

Libby continued tracing his spoon along the map. "San Patricio," he finally said. "Pretty little town, sits down in a valley. Pine trees and black soil. Don't fit in with the rest of New Mexico at all." He began nodding his head. "That's where they'll be headed. I'll make wager on it."

Though the marshal was anxious to get back on the trail, he was the one who suggested they spend a night in Bois d'Arc Hills. "It'll give the boy—and us—a chance to get some rest. Then, if he's feeling up to it, we can head out at first light."

"I'll be fine," Lyndon said. Meanwhile, he wanted to visit the local livery and see if he could arrange boarding for the old folks' mare. With proper care, the vet had told him, she was also going to fully recover.

"About time we had us some good news," Wisenhunt said.

T HEY RETURNED TO the site of the foiled shootout the following day. The neighboring farmer they had spoken to earlier was hitching the milk cow to his wagon and waved as they rode up. "How long you reckon before they'll be back and needing her?" he said.

"Hard to say," Libby replied. "Best you just consider her your property until you learn different."

The farmer asked no more questions, just cast a sad-eyed glance toward the ashes where the barn had once stood.

"Just as well take the chickens, too," the marshal said. "The boy here's done made arrangements for their horse."

As the farmer was attempting to get a rope around the stubborn cow's neck, Novak hurried into the house and returned with a jug of whiskey. "For your troubles," he said as he put it on the seat of the wagon.

"Y'all giving the impression they ain't coming back."

He got no response to his observation.

T HE LOGICAL THING to do, Libby said, was to start where the Ashtons were last seen. Standing near the tree where he had been shot, Lyndon pointed to the west. "They headed that way," he said.

All three knew that the first people they were eager to catch up to weren't the brothers.

Their search ended just before nightfall.

In a shallow gully they found the old woman sitting with her back to a boulder, her husband lying with his head in her lap. She was rocking gently and singing a church hymn, seemingly unaware of Wisenhunt as he approached, pulling the plug from his canteen.

"You got no cause to be afraid. We're here to help," he said, pouring a trickle of water onto her chapped lips. "You folks okay?"

There was a faint show of recognition as she stopped singing and looked up at the marshal. "We near froze last night," she said. As she spoke, her husband stirred and opened his eyes. "Praise the Lord," he said. "Ma, we're saved." Dried blood hid a cut across his cheek.

"We tried to tell those awful men we didn't have no money," she said, then went back to singing.

T HIS COULD BE the first miracle I ever witnessed," Wisenhunt told Sam. "I didn't think there was any chance we'd find them alive."

"So, what do we do now?" Novak said.

"Me and Lyndon will get them back to their place and see if that farmer knows someone to come and sit with them. You and Sam go ahead. We'll catch up quick as we can."

Once again, the old couple were riding double, her with her thin arms around Lyndon's waist, her husband behind Wisenhunt. This time, however, their spirits steadily rose as they neared home.

"I thought certain we was going to be dead," the whiskey maker said, "if not at the hands of those who took us, then from the coyotes or starving."

"How'd you come by that cut to your face?"

"One of them, the fella missing some of his fingers, done it while they was arguing about what to do with us. Somehow, the younger one managed to talk him out of shooting us and leaving us dead. It riled him so much he smacked me a good one before they rode off."

"They say anything about where they were going?"

"Nope, not that I heard said. I'm just praying it's someplace far away from me and my old lady."

CHAPTER EIGHTEEN

C HARLIE BOY SAT watching his brother sleep in the shade of a tall pine. It was midday and they had reached the edge of the picturesque San Patricio Valley but had decided not to continue into to town. They needed to rest. And thanks to the stubborn old coots they'd left on the side of the trail, they had no money.

Still, Dean woke with a smile on his face. "I was having myself a dream," he said.

"All you was doing was snoring. I was worried you would scare the horses."

Dean ignored him. "See, me and these two pretty ladies were drinking and having ourselves this conversation . . ."

Charlie Boy cut his brother short, tossing a dried pinecone at his head. "Hush and concentrate for a minute," he said. "What is it you figure we're going to do? We can't just keep on running everywhere and getting nowhere."

Dean got to his feet and began brushing pine needles from his britches. His smile was gone.

From their vantage point they could see the town below, with its neat rows of buildings, a towering church spire, and buggies and wagons making their way along the main street. There was the faint clanging sound of a blacksmith's hammer and a school bell ringing. The sweet scent of pine wafted through the late-summer breeze.

"Make yourself presentable as possible and ride into town," Dean said. "See what stores look like they might be worth robbing once it gets dark."

"You ain't coming?"

"Best just one of us makes an appearance in daylight. If anybody inquires, you're on your way to visit kinfolk. While you're gone, I'm going to try and get back to my dreaming."

THEY WAITED UNTIL well past midnight before making their way to the edge of town. Even the saloon had snuffed out its porch lantern and locked the door. The street was dark and empty. Aside from the barking of a lonesome dog somewhere in the distance and a couple of stray cats fighting over a dead rat, there was nothing but silence.

"A peaceful little place, ain't it?" Dean said as they left their horses and began making their way down an alley.

Earlier, Charlie Boy had seen that the local hardware, located in the middle of town, and the feed store, down near the livery, were the two most busy establishments. A small ladies' dress shop seemed to be drawing a considerable number of customers, but he'd judged it too sissified to consider.

They decided on robbing the hardware store.

Breaking the lock on the flimsy back door was easy and they quickly began to feel their way along shelves filled with everything from carpentry needs to work clothes. Dean stopped when his bad hand ran across a row of pocketknives, picked one, and stuffed it in his pocket. "We're looking for the cash register," he whispered. "It'll likely be up toward the front."

There was the brief sound of a small bell when the drawer slid out, revealing neat rows of bills and a tray filled with coins. "Good to see the owner didn't bother making a deposit at the bank," Dean said as he felt along the counter for something to put the money in.

As he did so, the glow of a candle appeared at the top of the nearby stairs. "Who's there?" a loud voice called out. When he got no reply, he fired a pistol shot down into the darkness.

On his visit to town, Charlie Boy had failed to learn that the store owner lived on the second floor of his establishment.

In his frantic haste to find cover, Dean spilled the tray of coins. As pennies and dimes bounced across the wooden floor, Charlie Boy ducked beneath the counter. A second shot came from the top of the stairs. "If you're here to try robbing me," the owner yelled, "it's going to get you killed."

In the sheriff's office down the street, the night deputy was awakened by the shots and, once he decided they hadn't come from late-night drunks showing their displeasure over the closing of the saloon, pulled on his boots.

Dean made his way to the edge of the stairs and waited motionless for the owner to come down. He held his breath, making no sound except for the rustle of his trousers as he reached into his pocket for the knife.

Barefoot and in his long johns, the owner slowly made his way down the stairs, his pistol pointed in the direction of his cash register. "I figure I know where you are," he said, "so I'm going to start shooting serious now." As he spoke, he reached to step closer to where Dean was hiding.

His eyes having adjusted to the dark, Charlie Boy watched as his brother quickly got to his feet, reached through the rails, and buried the knife blade deep into the owner's thigh. There was a loud groan, then the pistol dropped, and the shop owner fell forward. By the time he reached the bottom of the stairs he was unconscious and bleeding badly.

Charlie Boy had come out of hiding just as the deputy burst through the door, pointing his Peacemaker and ordering him to put his hands over his head. Before he could raise his arms, a shot came from the dark corner near the stairwell. The deputy's hat flew away as he grabbed his chest, then slowly went to his knees.

"We best get out of here . . . fast," Dean called out as he holstered his pistol. Charlie Boy yanked the drawer from the cash register, then ran toward the back door, knocking over a barrel of brooms as he followed his brother.

Even as lanterns were coming to life in nearby houses, the brothers were well on their way out of town.

T HEY RODE THROUGH the night, not stopping until daylight. Finally arriving at a small stream, they decided to let their horses rest and drink. Dean sat on a fallen tree trunk and counted the money. "Twenty-seven dollars," he said.

"Would have been more if you hadn't been clumsy and spilled all the coins," Charlie Boy replied.

Then, almost as an afterthought, he added, "Brother, we've got to stop killing people or we're going to soon have more lawmen chasing after us than you can shake a stick at."

I T WAS TWO days later when Sam Libby walked into the sheriff's office. His guess that the Ashton brothers had headed to San Patricio was quickly confirmed when he and Novak overheard a conversation in the café where they had stopped to eat.

"I'm told you had some troubles a few nights ago," he said to the young lawman who looked up from his desk.

"Who might you be?"

Carl stepped forward and gave his name. "We've been hired as bounty hunters and are looking for a couple of men we have reason to believe were headed this way," he said. "Could be the same boys—they're brothers—who were the cause of your problems. We've been trailing them from Texas, where they did some killings. And a while back they terrorized an old farming couple north of here."

The sheriff stood and extended a hand to Novak. "Name's Judson Wilson," he said. "Most folks call me Sheriff Jud. From what you say, we could have a common interest. Until you walked in, I didn't know the slightest where to even start figuring this out."

"We only heard bits and pieces down at the café," Libby said. "What happened?"

"My deputy got himself killed trying to stop a robbery down at the hardware store. The owner's laid up with a bad knife wound."

"Nobody seen anything?"

"Nobody but my deputy, God rest his soul. I'm on my way to speak a few words at his funeral this afternoon. I was just sitting here, writing down what I want to say, when you walked in." He was shaking his head as he spoke. "This kind of thing ain't usual for San Patricio. Last time I even arrested anybody it was an old drunk who was stealing folks' laying hens."

"The man who got stabbed," Libby said. "He tell you anything useful?"

"Said it was too dark and he was scared out of his wits. Hadn't never been robbed before. He's taken to bed over at his place, above the hardware store."

"Mind us paying him a visit?"

"I imagine he'd appreciate the company." As Libby and Novak turned to leave, he returned to his writing but looked up as they reached the door. "Bounty hunters, huh? Reckon why there ain't nobody wearing a badge doing the chasing?"

"That," said Libby with a slight shrug, "ain't none of our business."

* * *

THOUGH THERE WAS a "Closed" sign in the window, the door to the hardware store was unlocked. Novak and Libby made their way up the stairs and found the owner sitting up in bed, sipping from a glass of bourbon. "You boys aren't here to rob me, too, are you?"

Novak smiled and quickly introduced himself and his partner. After only a few minutes they realized they would learn nothing more than what the sheriff had already told them.

"I hope you boys catch who done this," the owner said. "They made off with might near a hundred dollars. Maybe more. And that don't count all the change that's scattered on the floor downstairs."

WHEN THE DEPUTY'S funeral was about to get under way, the café was deserted except for Novak and Libby. They drank sweet tea and watched as people paraded toward the church. A bell was ringing, signaling it was time to bid the deputy farewell.

"I can't figure why we're having such a hard time getting this over with," Sam said. "My first thinking was that the Ashtons were dumb and would be easy to catch. Now I'm of a mind they're plain lucky—and crazy as outhouse rats. That's what's making the job so hard. There's no way to figure their thinking. Killing a lawman . . . stabbing that old fool back there in the hardware store . . . blowing up those fellas with dynamite back in Fort Worth . . . They're meaner than snakes."

Novak slammed his hand against the top of the table. "You forgot to mention they also killed my wife," he said. "I'll thank you not to lose sight of that. That and that alone is the cause for me being here, riding with you, putting up with your high-and-mighty attitude and your sick choice of earning a living.

"Truth be known, I don't give a dime's worth of spit about those men who died in Fort Worth . . . didn't know the deputy . . . and am of a mind that lying store owner probably got at least a little of what was coming to him."

"Carl, I wasn't meaning disrespect—"

"Now's as good a time as any for us having a conversation that's needed," Novak said. He was clearly angry. "When we do catch up to them—and we will— it'll be me doing the killing. That's a job that's mine and only mine. You go ahead and collect your pay for it when it's done. That's fine with me. But I'm the one who's going to finish this if I have to do it with my bare hands. You'll do well to remember that and not get in my way."

Libby couldn't summon a reply to the sudden outburst. Instead, he took another drink of his tea and stared out the window at the passing funeral goers. The tension only eased when he saw two horses moving in their direction.

"Looks like the marshal and his little buddy have caught up with us," he said.

B OUNTY HUNTERS?" WISENHUNT chuckled, then shook his head. "You boys come riding into town and the first thing you do is go lying to the sheriff?"

"Didn't seem a smart thing to mention Sam being a hired killer," Carl said.

Lyndon was enjoying the banter, glad everyone was back together. The pain in his side had lessened and he was no longer experiencing nightmares or flashes of fever. "I'm guessing the boy's put on ten pounds the way that grateful old lady was feeding him before we left," the marshal said.

"They okay?" Novak said.

"Neighbor ladies are staying with them. There was a widow woman who took a real shine to the boy, changing his bandages and always asking what she could fetch for him. When we were getting ready to leave, she told him she hoped he would be coming back soon."

Blushing, Williamson joined the conversation. "Their cow and chickens have been returned," he said, "and I heard talk about a barn raising before the weather turns cold. The old man's already back to making whiskey, promising a free jug to everyone who helped them out."

Sam and Carl briefly recounted the recent events in San Patricio, explaining that the deputy sheriff was to be buried later in the day. They had no doubt he was killed by the Ashtons.

"And I'm betting we've got no idea where they're headed," Wisenhunt said.

"Not even a decent guess," Sam said.

The marshal rolled his eyes. "Now, ain't that a big surprise." He got to his feet and began massaging his hips. "I'm going to be proud when all this horseback riding comes to an end," he said. "Guess I better go over to his office and wait for the sheriff to get back.

Need him to know you 'bounty hunting' fellas can be trusted."

I'M GOING BACK to Texas." Charlie Boy had taken a deep breath and set his jaw firmly before making the announcement to his brother. "I'm tired of this country, tired of getting followed, and tired of us using your bad ideas." He expected Dean to take a swing at him, so stepped back.

Instead, his brother leaned against the trunk of a tree, his arms folded, and considered the idea. "Could be that would work," he finally said. "These folks chasing us, whoever they are, wouldn't likely expect us doubling back. Texas is a big place, where folks can get themselves lost pretty easy if they're so inclined."

"You got any particular place in mind? Can't be somewhere we've done been."

"The Panhandle might not be bad. The Comanches are mostly gone now, so it's safe. I hear there's big cattle ranches up there where a man can get work. Won't nobody know us."

"Right now," Charlie Boy said, "living in a bunkhouse and eating stove-cooked food sounds good to me."

"Then the Panhandle is where we'll head. First, though, we'll need to steal us some fresh horses. These we've got are about wore out."

Two nights later, a sheep farmer and his wife were awakened by a noise out in their barn. After arming himself with a shotgun, the husband went out to check and soon returned to say their horses were gone.

CHAPTER NINETEEN

I T WAS MARSHAL Wisenhunt who finally put what everyone had been thinking into words.

They had been in San Patricio for several days, making no headway on a new plan for tracking the Ashton brothers. They met several times in Sheriff Wilson's office, drinking coffee by day and whiskey at night, hoping someone could come up with an idea. No one had.

"We've got pretty much open country around here," Wilson said. "Miles of it. Whichever way they went, they're not likely to be noticed if they don't want to be. They could have ridden in any direction and traveled a long way by now. And there's hiding places everywhere. Caves, creek beds hid by thick undergrowth. Even if I was to get up a posse—and it wouldn't be hard, seeing as how folks here felt about my deputy—I wouldn't know which way to send them."

"So, we just sit here?" Novak said. "Just give up after coming all this way?"

It was then that Wisenhunt spoke his piece. "It's time we head home," he said.

A silence fell over the room before he looked squarely at Novak and continued. "We've done been gone too long. You've got a daughter back in Wolf Creek who needs to see her daddy. Lyndon's folks are no doubt worried sick about him. I've got a job I need to be seeing to. And Sam knows there will always be other work waiting.

"I ain't saying we're to give up. That's the last thing I want. As soon as I get back, I'm going to send out telegrams to every law office I can think of, asking them to be on the lookout. The sheriff here can do the same. I'll contact the governor's office in Austin about getting a 'Wanted' poster printed up and seeing that it's circulated.

"I've thought hard on this. Sooner or later, the good Lord will bless us with some luck and we'll hear something. Then we saddle up and go after them again. But for now, I think we ought to get ourselves back to some home cooking."

When there was no reply, he added a postscript. "No call to decide right now. Think on it, sleep on it."

Before Wisenhunt finished, Novak was on his feet and rushing for the door. When Lyndon left his chair to follow, the marshal motioned for him to sit. "Leave him be," he said. "He's got thinking to do. His decision's going to be the hardest."

NIGHT HAD FALLEN and the only sounds interrupting the stillness were the mingled voices coming from inside the saloon. Novak's first inclination was to get drunk, but he walked on past. He went by the café but felt no urge for supper. A lantern glowed in the upstairs window of the hardware and he briefly wondered how the injured owner was faring, but truth be known, he didn't really care. All of the other businesses in town were closed and dark, resting quietly at the end of another business day.

Soon he was on the edge of town, walking toward a grassy area where earlier in the day children had played while their mothers kept watch. Now it, too, was empty and quiet. He approached a stone bench and sat. Closing his eyes, he was soon thinking of his daughter, Lucy, sitting at Belinda Turner's dinner table, happily talking of something funny that had happened at school, then singing again with the church choir, or cuddling next to him as he read her a bedtime story.

Then he began whispering to his late wife. "I tried, Frieda. God knows I tried best I know how," he said, "but I've failed you and I'm so sorry. I just hope I can one day find a way to make it up to you."

The moon was high and Novak was still deep in thought when he felt someone sit next to him. "You figure to sit out here all night?" Libby asked.

"Just thinking, like Del told us."

Sam turned to face him. "I know you don't think highly of me, and rightfully so," he said, "but I do want you to know I feel bad about you losing your wife. I'm sorry for what happened to her. It ain't the natural order for a man to lose somebody so much a part of his heart and soul.

"Me, I've been doing this so long I've tried to teach myself not to let feelings get in the way, not to let anybody get close like you've done. At least you've got memories. I got nothing. I want you to know I've seen the pain you're feeling and have come to appreciate your suffering. You're a good man who tried hard to set things right. We all have. There's no shame to be had in not getting it done.

"The marshal's right. It's time we head back.

"But I just want you to know I'm not giving up until we find those men and see you and your wife get the justice owed you. And it's not just about the money, no matter what you're thinking. It'll happen, Carl. It's just going to take longer than we expected."

They sat together in silence for a time, counting stars and watching the moon disappear into the clouds. Finally, Novak turned and extend his hand.

The next morning, he told Wisenhunt he agreed it was time to go home.

T HEY WERE STANDING on the rim of the vast canyon, shielding their eyes against the warm sun as they looked down into the winding crevice. "It looks like somebody tried ripping the world apart," Charlie Boy said. "Never seen anything like it."

Palo Duro Canyon was wide and deep and extended as far as the eye could see. Its basin was big enough to plant fields of grain and cotton or for livestock to roam and graze. It was a sunken world, filled with trees and grass and meandering streams.

"From what I been told," Dean said, "there was a time when the Comanches made it their home, back when they were still peeling scalps off white folks.

They hunted buffalo that ran in big herds down there. It was their home . . . until soldiers came and ran them off to the reservations up in Indian Territory."

"How is it you know all this history?"

"You were too young to know Uncle Teddy. He passed when you was just learning to walk good. He used to work up this way and told me stories. He rode for a rich man who settled here and set up a cattle-stealing operation a lot like what Rafe Tompkins now has. Only a lot bigger. Stealing ranchers' stock, herding them down into the canyon for rebranding, then selling to trail drivers headed up to Kansas and over into New Mexico."

"Reckon they're still operating and looking to hire?"

Dean shook his head. "Nope. The ranchers finally had their fill and organized to put it to an end. Story I was told was that there was this big raid with everybody shooting. Most of the cattle thieves were killed, including the boss. Uncle Teddy said bodies of cowboys were scattered all over, like the end of a war battle. Then they were gathered into a big pile and set afire.

"Uncle Teddy was one of the few who lived to tell about it. Said he escaped by climbing one of those steep walls, then running until he finally dropped. He claimed he was later told the whole canyon is now haunted by the ghosts of his dead friends. Whether that's true or not, I can't rightly say."

"I ain't interested in finding out," Charlie Boy said. "I'd just as soon we didn't stay here too long. Where we heading now?"

"Uncle spoke of a little town about a half day's ride north. It's called Tascosa. Might be as good a place as any for us to get ourselves reacquainted with civilization."

THE BROTHERS HAD reached the Texas Panhandle in just under a week, often traveling at night and resting during the day. They were careful to avoid towns, even small farms and ranches, along the way. Their new horses, a pair of spry young palominos, had made the ride easier. Squirrels and rabbits, cooked over an open fire at the end of a green tree branch, kept them from going hungry, and their drinking water came from ponds and streams along the way.

"We still got our money," Dean said as they rode away from the canyon, "and I'm figuring on spending some of it on a big ol' plate of meat loaf and mashed potatoes. Maybe even a slice of pie. Then we'll need to find us a place that serves whiskey."

Charlie Boy couldn't recall the last time he had seen Dean completely sober. He'd not had a drink throughout their trip and seemed far less tense and quick to anger. Though Charlie Boy knew better, he hoped his brother would stay that way.

The sad-eyed waitress at the Bluebonnet Café had no meat loaf but offered a double serving of chicken and dumplings instead. A fresh pecan pie had just come out of the oven and was cooling in the kitchen. She said nothing more to the strangers until they had finished their meal.

"If it's liquor you're now wanting," she said, "the saloon got burned down during a town ruckus a while back. While it's getting rebuilt, the only place to get a drink is right where you're sitting." She pointed to a row of mason jars on a shelf behind the counter. "My prices are the same as what they charged down the street."

Dean pulled money from his pocket and asked that she bring one of the jars to the table. "Pick us a full one," he said.

Charlie Boy glanced around the room to be sure it was empty except for him, his brother, and the waitress. He was relieved to see no other customers had come in.

Reading his brother's mind, Dean leaned back in his chair and smiled. "Don't worry, little brother. I'll not misbehave." An hour later he was pleasantly drunk, needing help from both Charlie Boy and the waitress to make it onto the front porch.

"I ain't sleeping under the stars tonight," he mumbled as the waitress placed his hat on his head.

"There's a little shed out back of the livery," she said, "and a little hotel down the street. My daddy runs it. It'll cost you fifty cents a night, a little more if you're thinking about hot-water bathing—which I strongly suggest. Breakfast serving starts at sunup. You'll like the way I cook ham and eggs."

Dean gave her a crooked smile and blew her a kiss, then began staggering down the steps. "Don't none of them ghosts come up out of the canyon at night, do they?" he asked.

She had no idea what he was talking about.

As they made their way down the street, he lost his grip on Charlie Boy's arm and fell to his knees. He was laughing as he got up and dusted his britches. "Seems a right friendly town, don't it?" he said.

So far, his brother thought to himself.

At the moment, he was more concerned with getting Dean to bed and figuring what to do with their horses still standing at the café's hitching post.

PART THREE

CHAPTER TWENTY

Fall 1866

DESPITE THE NIP in the early-morning air, Carl Novak was sweating as he stacked the last few bales of hay in the barn. Lyndon's friend Billy Wayne had done a good job seeing to things on the farm during his absence, leaving little that needed to be done upon his return except enjoy being home. Echo, glad to have him back, rarely let him out of his sight, following his every move by day and sleeping at the foot of his bed at night. Dawn, freed to graze in the pasture, was putting on the weight she had lost during the long and tedious journey. Aside from a visit to the farrier in Wolf Creek for a shoeing, she had rarely left the farm since their return.

Best of all, Lucy was talking.

Upon his return, Novak had ridden straight to Doc Turner's house. That he looked tired, had several days' growth of whiskers, and was covered in trail dust didn't seem to matter to the little girl who was helping Belinda hang out the wash when she saw him.

A smile burst across his face when he heard the childlike scream of delight and the words, "My daddy's back."

Belinda watched the happy reunion from beneath her clothesline, giving father and daughter time for hugs and kisses before she approached. "It's good to see you back, Carl. Lucy's missed you so much."

He was jubilant. "She's talking a blue streak, just like you and the doc said she would. I can't tell you how grateful I am," he said.

"One morning, out of the blue, she walked into the kitchen for breakfast and announced that she was ready to go back to school and start practicing with the choir again. Except to sleep, she hasn't quit talking since. She still cries on occasion and sometimes has a bad dream, but I think she'll be fine, especially now that you're home." She gently put her hand on his arm. "Lucy's going to grow up to be a fine young lady . . . just like her momma."

She could sense Novak's sudden discomfort. And his next question. "Occasionally, she talks some about Frieda, asking questions there really aren't any good answers for. But, mostly, she's talked about you and home, when you would be back, when she could go see Echo. In fact, she and I hitched up the buggy and rode out to the farm a couple of times so she could visit the dog and see that the pumpkins we planted were being properly cared for. I've promised her we'd bake pies for the Harvest Festival."

At the Williamson farm, Lyndon's mother burst

into tears when he approached her as she was feeding her hens. She dropped her seed pail and rushed to him, arms outspread, stopping only when he warned her that there was still considerable tenderness where he'd been shot.

By the time she demanded that he remove his shirt and show her his wound, his father had joined them. "Who was it shot you, son?"

"I'll tell you about it later," Lyndon said as he rebuttoned his shirt and tucked the tail into his pants. "I'm about healed and feeling fine. Except for being hungry enough to eat one of them chickens even before you wring its neck and pluck the feathers."

Mama Williamson's tears had turned to laughter by the time they all walked toward the house,

"I see you brought a new horse home," the father said.

"Yep, we met up over in New Mexico. I'm thinking I'll call her Fire." There would be time later for Lyndon to explain why. For the moment he thought he could already smell his mother's cooking even though she hadn't yet lit the stove.

In his Cinco Gap office, Marshal Wisenhunt was rearranging the desk that the deputy had turned into a mound of old newspapers, a pair of oily work gloves, and useless pieces of mail. When he finally had things back to his liking, he pulled off his boots, leaned back in his chair, and locked his hands behind his neck. "Tan my tired backside if it ain't good being home," he said aloud, though he was the only person in the room. Then he began to consider the proper wording for the telegrams he had promised to send.

The only one unhappy about the homecoming was Rafe Tompkins.

Sam declined Novak's offer to stay at the farm for a few days to rest himself and his horse. "I'd just as soon get this over quick as possible," he said. "Enjoy visiting with your child," he said, "but remember, we're not done yet."

Before heading in the direction of the canyon, he leaned across his saddle and placed a piece of paper in the pocket of Carl's shirt.

MINUTES AFTER LIBBY'S arrival, Tompkins removed his sombrero, threw it into the dirt, then kicked it away as he unleashed a stream of curses. "I was told you were good at this sort of thing, the best. And here you come with your tail tucked between your legs, telling me them brothers are still breathing fresh air? What's a man to think?"

He only calmed when Libby assured him there would be no further payment due until he completed the assignment. He quickly recapped his travels into New Mexico, leaving out the fact he had been accompanied by the marshal, and promised to return to the hunt soon.

"Now," he said as he fitted his boot into a stirrup, "I've got two things to say to you before I take my leave. First, I didn't come here with my tail between my legs. Second, the next time you see me, have my money ready, because the job will have been finished."

Tompkins picked up his sombrero and was dusting it off as Libby rode away.

His new foreman, having quickly grown weary of the boss's constant tantrums, and planning to give notice, had overheard the exchange. He approached Tompkins, grinning. "Don't seem he likes you too much. I'm guessing if I was to offer him the fifty cents I've got in my pocket, he'd gladly hire out to shoot you dead. Then give me back change."

There was no longer need for him to turn in his resignation.

"Gather your belongings while I figure what pay's due you," Tompkins told him before stomping away. "You're fired."

I N THE WEEKS since returning, Novak had made a renewed effort to join more community activities. He felt it would make his daughter happy. A couple of times they rode into town to have dinner with the doctor and Belinda, whom Lucy had come to look on as a big sister. On occasion, he even stopped to play dominoes with the men who regularly gathered in front of the feed store. Attending church each Sunday, Carl sat proudly among the congregation, his daughter smiling at him from the choir loft.

They spent a pleasant weekend mingling with townspeople at the annual fall Harvest Festival, sampling the freshly baked cakes and pies, joining in the silly games, and listening to the music of a family of gifted fiddle players. Lucy even urged him to his feet and led him into the roped area in front of the bandstand when a daddy-daughter dance was announced. On the final night of the festival, soon after she and Belinda were named runners-up in the pie-baking competition, Lucy stood on the steps of the bandstand and sang a solo that received a roar of applause from those in attendance. People were still shaking Novak's hand and praising his daughter's talent as they got ready to return to the farm.

Some of the anger that had haunted him since Frieda's murder seemed to have quieted. Or he had at least pushed it far down into a place where it wasn't so quickly felt. There were times, mostly when he was helping Lucy with school lessons or listening to her sing while getting ready for bed, when things felt almost normal. Even his early-morning visits to his wife's gravesite had become more an exercise of fond recollection than one that gave rise to a new wave of agony and bitter loneliness.

When he'd tried to explain his feelings to Belinda one evening as they sat on the doctor's porch after supper, she told him it was a sign that his heart was mending.

All that changed the morning Marshal Wisenhunt reined his bay up in front of the farmhouse. He wasn't smiling. "Got coffee brewed?" he said as Carl greeted him. They were the first words the marshal had spoken to him since they had returned from New Mexico.

I'VE RECENTLY HAD correspondence from the sheriff up in Tascosa," he said as they sat at the kitchen table. "Fella name of Jake Hollister. He first sent me a telegram a few weeks back, then I got a letter from him yesterday. After sleeping on it, I decided it was time we visited."

He pulled an envelope from the pocket of his jacket and pushed it toward Novak.

"The telegram first," the marshal said.

Carl mouthed the words as he read.

KNOW WHEREABOUTS OF PEOPLE YOU'RE
LOOKING FOR . . . LETTER TO FOLLOW . . .

He folded the yellow sheet and picked up the letter. It was written in a childlike scrawl, and its spelling and punctuation would have made Lucy laugh. The contents, however, caused Novak to begin nervously biting at his lower lip.

I have lately got to know a man who does work for a rancher near here who had a good crop of calfs this year. We are not friends. He is a hard drinker and a mean one. He gets into fites ever time he comes to town. On several occasions I've locked him up in my jail until he gets sober and his brother comes and gits him. I am always proud to be rid of him since all he does is hollar and cuss when he wakes up. He claims to go by the name of Bill Smith but I don't think it is true.

He's got fingers gone on one hand. Im sorry to say I didn't read the poster sent to my office till yesterday. I have been busy. Next time I see him I will keep him locked up longer. Rite me back and tell me your thinking.

When Carl didn't respond, Wisenhunt spoke. "I hope he's a better lawman than he is at writing. Whoever done his teaching ought to be plumb ashamed."

Novak felt the muscles in his shoulders tighten as

he reread the letter. He was unaware that he was grinding his teeth. "It's them," he finally said.

"Seems a good possibility. I just thought you needed to know."

The bitter taste of bile rose in his throat and his breathing came in short bursts. Only minutes earlier, he'd been happy and hadn't even thought about the Ashton brothers for weeks. And now, suddenly, they were back, their names ringing in his ears and a vision of their cruelty as vivid as if it had been carried out yesterday. He cursed and got to his feet, surprised that his legs felt suddenly weak.

"I could send the proper papers up to the sheriff, asking him to arrest them and lock them up until they could stand before a judge," Wisenhunt said. "I've got no doubt they'd get sent off to prison. I'd be happy to testify against them myself. Could be a judge might even see fit to having them hang."

Carl's response didn't surprise him. "It's me who's going to kill them," he said.

Arguing was futile but the marshal tried. "You've come back home and made yourself a good life, Carl. Your daughter's happy and pretty as a button, singing like an angel. You need to think about taking good care of her, not chasing off after men who ain't worth rat spit. What if you get yourself killed?"

"I made a promise and I'm keeping it."

"That's what I figured," the marshal said, sighing as he nodded. "If your mind's made up, I'm coming along. But you've got to agree we don't tell young Lyndon. He's done all the atoning he needs to. Besides, his folks would skin our hides if we was to put him in harm's way again."

Carl agreed. "But Sam will want to know."

"I don't have the foggiest notion how to reach out to him."

"I do," Novak said. He went to the drawer of the small desk where Lucy did her studying and pulled out the folded note Sam Libby had given him. "He wanted it known how he could be contacted."

"Okay, that's good," the marshal said. "Truth is, I expect if we don't tell him, he's likely to kill us—free for nothing—just to keep in practice."

THE BUNKHOUSE OF Sundown Ranch was lit only by a low-burning lantern on a table at one end of the room. A couple of cowboys were playing a midnight game of cards while most of the men were sleeping.

Their whispers and the nearby chorus of snoring was suddenly interrupted when Sheriff Hollister burst through the door, waving a rifle. Three men he had deputized earlier in the day followed. They were carrying out instructions outlined in a telegram from Wisenhunt.

Hollister and his men hurriedly went from bunk to bunk, looking for the two men he had been asked to take into custody.

He first found Charlie Boy, still asleep despite the commotion, and yanked him into a sitting position. "Get your pants and boots on, then place your hands behind your back," the sheriff said. While a deputy was wrapping leather straps around his wrists, Hollister continued his search.

It took several minutes to find the other brother.

Dean, realizing what was happening, had slipped from his bed and was hiding beneath it.

"You ain't fooling nobody," Hollister said as a deputy dragged the elder Ashton to the center of the room. "Put your hands over your head or get yourself shot."

Dean feigned surprise and innocence. "I ain't drunk a drop tonight, Sheriff," he said. "You got no good cause to arrest me."

Nervously, Hollister swung his rifle, striking Ashton on the side of the head with the barrel. "I've got papers saying I've got plenty of reason," he said as his prisoner's hands were being tied.

While the stunned cowhands looked on, the brothers were led outside to two waiting horses. Alerted to the planned raid earlier in the day, the ranch owner watched from a distance. "Good riddance," he whispered as the raiding party rode away. He could hear Dean Ashton cursing long after they had disappeared into the night.

B ELINDA HAD NO more success persuading Novak to abandon his plan than the marshal had. Ultimately, the best she could do was readily agree to look after Lucy in his absence.

"I've explained to her as best I could that I'll not be gone long this time," he said as they walked into the yard after supper. "Truth be known, I think she's excited about coming to visit you again."

"Don't be a fool, Mr. Novak. She's scared out of her wits that her daddy's going off and might not come back."

"Del Wisenhunt's already said the Ashton brothers have been arrested and are in jail," he said. "I just want to see for myself and say my piece to the judge. Once that's done, I'll be back and not leave again. That's what I promised Lucy."

"Can you make the same promise to me?" She gently took his hand in hers as she posed the question.

Novak felt a sudden rush of mixed emotions—guilt over lying to her about the true purpose of his journey, appreciation for her concern for his daughter, and something else, deep inside, that he wasn't sure about.

"I promise," he finally said.

As he spoke, the sound of Dr. Turner tuning his piano came from inside. "Appears we're going to be entertained," Belinda said. "My daddy's playing, such as it is, and your daughter's fine singing."

N OVAK AND DAWN were waiting for the marshal before sunup. He had alerted Lyndon's friend Billy Wayne to tend to the farm, swearing him to secrecy. At Belinda's suggestion, Echo would stay at the doctor's house.

"You ever go to bed?" Wisenhunt said as he emerged, coffee cup in one hand, his hat in the other. "I've still got to walk down to the livery and saddle up."

"How long a ride you think we're looking at?"

"Four days, maybe less if you're of a mind to mistreat your horse."

"Four's fine. I brought us food and a cooking skillet. And a pan for making coffee."

Wisenhunt laughed as he stepped off the porch. "If you wasn't so ornery and butt ugly," he said, "I'd consider proposing we get ourselves married."

THEY RODE THE first day in silence, both men deep in thought. Novak wondered how he would accomplish his mission with the Ashtons in jail, the marshal thinking he hadn't been totally honest about his reason for coming along.

Wisenhunt knew his friend wasn't thinking straight, hadn't since the death of his wife. Neither was he a cold-blooded killer despite his resolve. If allowed to carry out his plan, he might well end up in jail himself. Or worse, be killed.

The marshal was determined to prevent both. He just wasn't sure how.

CHAPTER TWENTY-ONE

S HERIFF HOLLISTER WAS feeling good about the arrests and the ease with which they had been carried out. He had assigned a rotation of deputies to sit outside the brothers' cell, each with a rifle in his lap, to watch their every move. He checked on the prisoners regularly himself, when he wasn't in the café or out front of the livery, boasting about the greatest accomplishment of his otherwise routine career.

If he was to be believed, the captured killers in his jail were to be compared to wild animals. "Mean and bloodthirsty," he called them.

In truth, the jailed Ashtons were remarkably subdued. Sober, Dean wasn't swearing or yelling threats, and his brother, looking scared and distraught, spent most of his time lying quietly on his bunk.

In addition to notifying Marshal Wisenhunt of the arrests, Hollister had dispatched one of his deputies to locate the circuit judge who occasionally visited Tascosa, and ask how soon a trial might be held. The sheriff was anxious to be rid of the prisoners as quickly as possible, before they could do something that would tarnish the shine of his newfound reputation.

Only late at night, when their guard would doze, did the brothers talk.

"Unless we figure us a way to get out of here," Charlie Boy whispered, "we're for sure going to hang. They're blaming us for killing a whole bunch of people, particularly that woman back in Wolf Creek."

Dean grimaced as he rubbed the knot on the side of his head caused by Hollister's rifle. "I ain't hanging for nobody," he said.

"You got us a plan?"

"I'm thinking, but it ain't that easy with my head busted up like it is."

N OVAK AND THE marshal were still a day's ride from Tascosa and had made camp on the edge of a pecan grove. Their horses grazed in the fall's last traces of grass and drank from a nearby stream. The campfire cast dancing shadows in the trees and there was the aroma of coffee brewing. Both men had saddle blankets draped over their shoulders to ward off the chill.

The time had arrived, Wisenhunt decided, to speak plainly.

"Before we ride out in the morning," he said, "I'll be needing your sidearm and your rifle."

Novak looked perplexed. "Why's that?"

"Son, I can't allow you to walk into that jail tomorrow and start shooting it up, killing people for the pure meanness of it. I understand your feelings about these people, I honest-to-God do. If I was in your shoes, I'd likely feel the same. But I'd hope I had a friend who would make me stop a minute and do some hard thinking.

"Whether you know it or not, I'm that friend, and no way am I allowing you to do something that's crazy and most likely to get you in serious trouble."

"What gives you that right to make my decisions?"

"This badge I've been wearing since you was wearing knickers and your ma was wiping snot off your nose. The job I signed on for is to see laws don't needlessly get broken, by friend or foe. One of us needs to be thinking straight, and right now it ain't you."

"That's why you came along? To do my thinking for me?"

"Something like that," the marshal said. With that, he turned away and poked a stick at the fire.

The discussion ended, the two sat in silence as the campfire faded to nothing but a small bed of sparkling embers.

Novak was busying himself washing coffee grounds from the pot and Wisenhunt was spreading his bedroll when they heard a familiar voice.

"Hello the camp," Sam Libby called out before walking out of the shadows. As usual, he was dressed as if he was going courting.

He nodded at the marshal, then shook Carl's hand. "My friend at the post office alerted me I had a letter from you," he said to the marshal, "and I had a good idea what it was going to say. I left as soon as I read your news and been catching up with you boys ever since."

He left to get the horse he'd tethered in the trees nearby.

Carl glanced over at the marshal. "I reckon you're going to be asking for his gun as well," he said.

"Nope," Wisenhunt said. "I ain't figuring on interfering with him doing what he hired out to do. Can't say I admire the line of work he's chosen, but if he intends on breaking the law, I expect he'll do it in a way that ain't stupid and would get him caught. Knowing him, he's thought out a way to have me looking the other direction at the proper time.

"Plus, he ain't my friend."

T HE FOLLOWING MORNING, as they rode toward Tascosa, Libby couldn't help but notice Novak's empty holster and the tension between him and the marshal. He had a clear recollection of Novak insisting that he be the one to kill the Ashtons but didn't think it was the time to mention it. Instead, he only asked questions about why the brothers had ended up in this part of the country and how their arrests had transpired.

Wisenhunt had taken charge. "When we arrive," he said, "the talking will be between me and the sheriff. I'll explain that Carl has accompanied me since he's the husband of the woman they murdered and has come to say his piece to the judge."

He then turned to Libby. "Seeing that I wasn't really expecting you, explaining your presence won't be as easy. I suggest you keep yourself scarce until I can get me a story straight. Maybe go visit the town barber and get yourself all prettied up and smelling good."

Libby offered no argument. Novak only nodded before speaking. "I just want to see them, look them in the eye."

"I figure that will be allowed," the marshal said.

S HERIFF HOLLISTER WAS delighted to see Wisenhunt and Novak enter his office, quickly getting to his feet and shaking their hands. "It's a pleasure to meet you and I thank you for coming all this way, though it wasn't necessary." He was talking so fast his words were running together.

"Just wanted to see if I could be of any help," the marshal said. "I've been after these two for a long time. We wanted to come and thank you personally for your good work catching them."

Hollister had a wide smile on his face. "Want to see them?"

"That's one of the reasons we've come," Wisenhunt said as they were being led down a narrow hallway toward the jail cells. "How long you been the sheriff?"

"Coming up on a year since I was elected," Hollister said. "My daddy was the sheriff before me."

"I reckon he must be real proud," Wisenhunt said. "How old are you?"

"I'll turn twenty-three come January."

Novak thought he saw the marshal roll his eyes as Hollister unlocked a door.

"Mostly," the sheriff said, "we just get Saturday-night drunks in here. Sometimes a cattle thief. But nothing like these two."

"Real celebrities, I reckon," Novak said. The sheriff missed the sarcasm in his observation. Wisenhunt didn't and put a steadying hand on his shoulder.

D EAN ASHTON HAD his back to them, standing on tiptoe in an attempt to look out a barred window, when they reached the cell. Charlie Boy was sleeping.

"Got you boys some visitors," the sheriff said as he raked the barrel of his pistol across the bars, creating a loud noise.

Dean turned and his eyes went quickly past the marshal to Novak. "I don't see you wearing no badge," he said. "Who are you?"

"Somebody who wishes he'd met you a long time ago . . . back in Wolf Creek."

Carl glared through the bars, his heart suddenly beating so swiftly he could feel it beneath his shirt. The man who had so dramatically changed his life was not at all what he had long envisioned. He was short and skinny and not at all menacing-looking until one looked directly into his eyes. It was his dull, cold stare that spoke to who Dean Ashton was.

"My deputy says the judge plans on being here in a couple of days," Hollister said. "He'll be arriving from Fort Worth."

The marshal had seen no courthouse on their ride into town and asked where the trial would be held.

"There's a big meeting room in the back of the

feed store," Hollister said. "We have our town meetings there on occasion. That's where we'll set up for the judge, and a jury if he's wants one. Then we'll shackle these two and march them down to meet their fate.

"Knowing the judge and his busy schedule, I don't expect it to take long. My guess is we'll soon be getting ready to have us a hanging."

CHARLIE BOY, WHO had pretended to sleep through the brief exchange, got to his feet and watched the sheriff and his visitors walk away. He then moved to his brother's side.

"They're gonna kill us, ain't they?" he said.

"I expect so," Dean said, "unless we kill them first."

His brother smiled ever so slightly. "You've got us a plan, don't you?"

"I'm thinking on it."

LIBBY WAS HALF-FINISHED with his ham and collard greens when the others reached the café. Anxious to hear what they had learned, he waved them to the table.

"Boy, you smell pretty," the marshal said. "Is it the barbering talcum or them stewed greens giving off that aroma?"

Sam ignored him and continued eating while they waited for the waitress to take their orders. Finally, he said, "Well, am I going to have to ask?"

Novak explained to him that the judge was expected to be in Tascosa in the next couple of days. In the meantime, the Ashtons were securely locked up and being closely watched. Only when Carl mentioned that they would be walked from the jail to the back room of the feed store for the trial did Libby lift his head.

The marshal could see Sam's mind working. Novak expected him to issue some kind of warning. Instead, all Wisenhunt mentioned was that the sheriff had recommended they consider staying at the livery while in town. "He said it's more reasonably priced and we're less likely to catch something than if we stayed at the hotel."

That evening a chilling wind blew in and flurries of the first snow of the season began to fall just as the sun was going down. Still, after the horses were bedded down and they were shown where their cots were located, Wisenhunt pulled on his jacket to sit alone outside and light his pipe.

"I keep coffee going until I head off to bed," the owner told him, "so help yourself. All I ask is you rinse out the pot when you're done."

Inside, Libby polished his boots while Novak read an account of the brothers' arrest in a week-old issue of the *Tascosa News*. The story read like it had been written by an aspiring dime novelist.

"You going to explain to me why you're not wearing your sidearm?" Libby finally said.

Reluctantly, Carl told of the marshal's concern. "Could be he was right to give me warning. The way I felt when I saw them in the jail today, I could have shot both of them without giving it a second thought."

"And the next thing you knew, you would be sitting in a cell yourself, waiting to meet the circuit judge. To my thinking, the marshal did you a favor."

"I'm not leaving here with them still alive," Novak said.

"It'll be hard. Only once did I ever shoot a man already locked up," Libby said, "and that was only after breaking him out first." Unknown to Carl and the marshal, he had already walked the route from the jail to the feed store and visited the room where the trial would be conducted. The jail itself, he noted, was a fortress of thick limestone walls, the doors made of oak and iron. "We're not getting inside without an invitation.

"The way I'm thinking is the only chance to do it is when they're being taken down the street. By my count it'll be a little more than two hundred paces. But if the sheriff's a thinking man, he'll have them surrounded by deputies for their protection.

"It won't be easy, getting off two shots that hit their marks, then getting away before you get shot yourself."

"But it's possible?"

"Barely. Even if I give you my gun and have your getaway horse waiting, it's not a plan I'd recommend. Not sure I could even do it myself. You want my advice: let nature take its course and be satisfied. The judge will find them guilty—I'll bet on that—then we can stay around and enjoy ourselves watching them hang."

"What about when they get taken back to jail to wait while the gallows are made for the hanging?"

Libby could see that Novak was not giving up easily. "Then," he said, "we do some more thinking."

THE FOLLOWING DAY passed slowly. Carl groomed Dawn, drank cup after cup of the livery owner's coffee, and stood in the doorway watching as the snowfall got heavier. He thought about walking the route from the jail to the feed store as Libby had done, but decided against it. From where he stood, he could see there were no good hiding places along the route, just the street and sidewalks.

By the time Sheriff Hollister visited the livery to inform them that the judge would definitely be arriving the following day, Novak had dismissed any plan to try to kill the brothers in the Tascosa street.

After Hollister left, the marshal joined Carl in the doorway. "Appears you're doing some deep thinking," he said.

"Just admiring the snow."

"Winter comes earlier up this way," Wisenhunt said, reaching out a hand to catch the flakes. "I'm glad all this is about over and we can soon head back home. I got firewood that needs chopping."

Novak, still lost in thought, sipped at his coffee and didn't reply.

HOLLISTER AND HIS deputies had been pleasantly surprised at the docile behavior of their prisoners. Neither had raised any ruckus since being put into their cell, and they even made a point to voice their appreciation when their meals were delivered each afternoon. When the door was opened so their odorous slop bucket could be emptied, they dutifully stood in the back of the cell, their arms raised and their faces to the wall.

Earlier in the day, Dean had been very polite when asking for an extra blanket to ward off the sudden cold.

The sheriff, no longer feeling the need to make hourly checks, had stopped sleeping in his office and was going home nights to the comfort of his own bed.

The calm, however, ended in the wee hours of the morning the circuit judge was due to arrive.

The guard assigned to watch the prisoners was sleeping, his chin resting against his chest, his rifle dangling loosely across his lap. The lantern sitting on the floor beside him had gone out, leaving the hallway in darkness.

In their cell, Dean and Charlie Boy busied themselves carefully tearing the blanket into slender strips. They removed the cotton from inside their pillows and placed it and the cloth strips in a pile in the middle of the cell. They added pieces torn from the legs of their long johns and the bandanna that was wrapped around Dean's injured head.

"Get ready, little brother," Dean said as he reached into his boot and pulled out a lone match he'd been hiding there since dynamiting the tent in Fort Worth.

With their backs to the sleeping guard, the match's small glow went unnoticed. As did the flame that began as just a flicker but quickly grew. As they fanned the small fire with their hands, a cloud of gray smoke soon filled the cell and was floating into the hallway.

"Help! Get us out of here. The place is on fire,"

Dean began yelling. "We're gonna die." Charlie Boy continued to fan as the smoke began turning black.

In a daze, the guard stumbled to his feet, his rifle falling to the floor as he frantically searched for his keys.

"Hurry, or we're gonna be burned up," Dean yelled. As an afterthought, he added a plaintive "please."

As soon as the barred door swung open, the second phase of Ashton's plan went into effect. Charlie Boy grabbed the panicked guard, pulling his arms behind him as Dean began to pummel his face. In short order, the deputy was unconscious and lying on the floor, his body obscured by a blanket of smoke.

Charlie Boy, coughing wildly, reached into the haze and found the lawman's pistol while Dean ran into the hall and picked up the rifle.

In seconds they were out the back door into fresh, cold air and ankle-deep in the snow covering the alley.

Minutes later, Novak thought he heard faint movement in the corral out back of the livery but dismissed it in his half-awake state. He pulled his blanket tighter against his chin and returned to the pleasant dream he was having about his daughter, singing a new song she had learned from Belinda.

T HE MORNING WAS still gray when Sheriff Hollister burst into the dimly lit livery. Only the marshal was awake, waiting for the coffee to brew.

"They're gone," Hollister said.

"What?"

"They broke out during the night. Set the place on fire and killed my deputy. Them or all the smoke he inhaled. I just found him dead on the floor of their cell, the door wide open. They took his guns . . ."

Wisenhunt was cussing so loudly that he didn't hear the rest of what the sheriff was saying. Libby and Novak, still in their long johns, were hurrying down the ladder from the loft to see what the commotion was about.

The sheriff's face was suddenly childlike and filled with defeat as he told them something bad had happened. They listened in stunned silence as he breathlessly repeated what he'd told Wisenhunt.

Libby went to the open doorway and looked out into the purple morning. The snow had ended, leaving a white blanket covering the street and rooftops.

"They won't be hard to track," he said. There was a hint of renewed excitement in his voice.

Nearby, Hollister stood motionless, as if frozen in place.

"If it was me," Wisenhunt told him, "I'd go roust my men and tell them you've got escaped prisoners to go after. And I'd do it pretty quick."

The sheriff turned and hurried into the cold as Libby and Novak were getting dressed. The marshal was already saddling the horses. "Should have figured they'd find a way to set something on fire," he said to the puzzled livery owner who was watching the frantic activity. "Those boys ought not be allowed to play with matches."

As they prepared to leave, Wisenhunt approached

Carl and handed him his pistol and rifle. "You're likely to be needing these," he said.

DETERMINING THE ASHTONS' escape route was easy. They followed the brothers' deep footprints that led from the alley to the corral, then could see the direction their horses had taken them.

"It'll be slow going," Novak said. "They can't be too far ahead of us."

"Gonna be slow going for us as well," Wisenhunt said as he pulled his hat low against his brow and kneed his mare into a faster gait.

They weren't going to wait for the sheriff and whatever posse he could assemble.

CHAPTER TWENTY-TWO

Sam Libby was the only one familiar with the region, having tracked a claim jumper into the Panhandle years earlier. "It's my recollection there's a big canyon ahead," he said as they continued to slowly follow the tracks.

"Reckon why they would head that way?" Novak said.

"Not likely they're using much logic right now," Wisenhunt said. "They're just running for their sorry lives."

By late morning the clouds had cleared and the sun was warming the countryside. The snow was beginning to melt, dripping from tree limbs and creating fast-running rivulets along rocky crevices.

They had reached the crest of a hill when Libby reined in his horse, shaded his eyes, and pointed to something in the distance. This time, the marshal had remembered his binoculars and reached back to his saddlebag.

"Appears it's a campsite," he said. "There's a teth-ered horse and a tent, but I don't see no fire burning."

They split up and approached carefully from dif-ferent directions, each with his pistol drawn. Finally, as they got near, Wisenhunt called out but got no answer. When they reached the opening of the tent, they saw why.

A body lay inside, blood still frozen on the back of the neck below where a single gunshot had torn away part of the scalp.

Libby and Novak rolled the body over and saw lifeless eyes staring up at them. The man's spectacles, resting crookedly against a swollen cheek, had been broken.

Wisenhunt bent closer, resting his hands on his knees. "Not somebody I've ever saw before," he said, "but if I was to guess, I'd bet my hat that's the judge."

Inside the tent, clothing and the contents of a leather briefcase were scattered about. The saddlebags were emptied, as was a scabbard that had once held a rifle.

"They've got themselves better armed now," Libby said.

N IGHT WAS APPROACHING as the brothers reached the rim of Palo Duro Canyon and began search-ing for the trail that would lead them to the basin. The coat and blanket they had taken from the judge's tent had felt good initially but now did little to protect them from the cold wind that had begun to swirl, stir-ring the remnants of snow that was banked against the rocks.

"All this work," Charlie Boy said, "and we're likely

going to freeze ourselves to death, trapped in this hole in the ground." When his brother didn't respond, he continued. "You figure there's truth to those stories about there being ghosts down there?"

"There ain't no ghosts. We're not going to freeze. And we're not getting ourselves trapped. We find us a proper place to hide and wait, then we pick off anybody following us."

The idea of more killing was suddenly of no concern to the younger brother. "That's your plan? We kill them before they kill us?"

"It is. And it's a good one if I say so myself."

S AM LIBBY AGREED just as soon as he saw the tracks leading into the canyon. "There's going to be enough moonlight for them to see us," he said. "With the rifles they've got, we'd be little more than target practice to a good shot. Best figure on waiting until daylight."

Since their presence would be no surprise, Novak began gathering wood for a campfire. "They might as well know we're here and staying until this is ended," Wisenhunt said as he watched Carl's fire come to life.

They left the saddles on their horses for what little warmth they would provide the animals and had brushed snow away for a place to build the fire and sit. Even as they huddled close to the flames, they were unable to ward off the dropping temperature.

"Whole world's freezing," the marshal said. "Even the birds gone to roost are likely shivering."

Libby got to his feet and walked to the edge of the canyon. Even in the dim light he was aware of its vastness, letting his eyes trace its wide and winding course. He realized that if the Ashtons were inclined, they could keep the chase going for days, riding for miles along the basin, hiding among its jagged nooks and in its thick stands of trees and underbrush. And, he knew, for those in pursuit, there was always the very real danger of ambush from behind the giant rocks that lined the canyon walls.

"We'll need to box them in," he said when he returned, "see they make their stand where they are instead of keeping on the move. Best thing for us to do is split up. I'll ride on up the rim a ways to get ahead of them. Carl, you position yourself at the head of the trail they took. The marshal can set himself up on the ledge so he'll have a good view of what's happening come sunup."

"What about the sheriff and his men?" Novak said.

Libby laughed. "With that Hollister fellow leading them, they're likely lost by now."

Wisenhunt nodded his approval of the plan. "Once we have daylight, we can find ourselves a way to close in without getting shot in the process," he added.

"Meanwhile, we'll also send them a hello," Libby said. "After you take your places, give me some time to get up into that grove of trees. When you hear me fire off a couple of shots, you do the same. If they're as dumb as I hope, they'll think they're surrounded and have no notion how many of us there are."

THE FIRST SHOT was still echoing through the night when a second was fired. Then, from different locations, there were a half dozen more.

From beneath a limestone outcrop, Charlie Boy

sat up abruptly and instinctively put his hands to his ears. "They're shooting at us," he said, "and it sounds like they're everywhere. The sheriff must have sent out a posse." There was a final pistol shot from near the entrance trail, then its slow-fading echo, before silence returned.

"No way they can see where we're at," Dean said. "They're just hoping to scare us."

"Well, I'd say they done good. I near wet myself when that first shot was fired. Reckon we should be shooting back?"

Dean Ashton felt a rush of excitement as he contemplated the beginning of a cat-and-mouse game, a matching of wits. "No need alerting them to where we are," he said. "They're just smarting off by telling us they're here."

He, too, had a plan. "We'll leave the horses so they'll be seen at first light. That'll make them think we're nearby," he said. "But before dawn we'll be split up, you in one direction, me in the other. Stay on this side of the canyon and find you a place high enough to hide and watch. When anybody shows himself, let him get close, then shoot him. I'll be doing the same."

"How many we gonna have to kill?"

"Every last one. Then we can ride on out of here free as birds."

They waited through the remainder of the night, but no more shots were fired.

D EL WISENHUNT'S LEGS ached from sitting in the cold night air. Still, he waited for light before moving around. As he stretched, he was aware of the

slight pops in his knees and felt a stiffness in his neck.
It was mornings that reminded him he was getting
old.

The outline of the canyon below was coming into
clearer view and he was amazed by its size. He wiped
the dew from his binoculars and began searching for
any signs of movement.

In the distance he saw the two horses that had
been stolen from the livery's corral, both standing
motionless in the shelter of two snow-covered boulders. They were still saddled. The brothers were nowhere to be seen.

Turning to look toward the trail, he could see that
Novak was slowly making his way into the canyon,
stopping to hide between rocks and behind trees as
he went. It pleased the marshal that he was being
careful.

The only other sign of life was a family of mule
deer nibbling on the leaves of low-hanging mesquite
limbs.

Libby, having found a ledge from which he could
view the trail the brothers would likely take should
they continue to run, was too far away to see.

"They ain't going to be climbing this steep wall,"
the marshal said to himself before he began making
his way down to join Novak.

He was just a few feet away before Carl was aware
of his presence. "I'm here to keep you company, son,
not shoot you," the marshal said.

"You got any idea where they are?"

"Haven't seen nothing yet, but what I think we
ought to try and do is flush them up the canyon in

Sam's direction. They'll no doubt be watching for us to come their way, so keep your head down."

With his warning came a rifle shot that ricocheted off the edge of a nearby rock into the morning sky. The deer bolted in the opposite direction while Novak and Wisenhunt hurried into a thick stand of mesquites.

"I reckon we now know where at least one of them is," the marshal said. A second shot, wild and into the treetops, indicated they weren't facing an expert marksman or a man with abundant patience.

"I betcha that's the young one," Wisenhunt whispered. "I figure him to be the more stupid of the two."

A half mile away, Dean Ashton was certain his stupid brother had fired far too quickly, no doubt missing his mark while also giving away his location. Lying prone on a ledge high on the canyon wall, he tried without success to see where his brother's shots had been aimed.

Crouched low to the wet ground, Novak waited for his breathing to return to normal. The anxiety he was feeling didn't surprise him, but the absence of the unbridled anger he'd nurtured for so long did. His goal remained the same, but he was no longer willing to risk his own life to achieve it. Strangely, he felt no rush, just a quiet determination.

Patience, the man sitting beside him had preached.

"Just staying here won't do us no good unless we hope he'll soon run out of ammunition," Wisenhunt said. As he spoke, he was surveying the landscape between them and the shooter. "One of us needs to stay here and keep his attention while the other sees if he can circle around."

"You stay," Novak said almost before the marshal completed his thought.

"Be careful, boy. Keep in mind there's more than one of them out there."

Novak was on his feet, ready to run toward a large mound of dirt and stone left by some ancient landslide. Wisenhunt braced his rifle against a tree trunk and fired a volley of shots in the general direction of the shooter who was probably the younger Ashton.

Charlie Boy ducked his head, praying he wasn't hit, and didn't see Novak race from the protection of the grove.

To add to the distraction, the marshal began calling out to their attacker. "You should have stayed in that nice warm cell," he yelled through cupped hands. "Dying out here in the middle of nowhere ain't going to be to your liking. No, sir, not one bit." He then fired another shot as Novak quickly disappeared into a maze of boulders.

Charlie Boy was shaking so badly that he dropped the judge's rifle and had to crawl to a ledge below to retrieve it. "I know my brother will think me a coward," he said to himself, "but I ain't dying like this. Ain't no sin not wanting to die."

He began to slowly crawl toward the top of the ridge as another of Wisenhunt's shots zinged harmlessly past. "Why don't you come on down here and turn yourself in so I don't have to be hauling your dead body down all them rocks?" the marshal yelled. Later, Charlie Boy thought he could hear him laughing.

When there was no return fire, the marshal moved from the shelter of the trees and started slowly moving toward the canyon wall.

NOVAK, SCRATCHED AND bruised by the sharp rocks and thorny underbrush, reached an outcrop directly below the gunman and was trying to determine a route that would take him to a place where he would have a clear shot. He was unaware that the Ashton brother had already deserted his place and was working his way higher up the cliff.

Charlie Boy had traveled no more than a hundred yards when he arrived at an opening partially covered by sagebrush and cactus. Looking closer, he realized it was a cave. He began talking to himself again. "Nobody's gonna look inside there for me. I can hide and be safe. Ain't no sin not wanting to die . . . ain't no sin . . ."

He was still babbling incoherently as he crawled on hands and knees into the welcome darkness.

NOVAK WAITED BENEATH the ledge for some time, listening for any movement from above. Nothing. Finally, he began edging his way up only to find that the man who had been shooting at him and the marshal was gone. All that remained was a scattering of spent shells and footprints in the mud that led higher onto the rim.

Following the shooter's route was easy. There were broken limbs on bushes where he had apparently stumbled and deep impressions in the patches of snow that remained in shaded spots. A boot, which had wedged between the rocks, was left behind.

He reached the mouth of the cave and pressed his back against the wall on one side of the entrance, holding his breath and listening. He waited several minutes before he spoke. "I know you're in there," he said, "and there's no way out except through me." He thought he detected movement but got no reply.

"I've come a long way to see you dead," Carl said. "Unless you're as cowardly as I suspect, you'll come out and face me."

Against the back wall of the shallow enclosure, Charlie Boy was gently rocking. "Ain't no coward . . . ain't no sin . . ."

His anger returned and patience gone, Novak entered the cave. A slight opening in the rocks above him provided enough light to see that the man he was after couldn't be too far away. Pressing his body to the wall and keeping in the dark, he waited for a shot. But none came.

Inching farther inside, he found Charlie Boy sitting with his knees against his chin. He held his rifle but it wasn't pointed.

Novak cocked his Winchester. "I've been waiting for this a long time," he said. "Since the day back when I returned home and found my wife dead."

Charlie Boy began frantically shaking his head. "Wasn't me killed her. My brother done it. He's the one likes killing. She was a nice lady, real nice. I begged him to let her be."

"But you didn't beg hard enough to see she lived. So, I'm blaming you." Novak cocked his rifle and pointed it at a spot just below Charlie Boy's chin.

* * *

As HE BEGAN slowly squeezing the trigger, he heard the marshal's voice behind him.

"You don't want to do that," Wisenhunt said. Despite his aching knees, he had managed to follow Carl up to the cave. "I've tried best I knew how to persuade you not to end things this way. Now I'm begging, for your own good. You think shooting him's gonna bring you peace, finally set everything right. But it won't, son. Trust me on that. It'll just give you the worst kind of nightmares you can imagine. They'll haunt for the rest of your days."

With that, the marshal quickly moved in front of Novak, pointed his pistol, and shot Charlie Boy.

Carl was speechless as he stood, watching the blood drip from what was left of Ashton's face. The sound of the shot still echoed and the smell of smoke and gunpowder filled the small enclosure.

Finally, Carl managed to form a single word. "Why . . . ?"

"A man gets to be my age," Wisenhunt said, "he don't do much sleeping. Because of it, he's not as likely to be tormented by the kind of nightmares I was speaking of."

CHAPTER TWENTY-THREE

DEAN ASHTON HAD settled into a small crevice midway up the side of the canyon wall, a secluded location that provided him a good view of anyone coming his way. The sun had risen into a cold, clear sky, so he could see for a half mile or more in each direction.

His plan was simply to sit and wait, let them come to him. There couldn't be too many of them. Three, he guessed from the direction of the gunfire during the night. A good marksman could easily deal with that many.

He still held out hope that his brother might be able to help, but since he'd not heard any shots fired in almost an hour, he was beginning to have doubts. Charlie Boy had never been dependable, so most likely he would have to deal with matters himself.

With the judge's blanket wrapped over his shoulders, he sat and watched.

Sam Libby, meanwhile, had tired of waiting and decided to return to the rim from where he could look down into the canyon and hopefully find out where the Ashtons were. Having borrowed the marshal's binoculars, he scanned the rocky terrain and saw that the brothers' horses hadn't moved. The Ashtons were on foot, no doubt planning an ambush.

Novak and the marshal left the cave and were making their way down the wall of jagged rocks. Carl hadn't spoken since they emerged into the daylight.

"Dean's likely somewhere up the way," Wisenhunt said, "hoping to get us in his sights. If we move around some and make enough racket, causing him to pay attention to us, it'll allow Sam to sneak up on him."

"Then we can get out of here," Novak said.

". . . and head home," the marshal added.

Neither said anything about what had transpired in the cave.

Finally, a glint from Novak's rifle barrel alerted Sam to their location. From a distance, he watched through the glasses as Novak and the marshal slowly made their way from one rock formation to another. He still had no idea where the brothers were hiding.

Carl and Wisenhunt were both out of breath when they reached level ground. They sat in the shelter of a boulder, both shivering. "We can't just keep playing hidey-seek," the marshal said. "We've got to call him out and make him show us where he's at."

He was surprised when Novak got to his feet and said, "I'll do it."

Eye level with the top edge of the big rock, he

squinted into the sun, cupped his hands to each side of his mouth, and called out. "Hey, Dean," he yelled. "It's Carl Novak here talking. I'm the man once married to the woman you killed."

He waited but there was no reply.

He raised his voice even higher. "Mighty sorry to inform you that your little brother's dead. He's laying up the way in a cave with his head blowed all to pieces."

Novak ducked behind the boulder just before a shot echoed through the canyon and chips of stone flew from just above his head. It angered Dean to learn he could expect no help from his brother.

"Appears you got his attention," Wisenhunt said. He made no mention of his surprise at the cold manner in which Novak had announced Charlie Boy's death.

Even before the sound of the shot died, Libby was quickly making his way back down into the canyon. "Got you," he said as excitement rushed through his veins. It was a feeling he'd experienced dozens of times before and never tired of. He was now doing what he did best. "This hunt is about to be over," he said.

He waited until he was closer to fire his first shot.

"Okay, Sam's got him sighted," the marshal said. Assuming Ashton was concerned about the shot that had come from another direction, he and Novak got to their feet and ran to new cover. "We just keep closing in," Wisenhunt whispered, "and soon he'll be trapped like a rabbit down a hole."

Carl reached out and gripped the marshal's arm. "Don't be sneaking up behind me this time," he said as he stood, then began running in the direction of a fallen tree trunk.

Up on the ledge, Ashton abandoned his hiding place and was frantically making his way toward the rim as a couple of shots from Libby zinged past his head. From his vantage point, Novak could see the direction Ashton was headed and began climbing over rocks and pulling himself up by the branches of bushes. With luck, he hoped they would meet on the canyon's rim.

Ashton arrived on level ground first and began running, his hat flying away. He reached a shallow gulley and fell into it. Breathing heavily and lying on his stomach in icy water, he attempted to steady his rifle on the edge of the sodden bank. He was aiming back in the direction of the rim when he saw the top of Novak's hat come into view.

Carl had just gotten to his feet when Ashton fired. There was a loud groan as a bullet tore into Novak's thigh, knocking him to the ground. His rifle fell away and he was immediately sick to his stomach.

With difficulty, Dean made his way out of the slippery gulley and walked toward his fallen target. There was a smile on his face as he cocked his rifle. He was taking aim when he felt something cold press against the back of his bare head and heard the click of a hammer being pulled back.

"Drop the rifle."

So intent had Ashton been on Novak, he hadn't heard Sam Libby come up behind him.

As Ashton let his weapon slide to the ground, Sam roughly pushed him to his knees. Then he looked toward Novak, who had managed to get to his feet, his hands pressed to his bleeding thigh. For several seconds the two men looked at each other, saying nothing.

"I haven't forgotten what you told me," Libby finally said. "I'm leaving the decision up to you."

Novak stared down at the shivering Ashton, mud covering his coat and pants, a look of spiteful defiance on his face. For a fleeting second, Carl saw the image of Frieda, helpless and terrified as she was about to die. Leaving his rifle where it lay, he pulled his pistol from his holster and limped closer.

Ashton was laughing as Novak pushed the barrel hard against his forehead and pulled the trigger.

There was a muffled sound, then steam rose from the gaping wound rose into the cold air as Dean's body swayed briefly, then fell forward.

"I'll concern myself with the nightmares later," Novak said. Then he passed out.

Libby, already wrapping his bandanna tightly around Carl's leg, had no idea what he was talking about.

S HERIFF HOLLISTER, FOLLOWED by six men he had deputized, arrived at the entrance to the canyon as Libby and Wisenhunt reached the top of the trail. Behind them, Novak was strapped tightly to his horse, his head nodding as he tried to remain conscious.

Hollister, doing his best to appear in charge, was demanding a detailed account of what had transpired, but Wisenhunt cut him short. "We've got a man needing to see a doctor," he said.

"And the brothers, they're dead?" Hollister said.

Libby nodded as he dug his bootheels into his horse's side.

"What about the bodies?"

"Leave 'em," Sam called back as they rode away.

IT WAS GETTING late and outside the livery the snow had again begun to fall. The temperature continued to drop, making a loud statement that winter had officially arrived. Wisenhunt and Libby mixed whiskey into their coffee as they celebrated the news from the doctor. Novak would be laid up for a time, but the bullet had been removed from his leg, the wound cleaned and stitched. No bones or muscle had been damaged. A generous consumption of alcohol had helped him through the agonizing ordeal.

"Doc says he's not to travel for a few days," Wisenhunt said, "so looks like it'll still be a while before we get home. What plans you got?"

"Guess once the weather clears, I'll go report my news to the man who wanted the Ashtons dead. That Tompkins fellow."

Wisenhunt attempted to hide his reaction to the name. "Don't worry yourself none," he said. "Far as me and Carl are concerned, you done your job and should be paid proper for it." He took a long drink of his coffee and stared silently at Libby for a long time. "You ever think about giving it up, maybe doing something like farming or raising cows, before you get yourself killed?"

Libby chuckled. "I'll retire when you do—which I expect will be the day somebody does preaching at your funeral."

"Nope, you're wrong about that. I've been think-ing about turning in my badge for a good while. Once we get back home, I've got one more thing that needs seeing to, then I'm done."

Libby reached for the whiskey. "Need any help?" he said.

PART FOUR

CHAPTER TWENTY-FOUR

Winter

THERE WAS SOME discussion about borrowing a wagon from the Tascosa livery owner for Novak to ride home in, but he had adamantly refused. He would return astride Dawn, he insisted, even if the pain made his eyes water. Reluctantly, he did agree to bring his walking cane along.

The day was cold and cloudless when he and the marshal arrived at the edge of Wolf Creek. Earlier, they had said goodbye to Libby, who still had a lengthy ride to meet with Rafe Tompkins.

"I'll be returning in a few days," he told Carl, "and I'd admire to meet that daughter you've spoken so much about. Maybe I'll get to hear her singing."

"Consider it a promise," Novak said as he shook Sam's hand.

As they watched him ride away, Wisenhunt chuckled. "He ain't a half-bad fellow for someone who enjoys killing folks." He immediately felt bad about his remark and glanced over at Novak to gauge his reaction. He was pleased to see Novak was also smiling.

"Let's get home," he said.

It was Echo who saw them first, and bounded off the front porch, barking as his tail wagged furiously. The doctor looked out the door, and quickly turned to call back into the house. "Miss Lucy," he said, "looks like you've got company."

Before dismounting, the marshal sat watching the happy reunion. Lucy accidentally knocked her daddy's cane away as she reached out to hug him. Then his hat fell away as he lifted her into his arms and returned her embrace. Wisenhunt wasn't sure whether the child was laughing or crying, only that she was happy.

Belinda stood on the porch next to her father, arms folded, with a smile on her face. "Good to have you home, Mr. Novak," she said. "Nice to see you as well, Marshal. Come in out of the cold. I've got coffee and biscuits in the kitchen."

Too excited to sit, Lucy stayed by her daddy's side, talking so fast it was difficult to catch every word. Echo settled into a spot under Carl's chair as his master patiently learned of things that had been happening at school, at church, and in the Turner home.

Before excusing himself to leave, Wisenhunt answered the question no one had wanted to ask. "Everything needing doing has been taken care of," he said as he reached across the table and stuffed two biscuits into the pocket of his jacket. "Treats for the horses," he said with a grin.

He offered no additional details about their journey, no further explanation. Still, for the moment, it seemed enough.

Later that evening, after Lucy had gone to bed, Belinda and Carl sat together by the fireplace, sipping hot cider. The doctor had been called out to check on a case of flu that had apparently taken a turn for the worse. For long periods of time, the only sounds in the room were the steady ticking of a nearby grandfather clock and the crackling of the fire.

"If you ever feel a need to talk about it," Belinda said, "I'll gladly listen."

Without thinking, Carl rubbed his aching leg. "Maybe someday," he said. "But not now."

I N RAFE TOMPKINS'S office, the mood was far different. "I'll gladly pay what's due you," he said as he poured himself another drink, "but I'm owed some details of what took place."

Libby was making an effort not to let his dislike of his host show. "I tracked them down. I found them. And, like you asked, I killed them."

"Where was it this took place?"

"Up near a town called Tascosa."

"I hope they suffered. Did they?"

"I imagine so. They died."

Libby's reluctance to engage in conversation angered Tompkins, but he tried not to let it show as he opened his strongbox and began counting money onto the arm of his chair. "I reckon you're tired," he said. "Maybe you would like to stay in the bunkhouse tonight and rest up. The cook's fixing a brisket for supper." When he saw no reaction, he said, "And I'll gladly share my whiskey."

The idea of spending any more time in the man's box-canyon hideaway than necessary was hardly appealing. He'd seen enough canyons to satisfy him for a lifetime. And enough of Tompkins.

Sam thought back to his conversation with the marshal, who mentioned having one more thing to take care of before retiring. Wisenhunt hadn't told him so, but Libby assumed it had something to do with putting the man's cattle rustling operation out of business. Maybe he should stay and see what he could learn.

"Sounds a sight better than sleeping in the cold," he said.

THE MARSHAL SAT alone at his desk, having sent his deputy home after he'd welcomed him back. Aside from the usual barroom fights and a dustup between two farmers over a cow breaking down a fence and trampling some lady's sweet peas and okra, things had been quiet in Cinco Gap. Wisenhunt had almost forgotten the sound.

It had grown dark long before he thought to light a lantern. The events of the past weeks were still fresh in his mind and he found himself wondering just what had been accomplished. The death of the Ashton brothers was, of course, no great loss. But no real gain either. Their being dead would not bring back any of the lives they had destroyed and damaged.

His friend Carl Novak was likely thinking he would now have some peace with them gone, but he doubted it. The best that had happened was that he had survived to return home to his daughter. Maybe that would ultimately suffice and they could live out a happy, peaceful life. He hoped so.

And what of himself? His journey with Novak had really not been about seeking justice or seeing that the law was upheld. The only danger he ever considered was that which might come to an innocent man like Novak. He had gone to protect him, from the Ashtons and from himself, and had, at least to some degree, succeeded. Maybe that was enough to even out his turning a blind eye to his sworn duty. He had killed a man he could have just as easily taken into custody, and felt no remorse. He had ridden with a hired killer and come to like him, even to admire his twisted credo. He had crossed the line.

Now, if the situation required it—and it most likely would—he was going to do it one more time before he turned in his badge.

He reached into a drawer, withdrew a piece of paper and the stub of a pencil, and began making a list.

E VERY BUNKHOUSE SAM had ever visited had been a rambunctious place, with cardplaying, swearing, secret drinking, and loud storytelling. This one was different, quieter and subdued. It was hardly a happy place, he decided as he watched the dozen hands dutifully go about getting ready for bed. He had had the same feeling when they gathered for supper earlier.

The few he tried to have a conversation with showed little interest.

It was well past midnight and he was still trying to

get to sleep when he heard noises out by one of the corrals. Looking out a window, he saw that a small herd of longhorns was being locked away. Soon a group of cowboys entered the bunkhouse, talking in whispers as they took off boots and gun belts and tossed hats into a corner. One went to his bunk, pulled a jug from beneath it, and began pouring whiskey into a half-dozen tin cups being held out to him.

Libby had returned to his bed and closed his eyes, listening.

"Fifteen head," one was saying. "All fat and full growed." Another mentioned that he was surprised there had been an exchange of gunfire during their torchlit raid. "Some fool guarding the pasture started up shooting at me," he said, "so I had to fire back. Didn't want to, but I think I might have killed him." Libby thought he heard a smattering of laughter from some of the others.

T OMPKINS WAS STANDING near the corral gate when Libby walked into the yard, pulling on his coat to ward off the cold morning wind. "Weather like this'll wake a man in a hurry," he said. "Get you some rest?"

"Except for when some of your boys showed up in the middle of the night," Libby said as he watched the newly arrived cattle moving from one busted hay bale to another. "Business appears to be good."

Tompkins ignored the observation. "There's coffee brewed up in the kitchen," he said.

"Thanks, but I best be on my way."

"Ride safe," Tompkins said, "and be sure you

don't go spending all that money in one place, you hear?"

Locating the two men Tompkins had sent to ambush him as he was leaving the canyon was easy. Just before reaching level ground, Libby turned his horse through a dense grove of trees and came up behind where they were waiting, each holding a rifle.

"My first choice is to shoot you where you stand," Sam said as he approached them. "But if you kindly drop those rifles and put up your hands, I'll give it some more thought."

Both men were slack-jawed, their hands shaking. "We were just doing what we was told," one said. "We were only gonna take your money and send you on your way. Wasn't nobody supposed to get killed."

Libby laughed. "You're a liar," he said, "but I'm going to say something to you that's gospel. Seeing as how you failed to get this job done, I'd suggest you both ride straight on out of here and look for work someplace else. Maybe you can find somebody else needing cattle stolen. But I don't think I'd want to be you, attempting to explain this to the man you're presently hired out to."

He picked up their Winchesters and began walking away. "But, if you are dumb enough to go back and see Rafe Tompkins," he said, "be sure and tell him I said it was a pleasure doing business with him."

CHAPTER TWENTY-FIVE

DEL WISENHUNT WAS pounding the top of his desk and laughing. "I'd like to have seen Tompkins's ugly face when he learned how you made him a fool. You got his money, got two of his rifles, and, most important, you got his goat. I can almost see him stomping around, cussing up a storm."

Libby leaned the two Winchesters against the marshal's desk. "I'm thinking I'll stay around for a little while," he said. "I promised to visit Carl's place and meet his little girl. Might see that my horse is shod and—"

"—most likely visit the hotel, where they got hot baths and lilac water at a reasonable price." Wisenhunt started laughing again. "Wouldn't hurt if you got a professional shave. And had somebody clean and polish them muddy boots."

Sam just nodded. "Sounds good. And if you've got a decent general store in this town, maybe I can buy me a clean shirt."

"From what you've told me, you can easily afford it."

Their good-natured banter continued at the café, where Libby paid for their bowls of chili and left a generous tip for the waitress.

They were walking back to the marshal's office when Sam finally admitted the reason he had stopped by. "You mentioned needing to settle something before you turn in your badge," he said, "and I'm guessing I have an idea what it might be. So, I'm reminding you I'd like to help." Then he added a thought he'd not planned on saying. "Doing something that has a good feel to it might be nice for a change."

The offer took the marshal by surprise. The idea of including a hired killer in his plan was absurd, a violation of every rule and code he'd sworn to live his professional life by. "Go get your horse tended and yourself prettied up," he said. "Let me do some thinking on it."

He gave Libby directions to Novak's farm.

"I'm not expecting pay," Sam said as he walked toward his horse.

Wisenhunt had already made up his mind but would wait awhile before admitting it. Sam Libby, he knew, would be far better in the battle ahead than a tired old town marshal with bad knees and poor eyesight.

CARL NOVAK WAS still walking with the cane and had accepted Cy Butler's offer to stay on for a while and help with the chores. He was sitting on the porch, stroking the fur on Echo's neck, when Libby arrived. He'd never imagined the day would come, but he was glad to see his visitor.

"Peaceful-looking place you've got here," Sam said.

"You come to visit or help with the milking?"

Libby ignored the question and nodded toward the cane leaning against the back of Novak's chair. "You mending okay?"

A voice from the nearby doorway answered the question. "Dr. Turner's looking after him and says he'll soon be good as new. My name's Lucy. What's yours?"

"Samuel Libby the Third. But most folks just call me Sam."

Lucy smiled. "You're my daddy's friend. I've heard him talking about you. In case you're wondering, the reason I'm not in school today is I'm staying home to take care of Daddy until he's feeling better. I can get you some coffee if you like. Oh, and I like your shirt." Before Sam could reply, she was off to the kitchen.

Novak gave his visitor a bemused look. "Samuel Libby the Third?" he said.

"I just made that part up about the Third, hoping to impress her. She's every bit as beautiful and grown-acting as you said."

They sat in the warmth of the morning sun, Carl talking about things on the farm, Sam again recounting his adventures at Rafe Tompkins's place. Lucy sat with them for a while but eventually left with Echo to gather the eggs.

"It's good you had her to come back to," Libby said. "I envy you that, I don't mind telling you."

SEVEN ROADS TO REVENGE

Not sure how to respond, Novak changed the subject. "You seen the marshal?"

"Visited him yesterday. That's one of the reasons I wanted to come see you. I'm concerned about something he's planning on doing."

"Retiring?"

"No, something he has in mind to do before he does that. I think he's going after Rafe Tompkins. Any chance you can talk him out of it?"

"Stubborn as he is? Not if his mind's set."

"That's what I figured. I'm going to be staying around for a while."

"You're welcome to bunk here," Carl said. "I got plenty of room. And Lucy will tell you she can take care of two easy as one."

"She's already told me something I was pleased to hear."

"That being?"

"That you referred to me as a friend. I appreciate that. "

As he spoke, Lucy returned, cradling a basket under one arm. "I got enough eggs to try baking us a cake," she said, "if I can find where Mama wrote down her recipe."

Sam glanced over at Novak as the child hurried into the house. For a moment, however brief, he saw that the sad, faraway look remained.

RAFE TOMPKINS WAS on a rampage unlike anything his workers had ever seen. Not heeding Libby's advice, the two would-be ambushers had returned to the canyon and thrown themselves on their boss's mercy. They got none. Tompkins threw a lit lantern at one and punched the other in the face before picking up a pistol from a nearby table and shooting them both.

"Ain't nobody a man can trust," he said before calling someone to come take the bodies away and see that the floors of his cabin were cleaned.

Throughout the day he stormed from the barn to the corrals, to the kitchen and back to his cabin to refill his glass and light another cigar. Then he would start the routine over, cussing and kicking at the dirt as he went. Men scattered from his path like frightened chickens. No one was safe from his rage, not even the cook, who he left in tears after telling her her cooking ought to be tossed into the pigsty instead of served at the table.

"I want that man and I want my money," he said repeatedly to anyone within earshot. "Can't nobody get them for me, I'll see to it myself." No one attempted to argue that he would most likely be shot dead by a hired gunman before he could even clear his holster.

He called a meeting for after dinner in the chow hall. Most of his men had only nervously picked at their food by the time he appeared. The cook remained in her kitchen, afraid to show her face. The boss was a bit unsteady, but had a determined look on his face. His speech was short.

"I've got one hundred dollars for the man who comes and tells me where to find Sam Libby," he said, then staggered out.

*   *   *

Promising Lucy he would return in time for her "special-company supper," Libby said he needed to return to see the marshal. Novak asked that Cy saddle Dawn, and rode with him despite doctor's orders and his daughter's pleas that he stay home.

"We'll have the dickens to pay when we get back," Sam said. "She's a feisty little thing, isn't she?"

"A spitting image of her mama," Carl said.

In Wisenhunt's office, they quickly realized there would be no persuading him to abandon his plan. In fact, when he laid it out for them, it was obvious it was something he had given long, hard thought to.

He pulled a stack of telegrams from his desk drawer and handed them to Sam, who read them one by one, then passed them to Novak. They were signed by sheriffs, marshals, Pinkerton agents, and even a couple of Texas Rangers. All expressed their willingness to participate.

"I ain't so feebleminded as to think I can pull this off by myself, or even with just a couple of greenhorn deputies," Wisenhunt said. "For what I want done, we'll need more folks. I aim to see not only Rafe Tompkins arrested, but every outlaw who ever helped him steal a cow or burn down somebody's barn."

Spreading a map, he showed where he had marked Xs at every location where cattle rustling had been reported in recent years. "They've done themselves considerable traveling," the marshal said, "so their lawbreaking covers a number of jurisdictions. Once I got that figured out, I contacted every lawman looking to solve cases. And some others, like the Rangers and Pinkerton folks, who just like flashing their badges and chasing after people. We're going to have us a sizable raiding party when the proper time comes."

He leaned forward and looked at Libby. "If you're of a mind," he said, "I'd like to have you ride with us. I figure you ain't one of Tompkins's favorite people these days anyway. All I require is you don't make mention of how you earn your living to any of the other lawmen who'll be coming."

"I can keep a secret," Sam said.

Novak reached for his cane and got to his feet. "I'm not so crippled up that I can't take part," he said. "I need to start repaying you for—"

The marshal needed only a moment before interrupting. "I was thinking if you're feeling up to it, I'd deputize you to help me with getting everything organized," he said, hoping it didn't sound like the afterthought it was.

CHAPTER TWENTY-SIX

IT'S A SHAME nobody's got themself a camera," Carl whispered to Sam Libby as they sat side by side in a pew at the Wolf Creek Family Church. Since Sam was staying at the farm, Lucy informed him, he would be required to attend Sunday services with her and her father. "Because," she proudly announced, "I'm going to be singing."

Novak was delighting at the irony of a child persuading a hired gunslinger to attend a church service. "I just hope lightning don't strike the place," he said.

The levity ended when his daughter stepped from the choir loft and smiled at the pastor before taking her place next to Bella Rawlings, the church's longtime piano player.

By the time Lucy reached the first chorus of "Angels from the Realm of Glory," Carl was finding breathing difficult. He was aware that those sitting around him were spellbound by the beauty of his daughter's voice. And in that moment, all the touchstone events of his life were rushing to mind. It was on the very spot where Lucy was standing that he and Frieda had exchanged their marriage vows. Where Lucy, then just a baby, had been christened. And, on the worst day of his life, where his wife's casket was placed so mourners could pass and bid her farewell.

And now this.

A young girl's voice had finally helped him understand what Marshal Wisenhunt, even Sam, had been trying to tell him. Standing in front of him, singing like the angels in her song, was his purpose, his reason to move on.

Libby leaned close to his ear when the song ended. "Now," he whispered, "I'm feeling even more envy."

Carl could only nod, the faraway look gone.

While members gathered around Lucy on the steps of the church, Belinda was the first to reach Carl. "Oh, my word," she said. "Wasn't she just marvelous?" Then, overwhelmed by the moment, she reached out and gave him a hug, then kissed him lightly on the cheek.

Standing beneath the nearby grape arbor, Libby and Dr. Turner were smiling.

ZEKE WHITLOCK HAD slept off a drunk in the alley behind the Wolf's Howl saloon and knew he was in a world of trouble. His boss, Mr. Tompkins, had sent him to pick up some rolls of barbed wire that had been shipped from back east and he made the mistake of stopping for a drink before heading back to the canyon. That error in judgment would, he knew, cost him dearly. The pounding in his head was nothing compared to the scolding he knew awaited him.

It took him the better part of an hour to locate his wagon, parked in back of the feed store, and more time throwing up the last of the cheap whiskey that had tasted so good only hours earlier. He gave up trying to find his hat.

He was slowly headed out of Wolf Creek, begging the mule to avoid as many holes in the street as possible, when his luck changed.

By the time he pulled up in front of the barn he was almost sober, waving to his fellow cowboys as he hurried across the yard toward Tompkins's cabin.

IT WAS HIM, I'm sure as I'm standing here. He was all duded up, standing out front of the church house."

Tompkins could smell the whiskey and residue of vomit from all the way across the room. "The church?" he said.

"Big as you please," Whitlock repeated, suddenly feeling light-headed. "Reckon it would be okay if I sit down for a minute?"

Ignoring the question, Tompkins said, "You're certain it was Sam Libby. Wasn't somebody who could have just looked like him to a man not seeing as well as he might if he'd not been drinking?"

"I can swear to it."

"Where did he go after church let out?"

"I didn't wait to see, knowing you were waiting for me to return with the barbed wire," Whitlock said as he stole a glance at the whiskey bottle sitting on the table by Tompkins's chair.

When told to leave, he was disappointed he'd been offered neither a drink nor the hundred dollars for finding Sam Libby. At least he hadn't received a cussing out that would have made his headache worse.

TOMPKINS'S MIND WAS racing. He had no idea why Libby would be in Wolf Creek—maybe courting a lady with some of his money—yet the news excited him. If, that is, his drunk cowhand could be believed. First, he would need to send a couple of others to Wolf Creek to see if what had been reported was true.

Two days later, he got the news he was hoping for. One of his men had seen Libby out front of the livery and later, while having his dinner, he had seen him go into the café.

"He was close enough I could have reached out and touched him," the young cowboy reported. "He smelled real nice."

"I want him hog-tied up and brought back here," Tompkins said.

He began considering which of his men to send to capture Libby and how best it could be accomplished. It worried him that the prospects and the past performances weren't encouraging. Sending cattle rustlers to go up against a hired gunslinger would be no easy task. His best option, he decided, was strength in numbers. He would send a half dozen, maybe more, to Wolf Creek. If a few died in the process, well, that was just the cost of doing business.

He was already considering ways he would kill Libby.

M ARSHAL WISENHUNT HAD been busy with plans of his own. For the third time of the morning, he checked the calendar on his wall. By the end of the week his fellow lawmen would begin arriving.

To keep his promise of involving Novak, he sent him to Fort Concho regularly to oversee preparations. Wagonloads of supplies and bedrolls were being moved into one of the large rooms that had somehow avoided serious decay. A few men from Wolf Creek, all sworn to secrecy, were hired to shore up the fences of the corral and make sure the water well was in working order. Soot was cleaned from the chimneys and firewood cut and stacked. Feed for the visitors' horses was stocked in.

The long-abandoned old fort was being made ready for guests.

A large map, which the marshal and Novak had labored over during several long nights, was spread across a dining room table that had been positioned in the middle of the meeting room. On it was a detailed drawing of the canyon, routes into it, and ways it could best be surrounded.

The atmosphere Wisenhunt wanted was that of a military staging area, reminiscent of the days when the place was alive with soldiers planning attacks on Indian camps. Novak found himself marveling at the marshal's attention to the slightest detail as he made ready for the last chapter of his law enforcement career.

Delighting in the activity was the fort's lone per-
manent resident. "Company's coming . . . company's
coming," Bubba Joe would happily chant as he followed Novak from room to room. "Gotta keep a
secret . . . company's coming."

"Once everyone has arrived," the marshal said,
"we'll show them hospitality of a good meal—
barbecuing a side of beef might be good if we can get
a rancher to donate one—then we'll set about decid-
ing our best course of action."

Bubba Joe repeatedly offered to cook his famous
chili.

A T THE MARSHAL's insistence, Libby stayed away.
Wisenhunt had assured him he would let him
know when he was needed. On the days Novak wasn't
at the fort, he spent time helping Cy Butler with his
chores. With the approach of winter turning everything dormant, there was little to do besides chopping wood, mucking out the barn, seeing that the
livestock was fed, and riding into town each afternoon to escort Lucy home from school.

He was surprised how easily he settled into the
routine, enjoying a peace and quiet he had all but
forgotten.

CHAPTER TWENTY-SEVEN

B RADY JACKSON, SHERIFF in Lindsey Junction, was the first to arrive, soon followed by Will McCall, who was the marshal in Singletary. Both had brought a deputy along. By day's end, the fort's corral was full and a dozen lawmen mingled inside, renewing friendships and swapping stories. The last to show up were a Pinkerton agent named Billingsley and two Texas Rangers, J. W. Heath and Buck Lewis, who seemed inclined to stay to themselves and speak only when spoken to.

Sheriff Jackson studied the map of the canyon for some time then scanned the layout of the meeting area and sleeping quarters. "General Lee himself couldn't have prepared better," he told Wisenhunt as he slapped him on the back. The marshal was quick to introduce Novak and credit him with overseeing much of the planning, stopping short of mentioning that he'd fought for the Union.

Most of the lawmen present were exchanging tales of farmers and ranchers back home who had cattle stolen or crops and outbuildings destroyed. One said he had a murder warrant in his saddlebag since a ranch hand, a cousin of his, had been shot and killed trying to protect his boss's herd. Another spoke of an elderly farmer who had been so badly pistol-whipped that he lost sight in one eye.

None had ever seen Rafe Tompkins, and they listened as Wisenhunt described him. "He's a mean-as-the-devil little man, not quite as big around the middle as me, and has what I'd call a weasel face. Most likely when you see him, he'll be wearing a big sombrero and smoking a cigar. Also, if we're lucky, he'll not be fully sober."

Novak, who had remained in the background during the conversations, stepped forward. "He's also a coward," he added. "Though he's the cause of all the miseries your people back home have experienced, he's always had others do his dirty work for him. They should pay just as dearly."

His statement made, he turned to go outside and check on progress at the fire pit and see that Bubba Joe had tended to everyone's horses.

As Novak left, Wisenhunt was opening a large box he'd brought from the general store days earlier and began handing out white bandannas. "Everybody is to wear one of these," he said. "If it turns out there's a lot of shooting, heaven forbid, I don't want us killing each other."

THE DAY WAS still cold but warming as Sam Libby rode into town. Except for when he heard Carl's nightly reports after he returned to the farm, he had given little thought to how he might figure into the marshal's plan. Recently, his days had been more carefree than he could recall, his most important responsibility seeing Lucy safely home each afternoon.

With her father not available to meet her, Belinda Turner had volunteered. She would be waiting in the schoolyard and they would walk the short distance to the doctor's house, where Lucy did her lessons while sweet-smelling cookies were being taken from the oven.

If he timed his arrival right, Sam, too, would enjoy Belinda's baking before they rode back to the farm.

It was a routine Tompkins's men had become familiar with.

THEY WERE HEADED home at an easy pace, Lucy pressed against Sam's back to block the cold wind, complaining about the difficulties of long division, when his horse made a sudden stop and nervously lifted its ears. Libby's hand was easing toward his pistol when two riders appeared from a stand of scrub oaks. Two others emerged from a nearby gulley.

Almost immediately they were joined by another pair, who came up from behind. All carried rifles.

"So nobody gets hurt," one of the men said to Libby, "it would be best if you put your hands high as you can reach." Terrified, Lucy began to cry as one of the men approached and removed Libby's Colt from its holster then lifted her from behind the saddle.

As his hands were being tied behind his back, Sam glared at the man who appeared to be in charge. "What's the cause for this?" he said.

"Mr. Tompkins is wanting to see you."

"Leave the child be. Let her get on home," Sam said, attempting to maintain an even tone of voice that hid his fury.

The simple request seemed to puzzle the gunmen, who obviously hadn't thought everything through before carrying out their assignment. The man who had lifted Lucy to the ground and was tightly gripping her shoulders seemed the most confused. "What are we supposed to do with the girl?" he said.

There were several seconds of silence before someone offered a solution. "Bring her with us."

T HOUGH HE HAD left the fort before dinner began, it was already dark by the time Carl reached the farm and found Cy Butler pacing on the porch, a lantern swinging at his side.

"They ain't here, Mr. Novak," he said. "Sam and Lucy, they didn't come home. I'm worried sick to my stomach. Reckon we should see the marshal?"

His question went unanswered as Carl yanked at Dawn's reins and galloped away toward Wolf Creek.

Belinda was washing the supper dishes when she heard him call her name. The doctor put down the book he was reading and went to the door. The look on Novak's face told him immediately that something was terribly wrong.

Belinda dried her hands as he quickly explained the situation. "Everything was fine when they left here earlier," she said. "Lucy had done her lessons and . . ." She burst into tears before she could complete her sentence.

"I'd advise seeing the marshal," Dr. Turner said, "but when I passed his office on my way home he wasn't there. Fact is, I haven't seen much of him lately."

"I know where to find him," Carl said. Then he asked a favor. "My horse is about worn out and I've got a hard ride to make. Can I borrow yours?"

The doctor was already pulling on his coat. "She's boarded down at the livery. I'll go help you get her saddled."

Belinda wiped her tears with her apron and called out to Novak as he and her father were leaving. "Bring her back safe," she said. "Please. I'll be praying until you do."

T HE INSIDE OF the small tack room in the rear of Rafe Tompkins's barn was pitch-dark and cold. Despite the fact Sam had given Lucy his coat to put over hers before his hands were tied, she was shivering. The maturity he had seen in her when they first met, then when she had stood in front of a church congregation and sung with such grace and confidence, was gone. She was now just a little girl, afraid, cold, and crying. "I want my daddy," she said over and over.

Beyond the door they could hear voices, one louder than the others. "I don't recall telling none of you pea brains to bring a child here," Tompkins yelled. There was a faint sound of something breaking. "I told you clear as I knew how that I wanted Sam Libby, not some little girl." Something else broke. "Who is she?"

No one answered.

After another loud stream of curses, Tompkins

seemed to calm. "I know what I'll do about him," he said. "Her, I'll just have to deal with later. Maybe a good night's sleep will help me to figure it out."

And then the barn suddenly went quiet, except for the sound of Lucy crying.

A T FORT CONCHO, the meal was finished, a fire blazed in the fireplace, and Wisenhunt was in front of the gathering, outlining plans for its attack the following day, when Novak burst into the room. He was limping badly but had discarded his cane. Though he had just come in from the cold, he was sweating profusely.

All eyes in the room followed him as he hurried toward the marshal. "I think they've got Lucy," he said, "and Sam Libby as well."

It took the stunned Wisenhunt a moment to fully comprehend what he was hearing, to realize who "they" were. Quickly, however, he knew Novak was talking about Tompkins's men. But why was Lucy involved?

Still breathing heavily, Carl explained how Libby had been staying at his farm and bringing his daughter home from school on days when he was working at the fort. "I can't say all the details—I don't know them—but I'm sure she's been taken." Then he added a final declaration. "I'm going to get her."

The marshal took a deep breath, and for a moment stared at his feet, absorbing the turn of events. Then, lifting his head, he addressed the others in the room. "Gentlemen, our plans just got changed," he said. "We're going out tonight."

CHAPTER TWENTY-EIGHT

B Y THE TIME torches were hastily constructed and the horses saddled, it had begun to sleet. The moon had disappeared behind a blanket of clouds and the temperature continued to drop. The marshal and Novak were leading the way, tiny crystals of ice beating a rhythm on the brims of their hats.

"You sure you're up to this?" Wisenhunt asked as the fort disappeared behind them. "It wasn't my intention for you to be involved in this."

Carl didn't immediately answer, fixing his eyes straight ahead. Finally, he said, "Things don't always go like we want. If she's harmed in the least I'll kill Tompkins in the worst way I can think of. Swear to God."

I N THE DARKENED tack room, Sam Libby was having the same thoughts. Mixed with his anger was the knowledge that he was responsible for putting his friend's daughter in harm's way. He cursed himself beneath his breath for letting his guard down. He had allowed himself to be seduced by a world unfamiliar to him, one of quiet comfort and friendly people. As he had embraced it, gotten comfortable with it, he had allowed this to happen.

He scooted closer to Lucy to provide what body warmth he could.

As he did so, a dim stream of light fell across the floor and the door opened. Rafe Tompkins, with a candle holder in one hand and a pistol in the other, stepped inside. "Couldn't sleep," he said, "so I thought I'd come visit." Even in the semidarkness, Libby could see the smirk on his face.

"You got no cause to keep the girl here," Sam said.

"I've been thinking about that. See, she don't mean nothing to me. I'm sorry to say I don't even know her name or who she belongs to. We'll just have to find a place to get rid of her after I've decided what I'm going to do with you."

"My guess is you've already made up your mind about that."

"Oh, I have. Most definitely. It's just how I'm going to do it and how long it's going to take that I haven't yet figured out. All I know at the moment is I want it to be painful as can be." He laughed, then said, "Maybe it would educate the young'un if she watched."

Libby spat a stream of profanities at Tompkins. "If it isn't me kills you for this, somebody else will. Sooner than you might think."

He regretted the statement as soon as it left his mouth.

Tompkins slammed the barrel of his pistol against Libby's cheek and kicked him hard in the stomach.

"That's just a taste. Something happening I need to know about?"

Groggy, Libby shook his head.

"I'm getting cold, so I'll be leaving you to it," Tompkins said as he moved away and shut the door. Libby heard the outside bolt slam into place as Lucy began to cry again.

Instead of returning to his cabin, Tompkins went directly to the bunkhouse and began rousing his men. "Sleeping's over," he said as he hurried about the room, shaking shoulders and lighting lanterns. "I've got a strong feeling we've got visitors coming," he said, "and want them welcomed properly."

He began ordering men to various locations where they were to stand guard. Two who he most trusted were told to bring a lantern and rifles and set up watch on the porch of his cabin.

T HE CLOSER THEY got to the canyon, the quieter the posse of lawmen became. Conversation ended and torches were doused as the first stage of Wisenhunt's plan was put into motion. One group of riders made their way toward the main trail leading down into the canyon while others split off and worked their way to take their places along the rim.

"I'm not sure we can do much good with it being so dark," Ranger Heath whispered to Novak and the marshal. "Maybe we should wait until sunup like you wanted. We've got them surrounded, so there's no way anybody can get out."

Novak was already making his way down a narrow trail next to the main entrance road.

"We've got folks who ain't interested in waiting," the marshal said as he hurried to catch up with Carl. Heath and his fellow Ranger, Lewis, headed toward the entrance.

The first shot came from the back side of the canyon. Then, in rapid reply, came a volley from up along the rim. Soon gunfire was coming from every direction.

"No more use for us sneaking," Wisenhunt said. "They know we're coming." A shot from a nearby ledge zinged past his head as he slapped a glove against his horse's rump. "I'll be proud if this is the last canyon I ever have to lay eyes on," he said.

The darkness worked to their advantage. Tompkins's men had no clear targets or any idea how many they were facing. Bending forward with his head against his horse's neck, Novak continued to move forward with Wisenhunt close behind. As they reached flat ground they could see flickers of light coming from the bunkhouse, where, in haste, lanterns had been left burning.

"We best go on foot from here," Carl said. There was an abandoned old water wagon partially hidden by bushes and they tied their horses to its rotting tongue. Then they crouched and listened.

The sleet was coming harder, covering the ground with a slick, white coat. Carl's leg throbbed and the marshal's knees ached. "Patience," Wisenhunt whispered. "We have to wait until it gets light."

TOMPKINS OPENED HIS front door only wide enough to peek outside and make sure his guards were still there. "Where are they?" he said.

"Sounds like they're everywhere. Seems we're surrounded. It's too dark to see much, but I'm guessing there's a sizable number of them." As he spoke, there was the echo of a half-dozen rifle shots from the opposite rim of the canyon. One bullet thudded against the chimney of the cabin, chipping away shards of limestone. Another raised ice and dirt from the frozen ground just feet away from a nearby hitching post. Tompkins was closing his door when he heard a loud groan from one of his men. He saw him drop his weapon and grab for his chest, then fall. The last words his boss heard before the man slammed the door were, "I'm shot."

Tompkins moved around inside on his hands and knees, blowing out the lanterns that had served as the target for the shooters and frantically rummaging in his desk for ammunition for his Colt. He couldn't risk getting to his feet and reaching for the rifle hanging on pegs above his door. Though the inside of his cabin was warm, he was shivering.

After the series of shots fired at the cabin, it suddenly became so quiet he could hear his own breathing.

Still on hands and knees, he slowly made his way to the back wall, where his safe was located. After several false starts, he managed to dial the correct numbers and removed his strongbox. The next thing he had to do was slip away from the house before it got light.

UP TOP, SHERIFF Brady Jackson had taken charge. The shooting was unnecessary, an overzealous act that did nothing but announce their presence and give away their locations. He rode around the canyon rim angrily instructing his fellow lawmen to hold their fire. "We can't even see nothing to be shooting at yet," he said. "Unless someone shoots at you and is close enough for you to see them, save your ammunition and concentrate on thinking how to work your way down the side. We ain't here for a shooting war unless they're the ones who start it. I'm betting by daylight, they'll be ready to surrender."

Most agreed with Brady's assessment. The two Rangers had only huffed and turned away, continuing to aim their rifles down into the canyon despite the fact they could detect no movement.

Tompkins's men, meanwhile, had no plan of attack. When they had been ordered out of the bunkhouse, their first thought was to find cover. They hid behind the dining hall, huddled under wagons, knelt behind haystacks, and used the corralled horses for shields. Though they focused on the faint outline of the rim surrounding them, they might as well have been looking down a well.

The earlier shots fired convinced them they were badly outnumbered. Some were already talking about saddling their horses and making a run for it once the sun came up. Others were ready to surrender, if they could see anyone they could give themselves up to. Only fools and the blindly loyal stood ready to fight it out.

IN THE BARN, Libby struggled to loosen the bindings on his wrist but with no success. Though she had not been tied up, Lucy's hands were so cold and numb she was unable to provide any help. Libby continued doing what he could to calm her. "You hear that shooting a while ago? That's people coming to help us. You just hang with me a little longer, be brave as you can, and soon as it gets light, you'll be headed home to your daddy."

He was pounding his boots against the floor in an effort to get feeling back in his feet when she asked if he promised.

"Lucy, I promise."

"I wouldn't be making promises you can't keep." It was Tompkins again. "Won't be no going home for anybody," he said. He was again in the doorway of the tack room, a pistol pointed at Sam and his strongbox cradled under his arm. He was wearing his sombrero.

He had slipped out the back window of his cabin and, crawling much of the way, made it safely to the barn.

Glaring down at Libby, he said, "I prefer shooting you dead right now, but since I'll need help from you and the young lady to get away, it'll have to wait."

A S DAWN ARRIVED, the sleet ended, leaving behind a shiny glaze of ice everywhere. The sky was clearing and members of the posse were getting their first look at the rambling compound down in the basin. The map Wisenhunt showed them hadn't done it justice.

"It's like a little town," Jackson said, "almost as big as mine back home."

His eyes roamed, stopping when he saw cattle huddled in three holding pens. They reminded him of why he was there just as shooting started nearby.

Several of the men had left the rim at first light and made their way into the basin. When two of Tompkins's men tried to run to better cover, they were quickly knocked to the ground, badly wounded by rifle shots. One, attempting to escape up the trail, was shot by J. W. Heath, who was amused when he saw the man was riding bareback, not having taken time to saddle his horse.

The firefight Brady Jackson and Wisenhunt had hoped might be avoided was in full force.

With gunfire exchanges all around, Carl Novak was focused on getting to Tompkins's cabin. Before it got light, he and the marshal had made their way through underbrush to the back door and waited for sunup to make their entrance. When they rushed inside, pistols drawn, they found the cabin empty.

They were standing in the middle of the room, about to holster guns, when the front door opened slightly and the guard who had remained on the porch nervously spoke. "Everything okay in there, Mr. Tompkins?"

The answer was Novak's shot, which went through the partially open door and into the man's chest.

As smoke from the gunshot filled the small room, Wisenhunt made his way over to the open window. "He snuck out," he said. "With all the shooting, he could already be dead."

Novak hoped not. Aside from his desperate need to find his daughter, killing Rafe Tompkins was a pleasure he wanted for himself.

By the time they stepped over the guard's body

and made their way onto the front porch, the shooting had abruptly stopped. They saw men emerging from their cover, hands raised, and slowly making their way toward the middle of the yard. Several appeared to be wounded. All were frightened as they walked past bodies of coworkers.

Lawmen advanced from all directions, surrounding them. The sun was still just peeking over the cliffs and it was over. The two Texas Rangers immediately took command, seeing that the prisoners were tied up and weapons collected. The dead got no notice.

Buck Lewis walked over to Wisenhunt and shook his hand. "We got this done in short order and without losing a single man," he said.

The marshal gave the Ranger a disgusted look. "This ain't finished," he said. "Far from it."

Lewis seemed puzzled.

"We still got a little girl and one of our own missing," the marshal said. "And unless one of them bodies laid out over there is Rafe Tompkins, the man who's the cause for all this, he still needs to be found."

CHAPTER TWENTY-NINE

IT WAS SHERIFF Jackson who first saw the barn door swing open and a man on horseback emerge. He was wearing a sombrero pulled tight against his forehead and in front of him in the saddle was a young girl, a pistol pointed at her head. The mare was tightly reined and moving slowly. "Ain't nobody here can shoot fast enough to keep me from pulling my trigger on this young lady first," Tompkins said, "so best everybody just stand back and let us be on our way."

It was Jackson who gave the order for everyone to lower their weapons.

Aware of the shooting that was under way, Tompkins had frantically sought a way to escape. Enraged by the situation, he had considered simply shooting Sam Libby in the face and being done with it, but knew the sound of gunfire from inside the barn would alert others to his presence. He cursed himself for not bringing his bowie knife so he could cut Libby's throat. Ultimately, he decided the best he could do was take a shovel from the wall and smash the blade to the side of Sam's head.

Then, for the first time since he was a young man, he saddled his own horse. "Miss, we're going to take us a ride," he said as he stepped over the unconscious Libby and roughly yanked Lucy to her feet. After lifting her into the saddle, he carefully emptied the contents of his strongbox into saddlebags.

When they rode out of the barn, the yard went silent. The trace of a smile crossed Tompkins's face as he watched weapons being lowered. Even his own men had never seen him appear so crazed. The only sound was the distant baying of cattle and the child's voice calling out to her father when she saw him standing nearby. Novak's pistol lay useless between his feet.

Tompkins eased on the reins and allowed his horse to move a few steps toward where Wisenhunt stood. The marshal looked up at the rider but didn't speak.

"I figure it's you to blame for starting all this needless ruckus," Tompkins said. "Couldn't be satisfied to mind your own business, could you?"

For several seconds the two men glared at each other. Then Tompkins moved his pistol from the girl's head, pointed it at the marshal's midsection, and fired two quick shots. As Wisenhunt struggled unsuccessfully to stay on his feet, the horse and its riders sped away toward the trail that would lead them from the canyon.

Novak was the first to the marshal's side, followed by Brady Jackson. Kneeling on the frozen ground,

they could see that Wisenhunt's eyes were already
glazed and beginning to roll back in his head. One
arm jerked slightly and he reached to gather a fistful
of muddy ice from the ground. Some strange reflex
had caused him to lose one of his boots. There was a
low groan, barely audible, then a soft sigh. And he
was dead.

Several of the lawmen carried the marshal's body
to the cabin as J. W. Heath helped Libby stay on his
feet as they exited the barn. The Ranger had cut away
the bindings and tied his white bandanna over the
deep gash in Sam's forehead.

"Where's Lucy?" he asked as Novak approached.
"She okay?"

"Not yet," Carl said.

THE ACTIVITY IN the canyon was at the same time
grim and frantic. One of the Pinkerton agents
was urging that a group go after Tompkins immediately before Novak halted the conversation. "I'll see
that's tended to," he said. "You just make sure the
marshal gets cared for properly and these men are
taken to jail. See that you watch them like a hawk,
and if anybody causes trouble on the way . . . shoot
him."

Rangers Lewis and Heath had already announced
they would be leading the caravan of cattle rustlers into
Wolf Creek. The death of Marshal Wisenhunt aside, it
had been a good day for the Texas Rangers. Lewis was
planning to send a telegram to headquarters, passing
along the news, as soon as they reached town.

Brady Jackson stepped out from the group. "This ain't something to take on alone," he said to the clearly enraged Novak. "Like it or not, I'm riding with you."

"Me too," said Sam Libby, his dizziness going away thanks to the cold, fresh air. He looked toward the cabin, where the marshal's limp body was being carried up the porch steps, then turned to Novak. "This time," he said, "we've got no agreement. If you're figuring on killing Tompkins before I do, you best be quick about it."

Soon they were on their way. "Even a blind fool can track him in this slush," Libby said as they reached the top of the canyon trail.

RAFE TOMPKINS HAD no destination in mind. Pushing his horse hard along the frozen terrain, he knew only that he needed to put as much distance as possible between him and the men he knew would soon follow.

Steam puffed from the horse's nostrils as she attempted to keep up the pace her rider demanded. Tompkins knew if he didn't rest the animal soon, she would be of no use. Reaching a creek bed that wound through a series of limestone overhangs, he stopped and dismounted.

Lucy's attitude had changed dramatically during the ride. In place of her tears was a look of disgust, her tears replaced by a growing anger. "My daddy's going to kill you for this," she said as her captor led her to a dry spot beneath a ledge.

"Not if I can kill him first," Tompkins said. "Who's your daddy?"

"He's Carl Novak and he was a soldier in the war before my momma died."

"Him and that Sam Libby know each other?"

"They're friends, real good friends. If my daddy don't come and kill you, Sam will. I remember him telling you that back in the barn."

Again, Tompkins wished he had killed Libby when he'd had the chance. "I'm tired of your sass," he told Lucy as he began wrapping a kerchief tightly over her mouth.

He was preparing to resume their aimless journey when he heard a distant noise. Hiding the horse in the shadows of the overhang, he knelt behind a large live oak and watched as a lengthy parade of horses and riders headed northward. Even from a distance, he recognized several of the men whose heads were hanging and their hands tied behind their backs. His men, those who hadn't been killed, were being taken to jail. Most likely in Wolf Creek.

"We'll not be heading that way," he said to himself, all the while aware that he had to keep moving toward some kind of safe shelter for the night. Already the freezing wind was kicking up again and dark clouds were moving back in, promising more moisture.

For a moment he imagined a warm fire and a bottle of good whiskey, and wondered where he might find both. It was as he lifted the girl into the saddle in front of him that he remembered hearing about an old abandoned fort that was somewhere not far to the south. Several of his men had mentioned seeing it when they had herded stolen cattle back from their midnight raids.

H E WAS SURPRISED to see smoke coming from a chimney and a faint light from a second-floor window as they approached what remained of Fort Concho. The rest of the building was dark and appeared to be deserted. A freezing mist began to fall as he rode closer.

"We'll see if there's anybody friendly waiting for weary travelers," he said. "But it don't really matter. If we ain't welcome, I'll just start shooting folks."

Such a drastic measure was not necessary. Bubba Joe hurried down the stairs soon after they let themselves in and broke into a wide smile. "Welcome," he said. "So glad to see you. Welcome, welcome, welcome."

Tompkins looked around the room and saw dishes still scattered on tables and windowsills and bedrolls that remained stretched across the floor. Of particular interest to him was the big map spread across a table. He recognized what it was immediately.

"Looks like you had yourself a party," he said.

"We did. Yes, we did, but everybody's gone now. Not coming back . . . They're gone . . ."

"Folks must have left out in a hurry."

"There's food left over if you're hungry. We cooked a cow in the yard . . . Yes, sir, they left real fast when my friend, the marshal, told them to . . . real fast. I helped saddle the horses."

The mention of food got Lucy's attention. Aside from Belinda's peanut butter cookies, she hadn't had anything to eat in two days. Moving near the fire-place, she warmed her hands until they were no longer stiff. Once feeling returned to her fingers, she ripped the kerchief from her mouth. "I'd appreciate some food, please," she said.

"I'll fix you both up a plate," Bubba Joe said. "Steak and boiled potatoes and some beans left in the pot . . . I don't know what all else."

"That would be good," Tompkins said. "You're a nice fellow."

As Bubba Joe left for the kitchen, Tompkins shot a look toward Lucy that without a single word sent a clear message: *Keep your mouth shut or else.*

T HE TRACKERS SAID little as they followed Tompkins's trail. "The way he appears to be running that horse," Carl said, "we should catch up to them soon."

They rode another mile before Sam moved his horse closer to Novak. Jackson rode ahead, eyes glued to the ground.

"I want you to know how sorry I'm feeling about all this," Libby said. "I've not done much apologizing in my day and don't really know how it's properly done, but I hope to make it up to you somehow. All this has been caused by me—the marshal, Lucy, everybody—and all I know to say is I didn't intend for none of it to happen."

"Good people don't make bad things happen," Novak said. "It's bad folks who cause bad things. And I don't view you as bad." As he spoke, he was rubbing his aching leg. Libby's head was throbbing so that he alternately closed one eye then the other in an effort to relieve the pain.

"You'll have to pardon my saying, but for men your age," Sheriff Jackson said, "you fellows ain't exactly pictures of good health."

Sam laughed for the first time since he and Lucy had been abducted by Tompkins's men. Novak also managed a smile. "We'll have plenty of time to heal up and rest once we get my little girl back and tend to the man who's got her," he said.

The tracks were beginning to fade as night approached and the mist dampened the ground. They reached the creek bed where Tompkins had stopped briefly, and for a long time Novak stood beneath the overhang, staring down at the small footprints that he knew were his daughter's.

"Seems she's okay if she's moving around like that," Libby said.

"For now," Carl replied.

They stood together beneath the ledge, avoiding the mist, which was turning back to frozen rain. Jackson offered to build a fire.

"We can't just sit here all night," Novak said. "What's your idea on how Tompkins is thinking? Where's he headed?"

"Seeing as how I figure him to be crazy with fear, it's hard to say what his mind's doing," Libby said. "I'll bet this: He ain't a man who'll want to rough it outside in weather like this. Being sissified as he seems, he'll be looking for a place he can be warm and stay dry."

"No farms around here that I know of," Jackson said. "For sure, there ain't no towns. Indians might have left some dugouts behind, but they won't do to make a man like Tompkins comfortable, even if he builds him a fire."

Libby waited for a couple of seconds, then said, "Indians were run off by the soldiers, weren't they? If I'm not mistaken, that old fort you boys visited ain't too far from where we're at."

Carl was stepping into a stirrup almost before Sam completed his thought. "I think I can find it," he said.

They resisted the urge to hurry their horses along since the way was dark and unfamiliar. Carl could almost hear the marshal reminding him to remain patient.

B UBBA JOE ADDED logs to the fire as his guests ate. "Is there a room with privacy where the girl can sleep?" Tompkins said.

"She's welcome to have my room," Bubba Joe said. "I'll bed down here by the fire."

"Does its door have a secure lock?"

The question seemed to puzzle Bubba Joe and he had to give it a minute's thought. "Yes," he finally said, "yes, there's a lock. I'll have to go find the key."

"Perfect," Tompkins said.

W HEN THEY REACHED the outer edges of the fort, the men dismounted and pulled rifles from the scabbards. Sheriff Jackson gave a hand signal to indicate he would go around by the corral and quickly disappeared into the dark. Libby stood silently, looking at the outline of the old building before pointing to what appeared to be a side entrance. "I'll enter from over there," he whispered, knowing that Novak would insist on going through the front door.

The men had already agreed they would do no shooting until certain Lucy was safe.

Inside, Tompkins was rummaging through cabinets and shelves in search of something to drink. "The marshal said there was to be no whiskey," Bubba Joe said, "but I've got beer I made myself." He pulled a hidden jar from over the washbasin and proudly passed it to his guest.

Tompkins took one taste and spat it on the floor. "I've taken medicine better than that," he said.

With a wounded look on his face, Bubba Joe left the kitchen to return to the fireplace. Behind him, he could hear Tompkins cursing as he continued searching. Outside, the wind was howling.

As the young man knelt to prepare himself a pallet in front of the fire, he felt a hand on his shoulder. He turned and was looking into a familiar face. He was about to speak when Novak put a finger to his lips. "Where's the little girl?" he asked.

Unsure what was happening but realizing it was serious, Bubba Joe cut his eyes toward the second floor. He waved a hand to indicate he would lead the way, pulling a key from his pocket as he began tiptoeing toward the stairs. "That man didn't like my beer," he quietly said. "He's got a real funny-looking hat."

Novak put a hand over his mouth to quiet him, but was too late.

Though he assumed Bubba Joe was entertaining himself with some nonsensical gibberish, Tompkins moved to the doorway to check. In the glow of the fire, he saw two shadows on the opposite side of the room. "Who's there?" he said as he pulled his Colt. Then, not waiting for a reply, he fired a series of sweeping shots into the room. "I'm waiting to hear an answer," he yelled into the darkness.

Novak pulled Bubba Joe behind an old divan and told him to lie flat on the floor. "Don't move or speak a word," he whispered into the frightened young man's ear. Then he began making his way toward the stairs.

Still standing in the doorway, Tompkins fired another shot at what he thought was movement. And as he did so, another shot from behind him splintered the doorframe above his head.

Tompkins went to his knees and pressed himself against the wall. "That you, Sam Libby? And maybe somebody by the name Novak? Come to kill me, have you?" He aimed his pistol at the lantern sitting on the table and fired. There was a slight explosion and the room turned pitch-dark. "Can't hit what you can't see," he said, then gave a maniacal laugh.

Novak took advantage of Tompkins's distraction and raced up the stairs. At the end of the hallway he saw a closed door and hurried to it, only to find it locked. He pressed his face against it and called his daughter's name.

"Daddy? Daddy, is that you?"

"I'm here to take you home," he said. "We'll be leaving shortly. But for a few more minutes I need you to stay in there. Don't come out until I tell you, okay? You hurt in any way?"

"Just scared. I'm so scared."

Brady Jackson, having found no entryway from his

vantage point, had come in through the front door. A shot from Tompkins grazed his shoulder before he had even stepped inside. He was looking for cover when he heard someone shout, "Three against one ain't hardly fair."

"We didn't come to be fair," Libby said as he pushed the barrel of his rifle into Tompkins's back. Jackson's arrival had provided him the opportunity to find his way across the room to the shooter. Resigned, Tompkins let his pistol drop to the floor. "I was just looking for some whiskey," he mumbled as he dropped his head.

Bubba Joe left his hiding place and lit a lamp. He was followed by Brady Jackson as he carefully made his way to the kitchen, where they found Libby standing over Tompkins, his rifle pointed at his head. Jackson turned to find Novak and tell him it was over.

Another lantern was lit and handed to Jackson as he headed toward the stairs.

With the shooting stopped, Carl assumed all was well and was trying to fit the key into the lock that separated him from his frightened daughter.

Jackson gently pushed him away, then smashed his boot against the door, knocking if from its hinges. They found Lucy hiding under the bed. Her face was dirty, her dress torn, and she smelled like the inside of a horse-barn tack room. She was beautiful.

Novak helped her from her hiding place and took her in his arms.

"I knew you would come," she said as she buried her face against his neck.

Jackson stood to the side, watching the reunion, a smile in his face. Novak noticed the blood that had soaked his sleeve.

"Looks worse than it is," Jackson said as he turned to go back downstairs. Novak, with his daughter still in his arms, followed.

R AFE TOMPKINS WAS sitting with his back against the wall, a small, pitiful-looking man. His sombrero lay on the floor beside him, crushed by Libby. He was staring off into some distant place. As Novak looked down on him, all the old rage came back. He thought of the horror his child had been put through, of the cold-blooded killing of his friend the marshal, and of all the lives that had been destroyed by this evil and godless man.

He let Lucy slip to the floor and asked Jackson to take her into the other room. "Let her warm by the fire before we leave," he said.

When she was out of sight, he pulled his pistol and stepped toward Tompkins. He had cocked the hammer when Libby reached out and took his arm.

"You don't want your daughter remembering it like this," he said. For a time, it was as if Novak hadn't heard him as he continued to stare at Tompkins, deep in thought, his pistol still pointed at the man's head.

"Go," Sam said. "Take Lucy home."

O UTSIDE, BUBBA JOE waited with their horses by the front steps. He was grinning after being told he could keep Tompkins's mare and saddle for himself. The sleet had turned to powdery snow and the wind had calmed. A full moon was beginning to emerge as the clouds drifted away. Novak climbed onto his horse and waited for Jackson to lift Lucy up to her place behind him. She was wrapped in one of the blankets from inside.

They were turning to leave when a final shot sounded inside the old building, causing Lucy to tighten her grip on her father's waist.

"What was that, Daddy?"

"Justice," he answered.

CHAPTER THIRTY

T HE FAMILY CHURCH was filled for Del Wisen-hunt's funeral. Those late arrivals who couldn't find seats stood silently outside, all dressed in their Sunday best. Several lawmen from other communities, some who had participated in the canyon raid, were there. The women of his hometown of Wolf Creek had arranged more flowers in front of the altar and near the casket than anyone could remember.

Carl Novak had been asked to deliver the eulogy, marking another milestone in his life. He spoke quietly of the marshal's love for the town and its people, his devotion to seeing that laws were respected, and of his wonderful sense of humor. Mostly, he talked of their friendship and how much he had learned from Wisenhunt in their time together.

After he spoke, Lucy sang. Wearing a new dress Belinda Turner had sewn for her, she was again the confident young girl she had been before the nightmare began. "Kids bounce back fast," Dr. Turner had told Carl. He was right.

Down the street, the jail was filled with Tompkins's men, awaiting trials that would most certainly find them soon taken away to prison. Those who weren't quarreling among themselves could hear the faint sounds of a piano and a child's voice.

Sam Libby was one of the last to arrive. Nobody had seen or heard from him since that terrible night at the fort. As was to be expected, he was among the best dressed.

He waited until the service was over and the caravan of mourners had followed the casket to the cemetery before approaching Novak. Over his shoulder were Rafe Tompkins's weathered saddlebags.

"When she's older and maybe thinking of going off to singing school," he said, "see that she gets this. I helped myself to enough to buy some new clothes, but it's mostly all there."

CARL HAD BEEN asked to visit Wisenhunt's office and collect his personal belongings. He persuaded Libby to accompany him. They didn't find much—a broken pocket watch, a pair of gloves, his corncob pipe, a rain slicker and hat hanging on a peg next to the door, spurs he never wore, and a harmonica nobody ever heard him play.

"Not much for a man to leave behind," Sam said.

As Novak pulled open a desk drawer, his eyes fell on a sealed envelope atop a stack of old wanted posters and the telegrams he had received from fellow lawmen.

On its front it read, *In Case I'm Dead*.

His hands were shaking as he unfolded the letter that had been written as part of Wisenhunt's preparations for the raid on the canyon and began to read:

I had been saying for a long time that I'd stop Rafe Tompkins and his cattle rustling even if it killed me. If it did, somebody's now reading this letter I'm writing.

First of all, this is not to be taken as a Last Will since I've got nothing much to leave or anybody to leave it to. It is more some favors that need asking.

Would somebody pick two of the best horses left behind in Tompkins's stable and take them to the old farmer we met on our ride out to New Mexico? I don't recollect his name, but I'm sure it was the Ashtons who stole from him and we made him a promise we would get his animals back. Promises are made to be kept. They also took his rifle, which I hope can be replaced.

My own horse, which still has plenty of get-up to her, I'd like given to Lyndon Williamson if he'll promise to take good care of her, which I know he will.

Lastly, my badge can be found in the wooden box on the corner of my desk. I've considered long and hard about who I'd like to see wear it after me. All I can say is it needs to be a man who has strong feelings about right and wrong and wants to see folks kept safe.

It's my wish he not be a mean-spirited man, but somebody who can show courage and good thinking when there's a call for it. I'm not talking just about

*breaking up Saturday-night fighting at the saloon,
but doing what's right for law-abiding folks.*

*My choice for the job is Carl Novak if he'll see fit
to take it, even though it don't pay that much and
he'll be woke up in the middle of the night more times
than he'll like.*

Carl handed the letter to Libby, then walked to the
window, where he looked out onto the main street.

After Sam finished reading, he turned to Novak.
"Well?"

"I'll need to do some thinking about it."

"While you're doing that," Libby said, "I ought to
be on my way before the weather turns bad again."
He stood and they shook hands, then walked into the
chilly afternoon.

Carl watched as the stranger who had become his
friend rode past the café, the dry goods store, and the
livery, then gradually disappeared on the road that
led away from town. He doubted he would ever see
him again.

He gathered Wisenhunt's belongings into a box,
except for the badge, which he put in his pocket. He
looked around the empty room for a minute, then
locked the door and left.

He had somewhere to be.

Belinda Turner had invited him and his daughter
to come for supper.

EPILOGUE

O F ALL THE tales the old saloon storyteller told in
exchange for his whiskey, it was the one about
Sam Libby, Carl Novak, and Marshal Del Wisenhunt
that people seemed to most enjoy. More so even than
his colorful recollections of Quantrill and his Raiders during the war. As long as he told of the long and
dangerous chase to catch up with the Ashton brothers and the ending of Rafe Tompkins's cattle rustling
empire, people were willing to sit and listen, buying
him drink after drink until he would finally nod off,
too drunk to remember anything more.

His stories always ended with Carl Novak agreeing
to become a lawman. What happened after that, he
had no idea and felt no need to make anything up.
The true story was good enough.

Since he was unaware, he didn't mention that Lucy
grew up and went off to a school back east that taught
young ladies how to become opera singers. Or that
Lyndon Williamson, who went on to make a good

living raising horses, collected money from the townspeople to purchase the largest headstone anybody
had ever seen and had it placed on Marshal Wisenhunt's gravesite.

Never a romantic, even after too much whiskey,
the old drunk made no mention of Novak and Belinda courting or that most in Wolf Creek figured
they would one day get married.

And when he was asked whatever happened to
Sam Libby, he admitted it was a mystery, that he
didn't have the slightest idea.

Ready to find
your next great read?

Let us help.

Visit prh.com/nextread

Penguin
Random
House